GODSPEED

GODSPEED

LYNN BREEDLOVE

ST. MARTIN'S PRESS NEW YORK

GODSPEED. Copyright © 2002 by Lynn Breedlove. All rights reserved. Printed in the United States of America. No part of this book may be used or reproduced in any manner whatsoever without written permission except in the case of brief quotations embodied in critical articles or reviews. For information, address St. Martin's Press, 175 Fifth Avenue, New York, N.Y. 10010.

www.stmartins.com

Lyrics from "Six Pack" by Black Flag reprinted by permission of Cesstone Music, Long Beach, CA.

Book design by Michelle McMillian

Photos courtesy of Chloe Sherman

Library of Congress Cataloging-in-Publication Data
Breedlove, Lynn
Godspeed / Lynn Breedlove.
p. cm.
ISBN 0-312-28680-5
1. Lesbians—Fiction. 2. Narcotic addicts—Fiction. 3. Bicycle messengers—Fiction.
I. Title.

PS3602.R44 G63 2002
813'.6—dc21
2001048864

First Edition: April 2002

10 9 8 7 6 5 4 3 2 1

For Anna Joy

In memory of Quij and Fiver
and Kathy Acker and Kris Kovick

Dedicated to the Hags

ACKNOWLEDGMENTS

Thanx for telling me to go on with my bad self. I can hardly stand the love and genius that make this art fag life possible:

Kathy Acker for teaching me about Bataille and de Sade at Edinburgh Castle where we could take your SF Art Institute class for free over beer, and turning me on to your agent, and encouraging me to plagiarize and jerk off while writing although Anna said it was her idea but really it was Genet's. Anna Joy for inspiring me and editing and listening and going to every show and being the most punk-ass femme dyke and teaching me how to feel and cry and be jealous and fuck and write. Mom and Dad for telling me I was good and smart and could write even though it would never make me any money. Colt for being a good son and giving me hope and being punk 'til death. Kegger for hilarious sayings I liberally stole and being my gorgeous hag boyfriend. Jen Millis for being brilliant and gorgeous and editing me and listening to me bitch and telling me to get over it and have some gratitude for getting published, and for loving me so perfectly. Sarah Seinberg for inspiration and writing that one part and letting everyone think I did. Michelle Tea for taking me on tour and cracking me up and being so prolific it's a dare to keep up. Sini Anderson for taking me on tour and loving me through thick and thin and taking spiritual nosedives off cliffs and being the mad poet. The entire Sisterspit gang for being the traveling microcosm of dyke genius poets. Sarah West for cracking me up you faggot and being a great roadie and my pal. Ida Acton for showing me how to box and telling brilliant stories all night on tour to stay awake. Marci Blackman for succeeding and showing us we can, and always being charming and dignified. Shar Rednour for being a femme mechanic and using me as your prop when showing how to fuck in high heels. Tara Jepson for being my hilarious cohost at queer open mike and running Lickety and bike rides and love. Jenny Shealy for being the excellent babe who always gives me a good reference, and vice versa. Stanya Kahn for being performance artist extraordinaire and making me believe I don't need to stick to the page. Harry Dodge and Silas Flipper for being my old pals since we were scary dykes, and being the terrible trio and letting me read at the Clam when I sucked and going to hollywood and making it. And also Mr. Flapper (see above) for being the teen idol that kept the babes coming to the shows and loving me even though we're both hardheaded bastards and being Mr Hope Springs Eternal. Leslie Mah for lying in the hospital bed with me and being the archivist and the punk diva rock goddess. Tantrum for learning all the lyrix and singing with me. Slade Bellum for validating my feelings sister. The babes of Lickety Split for holding down the fort and riding your asses off for the love of it. Rachel Hawkey for never finding fault with me even though I had plenty. Kriss De Jong for keeping Lickety and T8 going via computer genius and reading the manuscript to Eliot Daughtry at bedtime, and El for your coyote brain. Kris Kovick for being Mr One Breast and never giving up and always blowing sunshine up everyone's ass cuz we need it to carry on. Sheila tha Heala for keeping me alive, and runnin Lickety with Thelma and Louise on your head, and keeping the chi movin. Kayha Engler for being the most forgiving Eurobabe with unflagging integrity. Elitrea for being by my side in the trenches and for the squat vacation and for rapping some true shit. Anne Cvetcovich and Gretchen Phillips for being the genius couple of life. LV for letting us play for the best audience in the world. Kathleen Hanna for sending me small violins and telling me to quit smoking and fucking shit up grrl style now. Lunachicks for crackin my shit up and rocking severely. 7 Year Bitch for seriously rocking. Melissa York for being my vicarious cartoon drummer who's not afraid of being hokey. MDC for taking us on tour in europe and telling your fans to buy our shit and being PUNK AS FUCK. Jello Biafra for believing in T8 and puttin us out there. Ren for being coffee-acheiver Mom and making Biz who is gonna be the president of the United States and is the best godchild ever and changed my life. Jonathan Hevenstone for gently editing my egotistical ass. Teresa Theophano for making it happen. Sue Fehn for thirty loyal years, drunkles in the parking lot, playing army, wearing black. Missy Vice and Black Flag for teaching me Punkrock. Mrs. Allen, Miss Kirkpatrick, Professor McAuley for saying I could write good. Rosemary and Cindy and Kriss Ridste for coming out the other side with me. Chloe Transister. The name says it all. And everyone else who waited nine goddam years. Tribe 8 fans everywhere. Without you I am nothing.

Colt's heart, skull, and hard-luck tattoos by Leslie Mah.

Contest:
Find all the pop culture references and win a free blow job in the boyz bathroom. You pitch I catch.

Mom says to tell everyone this is a work of FICTION.

Don't nobody try this at home.

THE HAG ANTHEM

Goin' to a birthday party with tha fuckin' hags
Someone's gonna end up in a body bag
Mona's drivin'
Bad moon risin'
Ain't afraid o' dyin'
Cuz we're fuckin' hags

Get a forty-ouncer
Get a girl and bounce her
On the end of my dil-do
Ya callin' me a hoe?
That's what I am
My middle name is scam
I'm a hag

Ain't payin' no rent
I'd rather get bent
Let the landlord rot cuz I'm gonna squat right here
Don't come to visit me without a six-pack o' beer and a pack o'
*   cigarettes*

We'll be in heaven
Don't forget the spray paint
Turn up the L7
I'm a hag

United we stand divided we run
Cops would like to catch a hag but they never caught a one
We're too quick
Slick we got brains we're insane
Dealin' with the pigs would just be a pain
We got gigs to hit
Our pals are waitin' in the pit
so we can kick
the shit
Out o' the first muthafucka
that gives us any shit
We're fuckin' hags

Went to Headhopper's
She was bored
So we went dumpster divin' on our rad skateboards
We found some lamps and coffee machines
And a buncha other what I thought was kinda useless things
With which she's gonna build a motor
And skate to Petaluma
She's a hag

Cash gas or acid no one rides for free
'Less you're ridin' my face

Then maybe we'll see
that's what Jo said wavin' her gun
Left her car on the freeway now she's on the run
She's a hag

Julian Julian hitchmasta
hitchhiked all the way to Alaska
Her mama's worried 'bout her fate
Said "They're gonna chop you up and mail you all over the United
    States"
But her mama ain't a hag she's a hag

Crash jumped a fence
and sprained her ankle
Then she lost her wallet with three twenty-dollar bills
Other hags brought some ice 'stead o' callin' her a wanker
and assortments of prescriptions for the pain to kill
She's a hag

Mr. Quijas locked herself out and she was pissed
So she thought she'd wrap her hand up in a flannel shirt
Proceeded to smash the window with her fist
Since she saw it on TV she knew she couldn't get hurt
The blood began to squirt
All she could blurt
out was
I'm a hag
And I get into hag fixes
Used to gettin' eighty-sixed

Nothin' that a coupla sixers won't fix
I'm a hag
I go out taggin' with my sistahs
I go on hag adventures so I'll take my licks

I got bills to pay
I better go on GA
Or make 'em think I'm crazy and go on SSI
Wild look in my eye
Got my coat on backward
Look a little more dangerous than a mere slacker
I piss in my pants
I don't miss a chance
to make it look like I deserve some of the government's reserves
Cuz I'm a hag
I don't believe in workin'
and if I ever do its only cuz I'm hurtin'
You think I'm a beast
But I'm an artiste
If you act like a sucker you gonna get fleeced
Cuz you owe me motherfucker and that's cuz I'm a hag
I got nasty hag habits
And if you don't like it
why dontcha just bag it
I'm a hag
And I ain't got no respect
for no one but a hag except Becky Wreck
When I get stewed I get an attitude
If you say I'm rude that's an understatement dude

Cuz I'm lewd I'm rank I'm irreverent and malicious
When I'm comin' down off speed I'm downright vicious
I'm a hag (SF)
I'm a hag

By Lynnee Breedlove, 1993

PART ONE

BASTARD IN LOVE

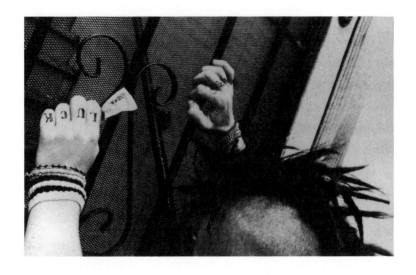

DAREDEVIL DELIVERY

OK, so you're breathing bus fumes and spices from restaurants and charred fish and raw sewage, and then you got cabs and buses whizzing in and out of the corner of your eye, but you keep looking straight ahead, because you got eyes all over your head. You take everything in, you don't miss nothing, the whole wide street and things coming at you from around corners as you round corners, and you can see things before they appear to the non-messenger eye, you can see through buildings, you can look down a cross street before you even get to it, half prophesy, half feel, half hear the way's clear. You have to if you want to survive and deliver the package on time.

Your head swivels back like Linda Blair when you change lanes, but it has to spin forward again in the next split second, because that's all the time it takes for an idiot in a half ton of steel to end your life, see. So you just cock your ear back and listen for something coming. You're a mutation, a monster genetically engineered to deliver in fifteen minutes what a car would take an hour to do.

And lights, you don't mind traffic lights, just traffic cops, and traffic. The question is not, is the light red, but can I make it across this intersection alive. You estimate the number of seconds it takes Car Driver's brain to register that his light is green, plus the second it takes him to put his foot on the gas and move into your lane, that's how much time you have to run the light.

Now peds are a different story, as they pose less of a threat to your physical safety, but they can slow you down and fuck you up with legal shit, so you want to miss hitting them. You keep stoking, weave here cut there, thread the needle right through the middle of them. If you slow down, they just take over and you have to stop, and a messenger can't be stopping for a lowly ped. When that little green man lights up for peds to go, they go, and they don't care about nothing but going, not you, not cars, not nothing, they just march right at each other like ants. You got to speed up when your light turns red, and scream, because only a bike messenger yelling NO BRAKES and barreling at them at high speeds will stop them, see.

You crouch, centered over the bike, pushing it from side to side under you. You just keep this smooth easy flow, rolling on the pedals in high gear. You always got two fingers on the brake, or one middle finger if you're passing a cop, so even if you're full speed, ready to run a red, you could squeeze the lever just in time for a dead stop, scare a ped good, make your rear wheel jump up high. Look at him real blasé like so what, and if he gives you any shit, you say, Get your fucking hand off my bike, ped.

And then you pull up on the grips, push down on the pedals, push-pull your whole body into the bike, blend into the machine until you're not straining or stretching, just striding gliding rolling in circles, it's all going in circles forward, you go faster, the circle gets longer, elliptical, just pistons up and down, pistons, and then you can fly down Nob Hill, but you got to go diagonal on the cable car tracks in the rain, don't touch the brakes. Wet metal will kill you. You don't want to eat it because the worst feeling is squeezing, squeezing brakes, and nothing's happening but you and your bike flying horizontal with the rubber side up. Extreme harshness.

So you don't brake in the rain. Concentrate more on steering out of the way of shit. You just fly, spitwads dotting your eye, squint and put your baseball cap on forward style. You got to be good, like me, the Artful Dodger, Masta of Disasta, cut around cars stacked up, the first rain bringing the road oil up, making it slick, washing broken glass to the side of the street where you want to ride. Brain-dead no-attention-paying motherfuckers pulling out in front of you, and you splitting lanes at twenty-five, swoop, whooping at peds, yelling, Jump, suit, jump. Sometimes you get a big load, sixty pounds on your back, stuffed in your gravy bag. Feels good, because every pound is extra cash.

Then you're home free, South of Market, no more cages boxing you in, you're just watching for potholes and glass, micro-geography, your eyes snapping up asphalt in tiles ahead of you, your front tire sucking up road through a funnel.

That's when the orange syringe cap on the street looms godlike. It disappears in a blur under wheels and feet. It rewinds and plays back again and again thirty times, the same piece of plastic, block after block, burning bush, big as shit, alert alert right there in the street, saying, Hi, you need to get fucked up.

And the ride that a second ago was your joy, your perfect freedom-fighter life, winds down in that insto-second to a reflex, your legs left alone with instinct and feel and a glassed-in quiet. Superimposed on the traffic and streets, blood mushrooms into a cylinder of liquid pleasure, poison, superman desire, larger than life and challenging death, and all you can think is, Do I have twenty cents to call up my man? And where will I get twenty dollars.

Package, what package?"

"You never dropped the package."

"I dropped the fucking package."

"They never got the package. Did you even pick UP the goddam package?"

"Yeah, I did. What the fuck."

"Well, where the hell is it then?"

They seem to think that I, Danger Dyke, have lost a package.

"I dunno. *Maybe* I lost it. How should I know."

"How should *you* know? Because that's your job, to deliver packages, you idiot."

So fired. Again.

Good thing there's a million messenger companies. So being fired all the time is no trauma. I always wanted to ride for the Church of the Warped Reality, which delivers pot. Plenty of fringe benefits. So I'm cruising the Tenderloin in search of the Church. I heard it's the office over the pool hall with the venetian blinds in the window.

Actually though, I like the stretches in between jobs, those days I ride, but not for money, when I go where I want, not where I'm told, and I got a couple bucks. I stay high. Go to Mount Tam with the boys, get drunk and ride dirt trails. Or go to UN Plaza, hang with the unofficially emancipated youth in front of the dirty upside-down hat on the sidewalk and say, Spare change? Me and my man, Fuckalot, whose whole life is bikes and punkrock music, we ride the tall bikes. Those are bikes she built so big, you have to run and jump to get on them, and then you are riding up ten-feet high, and everyone says, There go the tall bikes.

I stop in at the Regal where Ally works, slip a five in the slot, act like a customer. Butch it up, incognito, pass as a boy in my hoodie. "No unescorted ladies" is the Rules, but so what, they let me in because they like Ally. She's the queen of the Regal Show World.

I look her up and down so I blend in with the slimeballs. Stroll back and forth, lascivious drool, jaw slack in awe of her stretching up tall, all tits and red satin. Her tongue's running over her lips, her eyes narrow into eyelashy slits as she lures us inside.

"Wanna come inside?"

She sneaks me in the back. I slip into her booth, her side of the glass, out of customers' sight. She gets a bite from a sucker. He slithers into his shmegma-filled closet. It's freshly mopped with Pine Scent Janitor in a Drum. Mmmm. Delish. Sperm stench or ammonia overdose, I don't know how they can come swimming in air substitutes.

She winks at me quick and we switch places, she in her fake half-a-bed, brass with black sheets. I'm where the johns can't see me unbutton my jeans. It's hot, the sneakiness of it, what if security finds out or the customer, and she, she is the hottest, the tenderest angel in the lowest, most sordid place, and I'm in it with her. My heart's racing.

She says, "Oh he's cute, hope he's got lotsa money," in a vestigial accent groomed in working-class Southern Cal hamlets.

She snakes up close to the window, whore under glass, picks up the phone. It's a direct line to his closet, like she's visiting him in jail. I can't see him, but I know he's Idiot Boy, because she has to motion about ten times for him to pick up the phone. I wonder if he's got the coordination skills to jack off with the other hand. Sometimes they don't. It's just too much for them. Hold the phone. Jerk off. Pull twenties out of your wallet and slip them in the automatic slot so you can still see Miss Thang through the window, because if you don't keep the dead presidents flowing, the window goes black, and there you are with a hand fulla dick in the dark all alone.

"What's your name?" she purrs. The original kitten. "Come here, kiss me," she teases. Then all I can catch are snatches of porn.

She's breathing, "I want you to slide your tongue . . . touch my . . . move your cock between my tits." She pushes them together. "Squeeze . . . you're going to have to put five more dollars in the slot," she says in the same tone. "No, that will cost you twenty."

She's making him hold that nasty thought by staying breathy while she's talking dollar. I'm trying not to laugh out loud so he doesn't hear me. She's got him by the nads. He can't come until he slips her another five. This is great. Now he wants her to fist herself or put a banana up her butt or whatever perverted shit he's thinking in the throes of his wanking, and he can have it for a price. But he's bitching. He wants her to fuck herself with the phone for five bucks.

Yeah, fuck yourSELF with the fucking phone, dickwad, but no, she just says, "That will cost you fifty. You will ask nicely, not tell me, do you understand, sweetheart?"

Then she steers him back to the econo-fantasy, since that's all he's forking over.

"Now slide it in . . . flip me over." She's on her knees. "Push it in me. I want your big, fat . . . I want to feel you inside me. . . ."

She's undulating like she wants it. She's pouting real good. I like to watch her face. That's the sexy part. The guys like to look at her tang, because that's how they are, and so she spreads it and lubes it for them, so they can think of how good their dick would feel in there, and after a while I can't help staring at it, mesmerized by the shapes she makes it take.

She glances over her shoulder. "Move inside me." Her ass rolling hungry up to the glass. Girls screaming fuck me from video booths.

She hangs up the phone. In motherly tones she coos at him, "Now you want to marry me, don't you. They all do after they come."

She gets up and gets dressed, back in her G-string she slips. With alcohol, she sprays down her tits, wipes off the lube, and lights a smoke. She pushes me down, her tongue tracing my lips with clear honey drool. Spitglaze, like lip gloss. She steps back and looks at my mouth like it floats in a void, not attached to my face. She gets off on making me femme. Pulls up my hair in a hair don't. The worst torture for me who must, above all else, be a boy.

I let her, not with resignation, like when Mom stole my manhood by putting me in dresses, but with abject, willing love.

And Ally looks at me, not like she looks at Them, but desperate, pouring her guts out of crescent-moon eyes, green-laser worship verging on hate. I never been loved like that.

She hides me and opens the shutters to her boudoir, so she can peruse the sleaze parade and solicit more slime.

Slime: "What do you do in there?"
God: "It's a live sex show."

Slime: (Something shitty.)

God: (Laughs.)

Slave: "Honey, why don't you just kill 'em?"

God: "I want their money."

Dead serious about the business of pleasure. Like me.

But today I ain't paying for pleasure. That's why automatic pilot takes me out of the Tenderloin, right past the Regal to Frankie's.

Meow. Mee-aow."

I'm meowing up at Frankie's window because it attracts less attention than yelling Frankie. She drops the key out the window. I run upstairs. The curtains are drawn, and she's groggy.

"Whatever it is, just shut up. I'm sleeping."

I shut the door. She falls back in bed. I sit down, obedient, and wait until I'm sure she's asleep. She sleeps real light. Cocaine won't let her dream, so she doesn't breathe heavy and her chest doesn't heave, telltale. She doesn't even toss and turn. It's creepy. She just lies there, like dead. I have to watch her for a long time.

Then I get up and tippy-toe over to the fridge. Get the baggie out of the butter compartment. Put it on the counter. Get the bag of fresh points off the top of the fridge, tear it open, pull one out, nice and stealthy-like. Break a healthy chunk of mica off the half oh-zee. Real quiet. My hands are shaking. It looks like a lot, sitting in the cradle of the spoon. Aw fuck it. If I put some back now, she'll know I chipped off her stash. Dip the needle in the cup of water. Draw up twenty cc's and shoot it in the spoon. There's that *PHHHHT* when it hits the metal. Damn that was loud. Quick, turn around. Did it wake her up? Jesus, quit being so damn paranoid.

Frankie lying there like a cherub gives me a guilt pang. But if she wasn't so tight, I wouldn't have to steal my high. And she's always kicking me down, she's got plenty. She won't mind if I help myself to a tiny taste. It's not like I'm gonna ruin her with this one snib.

Should I put in some more water? Nah. It's better thick. Hits your heart all at once, woo. Roller coaster. OK, now mash it up with the plunger part. Look at that clear sparkly nectar. Yum. Roll up a teeny tiny ball of cotton. Aw shit, we're out of cotton. We'll just peel the paper off this here cigarette filter. Pinch off a few fibers. They say there's asbestos in this shit. Yeah, like I'm real worried about my fucking health.

Now lay the needle down flat and suck that pretty shit up until . . . *sssSSSST* . . . the fibers dry up, all white, and then hold the syringe up like a doctor does, upside down against the light.

Doctor Danger, the patient is ready. Pull the plunger down, push it up, just right. Give it a tap, get the bubble up by the needle for the vacuum effect, so it sucks blood into the rig when you hit the vein. People freak out about the bubble. They say it hits your heart and it's all over. Yeah, well, fuck that. It's so you can register. In thar, dude. You just gotta know what you're doing, is all.

Belt the bicep, and what a gorgeous bicep it is. For a junkie, not bad. Ride all day, shoot all night. A regular Annie Oakley. Vein's callused, but with a new needle, it ain't no thang. Slide that baby in, ouch, oh yeah, there it is, mushroom cloud of blood, red flower. OK, don't get excited and lose it, getting all shaky and shit. Push it in slow. . . . Wait, that's half the hit and I'm already tasting it. It's a lot. I should pull out.

What, and waste the rest? The blood clots in the needle and then you got a rig full of garbage. No fuck it, it's now or never. I'm driving it home.

That's it, there's your whole mouth playing that underwater steel drum with a hive of bumblebees in it, and there goes your scalp floating off the top of your head, 4,3,2,1, lift off, and a slow motion wave of reverb, echoes layering over each other in a thick pile carpet of artificial sound, saying *Mmmmm wawawa wayyy yay yang*.

Whoa shit. It's speeding up. Sound's going faster, it's not Bowie on the radio, now it's Alvin and the Chipmunks singing, Rebel, rebel your face is a mess. . . . You had to be a greedygut. You fucked up.

No, OK, OK, chill. Get on your knees. And what, pray? No, so your heart won't bust wide open, bozo. OK, that's not working, go prone, all the way down, flat on the floor.

Oh goodie. Here we go. Arms and legs bouncing. I can't believe I'm doing a fucking fish dance. I heard about this shit. This is harsh. Hey, you should yell Hey Frankie. Nah, you'd never live it down. Her seeing you do a fish dance. And so what. If you die, you die, whether she's watching or not. What's she gonna do. Nothing. Call 911, then you got cops and ambulances, and by that time you're dead, so you might as well die in peace with a shred of dignity.

OH Jesus. God. Hello? Can I stop with the spaz attack now? Without my face being froze sideways. What a bummer trying to get chicks with your face all sideways. Can't even flirt. Without blowing too many circuits. No brain damage, OK? OK, brain damage, fine, I don't care, just semi-retardation. Jesus fuck. Wait. Is it stopping? I'm slowing down. No more shock therapy. Thank you. It's stopping.

Damn, will you look at Frankie, sleeping through that whole shit. I could have fucking died.

THE WORLD ACCORDING TO JIM

I sleep restless. I dream I'm the beautiful pin-eyed junkie boy down the hall, and I'm kneeling butt naked with my jeans bunched around my boots. Someone's branding me with an iron. I wake up yelling.

It's already dark outside. I'm late. Fell asleep in my clothes again. Which makes getting out the door easy. All I got to do is chug a beer, shove another one in my pocket, pack of smokes, shades in case I'm still awake when morning comes. Jump on my bike and head for Babe Land.

In the lobby at the Regal, I shuffle around in front of the mirror where the guys straighten their ties when they come in, like the chicks give a shit—fixing my hair so it doesn't look fixed.

I'm waiting for Ally Cat. Love the Greco-Roman decor. The wild-eyed plaster-of-Paris head perched on a pedestal. And there's a half-naked armless but otherwise buff chick on another pedestal, fake chandeliers with flame bulbs, and gold-paint splats on the wall that are supposed to look like marble if you're post-come bleary. Who the fuck's idea was this, Walt Disney on estrogen? The six-foot-high pink neon sign's yelling REGAL: WHERE YOU ARE KING. That's good. I'd put that in my room. Throws a nice glow on your complexion when you're pasty.

I'm in a trance, eyes locked on the sign that says PRIVATE, STAFF ONLY. Waiting. Finally the door opens. She pokes her head out and hustles me in, smelling like lube and perfume. Her ass switches up the stairs in a see-through, flower-print next-to-nothing swishing around her all silky.

Up in the dressing room, there's a long mirror and a counter where her and her pals put on makeup. It would be a handy place to do rails and pour shots. She plops down on an overstuffed chair and sits me on the floor so my head's resting on the red-satin triangle of her G-string crotch. She introduces me to a naked girl. I don't want to look too hard and be disrespectful, and I know Ally's checking me out to see if I'm staring. I used to get nervous around naked chicks, but hanging around here I learned. You just look them right in the eye.

Ally spits her gum out and kisses me. The world disappears. I don't want to disappear in front of Naked Chick, so I stop kissing Ally and say, "Uh, when ya gettin' off?"

"When ya gonna get me off?"

"Such a card, a real joker."

"I'll be done in an hour."

"Hey, I know. Whyn'tcha gimme some money and I'll wait for ya at the bar."

"Right."

"I am. I will. What."

Blank stare.

"OK. How 'bout this. Gimme some money, and I'll get us some Chinese and bring it back here. I'll walk you home. We can chow down at your place."

"I'm sorry. But I do not see the difference between the first proposal and the second. Either way, I'm giving you money. Do I look stupid?"

"What."

I don't know why, but eventually she pulls a twenty out of her bra and presses it into my hand with this look like, You better not fuck me up, and I stuff it in my pocket with this look like, Don't worry baby, I won't.

I give her a kiss and run downstairs. I don't wipe off the lipstick until I get outside. There's a rule that girls who wear lipstick have, ever since my grandma. You can't wipe it off or that means you don't love them.

And this time I'm getting Chinese food. I'm going.

But I got this allergy to money, mainly twenty-dollar bills. They give me an itch, right in the crook of my arm. There's only one known cure, and it ain't Chinese food, if you know what I mean.

My old geezing buddy, Carlton, he spent ten years at Atascadero. Geezing, that's shooting up, and Atascadero, that's a prison for the criminally insane. Whenever Carlton wanted to get high, he'd say, I got an itch, and he'd get this maniacal smile that would always make me smile back, because that meant I'd have to steal twenty dollars out of the till at the gas station where I worked and send him out to get something good.

He always came back with something real good. That was in Oaktown, when the Hell's Angels used to make all the speed. They'd sell it to dealers and then send guys around to drop in on you unexpectedly. Hi, just me, big hairy killer-rapist for a friendly visit. How 'bout lining me up? And then, if they did a big line of your shit, and it was still pure and not cut with the required sixty-percent baby laxative, they'd tie you up and fix you with a gram of it, a "hotshot" is what it's called, which would kill you in twisty dance of death. They couldn't have you just running around selling that shit to people as is, because then everybody would be banging grams and dying, and then the federales would be forced by some rich OD's father to put a stop to the whole thing. Besides, the Angels wanted people to party, not die. Dead people don't buy drugs.

Anyway, one time Carlton came back with this lavender shit that was so good, it made my tang hot. Once you get something with a rush like that, you're never the same. Never satisfied. Always looking for that perfect ten minutes, and it never comes again. And way in the back of your mind, you know it's never going to come again, but that just doubles your resolve to find it.

See, with this itch, first it's a physical thing. When the holes on your vein start scabbing up, they make those super-tiny scabs, but they itch, like a tattoo healing. They are a tattoo, tracks are, the worst sort, because they don't make a pretty picture you can show off to your pals. Booting is an exclusive activity, so you only shoot up with members of the club, and the rest of the world just looks at you like you are demented, when, of course, what's the difference between putting it in your vein or your nose. I'll tell you. It's blood. Blood means life or death, and people in this world don't like facing life or death. That's an activity for the elite.

So OK. Then there's the mental itch, which is entirely kicked off by the physical itch. And that's the sneaky part, because just when you're all satisfied to take a break and sleep and eat and rest up for a day or two, along comes this itch in your arm that reminds you of the fun to be had, the whole time it's blocking out the grittiness and jaw grinding and fourteen pints of beer and the fifth of whiskey you had to drink to come down, so drunk you were stumbling all over the furniture but not actually falling down and closing your eyes, and all that irrigation still didn't wash down the cement bits and scum in your mouth from hours without swallowing. And that itch also blocks out and explains how you woke up next to Carlton, who was beating off and cackling, and the epic movies of sweaty Charlton Heston in a sheet you watched with Carlton's mom, while he cleaned out her wallet so you could get more speed, when all that poor old woman had in the world was her son and a pension check. Jesus H. Christ on a raft.

The thing about Carlton was, he was a murderer, and proud of it too. He bludgeoned a guy and his son to death after they picked him up hitchhiking. So, see, there you go, what Mom says about picking up hitchhikers is right after all. They all got out of the car to look at the view of the mountains, and Carlton picked up a rock and smashed the old man over the head with it, and the guy crumpled to the ground. When the kid turned around and saw his dad lying there, Carlton bashed him over the head too, to stop him from freaking out. I don't know. He never said why. He would always whip out the police report and show me, just facts, not whys and wherefores. When I'd ask him why, he'd just smile all crazy and say he didn't know.

But boy could he hit me and never miss, which is hard because I got the invisible veins, not the ropes he had. And he had the connection. My old girlfriend, Rocky, who used to score for us and hit me up, she was gone, so I had no choice, not knowing how to hit myself. I was scared I would miss the vein, which would mean a big red lump and no rush, because I was always shaking with antici . . . pation. So, you see, I just didn't have no choice.

Plus, once Carlton shot me up, I realized that Rocky had been cheating me, doing most of the bag and leaving me the cotton the whole time, and finally I was feeling the real thing. Fuck that bitch taking my money and putting it all in her arm. That figured, since she was the bastard that turned out my virginal ass, telling me with her bedroom eyes and big black pupils how this was gonna be better than sex, and come on just try it, didn't I trust her? A snake like that, that gets off sullying the tiny lamby children, of course she wouldn't be interested in satisfying my need once she had created it. No, the thrill of the fall behind her, she went right back to fixing her own jones, fuck me, because now I was just another hungry arm, in the way of her own high.

So I took responsibility and finally I was getting my propers. From a psycho killer, qu'est-ce que c'est. And it was good.

You see how this thing is so smart at showing your mind what it wants you to see and covering everything else up, or how it's always telling you this time will be different after the rush, but you don't give a shit if it's different or not, or if your brains get bashed out or not, because the rush is the fucking meaning of life. It's a trip to God. It puts a measly orgasm to shame. The trick is to get just the right amount, push it to the edge, so you almost overamp but not quite. So you just breathe hard, cough when it hits your heart, and your palms sweat, and you look in the mirror and your eyes are black as buttons, and you got that fresh-fucked blushy look, all intense and dreamy. Nobody telling you what to do, because you can't hear them with the blood river rushing in your ears. And you don't care, so they can never hurt you.

See, now, I'm normal and rational, but I've known plenty of dudes who like to flirt with death and overamp every time, or they're just not satisfied. The first time I saw a guy like that, I was in awe. He was the Evil Knievel of the needle. Evil Kneedle. I was the audience and he was the circus trick.

Everyone else kept drinking and playing cards, but I watched him. He put half a gram in the spoon, twice normal. He drew it up and put it in his arm so fast, it was like making breakfast, second nature. Could do it in his sleep. Then all of a sudden, he was moving real fast, peeling all his clothes off and sweating up a storm and fidgeting, but all the time sitting right there on the couch, not going anywhere. He was a sphere of motion particles, like the lights moving in a TV screen, hypnotizing you but you can't see them, you just see a picture of a cowboy. That's how it was, molecules jumping and zipping around in his body, sweatballs sprouting all over his face. Then he got up as calm as could be, walked over to the table, grabbed a chair, and asked us to deal him in, just like that. Like nothing.

Then there was Rena Sue Simms, she liked to turn on her portable tape recorder, bang a gram, and play it back later, just to hear herself flop around. I don't know how she survived it, over and over. But she sure is in lousy shape now. She walks jerky, and her face is twisted in a grimace you can't look at.

See, I seen a lot of people do a lot of skank and survive every duel with death like a high-noon sheriff, so I guess "speed kills" was just a lie. Anything anyone puts in a spoon, I bang it, and if they don't put enough, I bitch. I ain't scared. I just want to get as far out into the stratosphere as I can without breaking the sound barrier. Life's a train and I'm throwing myself in front of it. I got to get the most possible out of everything as fast as I can, always have, even soda pop. Mom used to go "slow down," but before she could finish talking, there was the empty bottle on the table. Sugar, speed, it's all sucked into the vortex called my body.

Some people get high to escape, but I got nothing to escape, no torturous childhood. Just my own self. I ain't running from or to, I just like running, like riding, that downhill whoosh, scariness, no rules, the danger that speed itself might take you out, that the speed of light might disintegrate you in a time machine you haven't got all the bugs out of yet, or else you survive, lonesome and free, orbiting the earth like Major Tom. Rapture.

I don't know why I want to go to the moon. Why it's more important than love. It's this thing, like breathing. No matter how long you hold your breath, you're gonna breathe again because your body decides it's so. That's the way it is with mainlining. It's the best of both worlds, control and being carried away. Yeah, you hold the spike, you put the power in your arm, and then the power seizes you by force, like a headless horseman grabbing you up. It's its own life force in your head, your blood, it's reflex killing thought and not needing thought to live. It's already alive. A syringe cap lying on the ground is all it takes to reanimate, charge you with a million volts. You just look at the rig, you don't even have to touch it, it galvanizes you like lightning, locks down your gaze and says, You are going to get high now motherfucker, nothing else matters so don't argue.

So you don't. You follow your body, all hot and rushy in anticipation, and do what your hands tell you to do.

HEDGEHOPPER KICKS DOWN

So I'm heading into the heart of the Tenderloin singing, "I love her, I love her, I love her, and when she comes, I'll swallow, I'll swallow, I'll swallow, and that is cuz I love her . . ." and I don't feel like going straight to the restaurant. I got plenty of time, so I take a detour, left on Turk Street, into the land of crack I roam, and lo I find myself at the house of Hedgehopper, notoriously nefarious dealer of marching powder.

I ring the bell. No answer. So I sit on the sidewalk and wait. There's always free entertainment here, nonstop street party in the unearthly light. People huddled in corners, passing pipes.

There's this nerdy guy with glasses, and floods showing his white socks and loafers. You wonder how he ever got into this mess, standing in the middle of the street, shouting, wooden, as if he never shouted before, "YA GOT ANY? YA GOT ANY? A DOLLAR THIRTY. THEY DON'T GOT ANY. YA GOT A DOLLAR THIRTY HIT? C'MON, PLEASE?" to no one and everyone, turning around and around.

They don't got any. But here comes a guy who does, and he starts smoking it up right in front of everybody, and they're getting hungry and fidgety, but he doesn't care, he's all happy and jumpy and chatting up a storm, working the party, mingling, dropping rocks in the end of a glass tube and lighting it, putting on a show.

The meat wagon glides by and shines the light on everyone, just so they know the Man is watching, and Make Whoopee disappears, along with everyone else who's got any. Those who don't got, we just sit and stare, like What. Whatchu gonna do. I ain't got none, so what you lookin' at, bacon boy.

I'm aiming to look nonchalant, but I'm getting squirmy under the scrutiny of the gestapo, when Hedgehopper comes skating up.

"Hoppa."

"Yeah. Whassup." She unlocks the gate and I hustle in behind her.

"Ya holdin'?"

"Yeah. What about it."

"I got some money."

"Well, halle-fuckin-lujah. You can pay me what you owe me then." She walks down the stairs, unlocks another door.

"How about frontin' me another bag first?"

She's looking straight ahead, walking fast down the hall so I have to skip to keep up.

"Fine. But you can't do it here. Last time you locked us in and wouldn't let anyone out for five hours, saying we was surrounded by the feds an' shit."

"Oh, that. Paranoia will destroy ya. Happens to the best of us, right?" I'm all laughing, punching her in the arm. "That was some good shit."

She spins around. "Good shit, my ass on stilts. You need to sleep more than two hours a week and eat something besides a six-pack once in a while. Fuck a buncha good shit. . . ."

"Hey, beer is food. OK, OK, I won't do it here. Killer, no prob."

She unlocks her door and we slide into her high-ceilinged practice studio with no windows, and egg crates and carpet all over the walls. "Just shut up talkin' so loud, will ya," she says.

I scrunch my fists down into my pockets and scuffle around, start poking around a tweak project she's got going there on her workbench. It's a perpetual work in progress. Buncha nuts and bolts and wire and scrap metal.

She starts yelling, "WHADDAYA. GET OUTTA THERE, WILL YA? Did I tell ya to mess with that shit? I got everything set up there. Jeez."

She hands me a bag of hag grounds and a syringe, and I'm trying to be polite and not make a break for it like my ass is on fire, but it is, so I start moseying backward toward the door saying, "Right on, thanks a lot. OK then, well, I guess I'll be seein' ya. . . ."

"This week would be nice. I'm not your fuckin' savings and loan." She's got her lips all pressed together like, what a fuckup, like she's not.

'Kay, right, yeah, later. I'm out the door whistling down the hall *la-la-lee-la* taking the stairs two at a time, jump on my bike, doin' da hump-dee-hump with my bike down Market Street. I know this bar on Sixteenth Street, I can do it in the bathroom.

Someone starts yelling from the sidewalk, "Hey bee-y-a-a-atch, you owe me twenty dollars, fucker."

"Fuck 'er? I don't even know 'er. *You* brought 'er, *you* fuck 'er." Then I look back, and it's that guy from last week who gave me a twenty to go score, and I said I'd be right back with the shit, and I just remembered I never did come back. Damn.

Oh well, when in doubt, show off. So I jump up and stand on

the crossbar, surfing with one foot wrapped around the seat post, standing tall, looking in bus windows, and he's yelling and I'm yelling and everyone's having a good old time, and then boom, I look, and there's a suit crossing the street right in front of me, so I jump on to the seat, just in time so I don't endo, that is, fly ass over tits across the handlebars through the intersection. But I'm not quick enough to miss the suit.

I don't run him over, I just sideswipe him, so I keep riding, and I look back to see if he's in one piece and he is. Now he's on the ground yelling *his* head off about fucking messengers, which I don't know why, because he could have been tore up from the floor up. I think I did a damn good job of saving his measly suit life.

So I'm zipping along at high speeds with angry customer and CEO dude both in the dust back there, so I can't slow down yet, and then of course it's lights flashing, sirens whooping, black-and-white Harley-Davidson in hot pursuit up my ass. I'm in demand today.

You know, you can kill all the hookers and crackheads you want in cold blood, and it's NO HUMANS INVOLVED. (The cops got an actual rubber stamp that says that. NHI. Oh yeah. Believe it.) But powerboy in a suit gets a scratch and they call out the National Guard, don't they.

So I'm thinking, Fuck it. I ain't indulging no cop fantasy of my arrest and incarceration. They'll never take me alive.

As I am the proud two-time winner of the Alley Cat Race, which requires an instinctual knowledge of one-way SOMA alleys, I figure I got a chance. I wing down Seventh Street the wrong way into five lanes of oncoming traffic, ignoring the law as no motorized vehicle can, but no, that doesn't lose Officer CHiPs, motor or no, he's above the law, and he wants to be a hero and follow me, so I whip down a back street through the hole in the fence, across the parking lot where folks live in boxes, and out the other side. Nope. Can't shake him. He's still whooping and flashing like a Gay Day Parade drag float. So OK. I hammer across Mission, down this tiny alley that cuts into what I'm hoping is lucky side-street number last, hang a left wrong way down the one-way once again, bunny hop the curb, and go flying into a pair of headlights. I can feel the fender whoosh by my leg, and I'm swooping out of the alley, dancing to the mellifluous strains of tires screeching, pig squealing, big bike crashing. See, the Law thinks he can ignore the law, but no one beats the law like a bicycle, chump.

Me, I'm cruising, smiling, heading for sanctuary in the toilet at Jack's bar.

SUBMISSION

I clean out the needle, holding it under running water, pulling the plunger back. I turn off the water, squirt the nastiness into the sink. Pink drops, bloody water. I flush the toilet for effect.

I can hit myself in the time it takes most girls to piss. Got to make it look real, or they start banging on the door and fuck up your whole high.

I roll down my sleeve, slip into my jacket, look in the mirror past the lipstick graffiti that says JOE SO FINE. Shit is good. I can tell by looking in my eyes. I'm fucked up, all warm and slow and fast. Blood's pounding in my ears *doozh . . . doozh . . . doozh.*

But you can't relax and enjoy. You got to face them, the public, some girl waiting to powder her nose in the little girls' room, she's right in your face when you open the door. Yeah baby, if I had any left, I'd powder your nose, alright.

You got to get out and look like James Dean, before they figure out what you're doing in there.

Funny, if you stay in the can too long, they figure you're banging dope, but if you hurry and open the door rushing your brains out with eyes like onyx marbles, they never get it. And you can't let them know, because if they know, they stare, and then you get paranoid, and it's twenty bucks down the drain.

So I stumble out into the light and sound. Everything's moving and flowing and loud. You can't separate the words out. Words are falling all over each other, yelling, talking, laughing, flirting, fighting, singing along with the jukebox, all tumbling into a pile of neon spears, surrounding me like a kaleidoscope tunnel, the curl of a wave I'm riding while staying perfectly dry. At the end of the tunnel is a circle of focus in which Rosemary's quietly tapping a pint of ale.

"JIM," she sails out my name like a floaty boat over the beery sea.

Damn, she spotted me. Now there's no sneaking out the door.

I slouch down, relax my jaw, and droop my eyelids Elvis style. I am not amping balls at all. I am cool, stoned, a bee charmer. You cannot see the atoms smashing out of my skin, you cannot feel the thermonuclear heat radiating off me, I'm an icy clear deep lake. No diving. No lifeguard on duty.

"D'ya wanna beer-r-r," she yells, waving an empty pint, so I nod yeah.

She draws it and hands it over. I slosh some down. My throat's too tight to chug it, but the wet's nice in my mouth. I lean on the jukebox, browsing, struggling to get more beer down.

Rosemary's back over at this end of the bar, trying to yell a conversation over the noise. I love her, and when I get drunk and we pass out together at her house, I try to get snuggly with her, even though she's devoutly straight and always pushes me away. But tonight I can't look at her. I can't let her see me like this.

I mumble, "Gotta go." My tongue doesn't know what to do, how to build words, so I keep them short.

She still doesn't get it. "Whatsh? Where're ya goin'?" Her Dublin accent gets thicker when she's had a few. The "sh" on the end of "whatsh" gets more pronounced.

I try again. Concentrate. Enunciate. I g-o-t-t-a g-o. It still runs together, sticky. No spit. Aw fuck it. I smile an apology and turn around, so I don't have to see her worry.

The night's like night, with invisible wet, and I glide to the bike, free of human interaction. What stress humanity is. The Krypto-brand U-lock comes apart in my hand. Everything's automatic. My leg slings over the seat and I coast down the sidewalk, bounce off the curb, resilient, slow like a Cadillac, with luxury suspension.

Rain fell while I was inside, and my tires go *kshhh* on the street. I'm alone, no cars drowning out little sounds. That means lateness. Frayed thread of memory slithers between my ears. Ally Cat. Oh shit. Oh fuck oh fuck oh fuck. I gotta fly. I gotta fly I gotta jam I gotta haul fuckin' ass. Blood's coursing in my temples, push down on the pedal, skip the wet metal, water's flinging itself in a stream up my legs, up my back, I haven't got around to winterizing my bike. I got to find her. Wonder if she waited, how much time went by while I was dinging around, out of my head, having fun serving myself when it's way more fun serving her. Left on Mission. Yeah, she's waiting, how late could it be? All I did was cop, roll over to Jack's bar, slam, and bail. What the hell.

You fucked up. You jerk, you're blowing it. She's gonna be pissed and throwing shade if she is there. Scared of that. And you deserve whatever she dishes out, junkie loser.

Ah shaddup. Come on, be there baby, come on, come on.

There's the root beer–metal flake '64 Chevy pickup parked by the liquor store, there's the guy getting out. The door opens like in a dream, I yell LOOGOUT and swerve, but the edge of the door catches my knuckle and the grip of my sawed-off handlebar, and I'm rag dollying. Flying up instead of across, silent, turning around in the air like an Olympic diver, horizontal on my back six feet up in the air, suspended beautifully, my arms stretched out to greet the gods, stargazing. The stars are out. There's no sound. SMACK. I hit the asphalt and everything gets real again. The sound starts up and nothing's slo-mo no more. And I'm thinking, *Hmm, I should give up the organ-donor life and wear a skid lid, like Mom says.*

A woman's gravel-truck voice dumps a load: "Are you OK?" Someone helps me up. Oh. I'm among friends. Good. I shake my head and start to hold a lecture on door opening, when out of the side of my eye, I see a guy step off the curb.

He says, "What are you doin'? What the fuck are you doin'?!"

I look at him and say, "I'm gettin' doored, what the fuck's it look like I'm doin'. Please, bitch." See, I don't think before I talk, is the thing. . . . That's a problem my mom always said I had. She said, "Plug in your brain before you turn on your mouth." But no, I do not heed words of wisdom. I open my big yap, and then I look at how glassy the man's eyes are as he rushes me, then in those eyes I see the need to kill things, then I smell the Night Train on his breath and feel the King Coma spittle mist my face, then I feel him clock me, scabby knuckled swollen fist, *then* I think I should have been more diplomatic. Definitely the wrong order.

I'm fumbling to get my lock out of my back pocket, heavy steel encased in black plastic, but I fall over my bike and he's coming after me again. I get the Krypto in my fist, high over my head.

He says, "Fucking HIT me, come on. . . ."

"I'm 'onna fuckin' kill you I'm 'onna cut your dick off and shove it down your throat, dogshit."

Just as I'm thinking, *Can I do it, yeah he's no match for me, him drunk and the Mr. Hyde serum flowing through me,* and I'm focusing on the exact point on the bridge of his nose where I will make contact, it's *Night of the Living Dead.* All his sleazy pals are circling me, lurching out of shadowy doorways.

Shit.

"O-OK everybody, back off, I got AIDS, man, you don't wanna get my blood on you, you'll die, just step off." This could very well be true, I don't know, but they don't give a shit. They're all Mr. Risk. I jump on my bike and take off yelling faggot. That always gets straight guys, because while you're making your getaway, they are scratching their heads wondering if that circle jerk they had five years ago makes them gay.

Then I'm riding, riding, in my getaway car that makes the wind that soothes my jaw, swept away from adversity by pedals that move legs that move pedals. I'm escaped, on my own, lugging stung pride.

What's up with kicking a guy when he's down.

What are you gonna tell Ally, why you ran away like a big chicken-shit?

Aw, she thinks that's smart, she thinks I'm a sensitive guy, she hates fights. So I could at least have an excuse for being late now, she'll feel sorry for me, and I'll get some good old petting and cooing. Then I could work it and say, You should have seen the other guy, and I'll tell her how I got him on the ground and was whacking him, slamming him with my Krypto, Teach you to abuse someone who's already been laid out and can't fend for themselves, *slam, slam, smack,* right in the head with my steel toe, until he wasn't moving. But she hates fights.

So here we are, Shmiegel Blow World. I run in and ask the bouncer if Sister Aqua Divina is there, because I got strict orders from Ally only to use her stage name, she don't want weirdos knowing anything about her real life, even people that work there, because stalkers would be lurking, and she would have to kill them, and she doesn't want to ruin a perfectly good dress, so I just always ask for Sister Aqua Divina. Anyway Fridge with a Head says she's gone, so I run out the door and jump on it all the way to her studio in North Beach, pumping up Columbus, park in front of Grant 'n' Green Blues Bar and ring her bell. She opens the window upstairs and leans out.

"What," she says.

"Hey, lemme in."

She closes the window. I wait around, whistle, *"The soul of a woman was created below. . . ."* Ring the doorbell again.

She leans out the window. "WHAT."

"Come on, honey. Lemme in."

She closes the window. I light a smoke. She opens the door and stands there looking at me, making no move to let me in.

"Hi, darlin'. Sorry I'm late, I got ambushed and—" I'm trying to step inside, but she doesn't budge.

"Get. Out."

"But baby, look, I'm bleedin'." I point to my eyebrow.

She body blocks me. "More than your eye is going to be bleeding if you try to take one more step inside this door."

Damn. My incredible charm is not working. What could be wrong? "Come on, cupcake, lemme explain. . . ."

"Don't explain. I understand perfectly. You are a fuckup. A liar, a cheat, and a speed fiend. And I have no use for the likes of your company. Good night," she says, and closes the door.

"But sweetums."

She's so cold, like an ice cream cone.

PAPER BOX

I'm a bike messenger in love with a stripper and I guess I always will be.

When I first saw her, she was standing naked on a stage strewn with boxers, bras, and beer bottles. Well, OK. It wasn't the *first* time I saw her. We hung in the same circles. But it was the first time I saw the gold light and heard the humming of a supernatural cosmic intelligence. See, Ally was just a stripper to put herself through college. In real life, she was a modern-day Joan of Arc.

She was in a postpunkshow trance.

The punkest band in history, named after a midwestern macro-brew, had just played, getting naked, roaring around, spitting on everyone, getting spat on, and yelling in harmony, "TONIGHT . . . WE'RE GONNA . . . FUCK SHIT UP. . . ." Three lead singers, two girls and a naked, ill-endowed boy with all-American good looks, clawing his naked chest bloody, and Ally was the queen of them all. Between them, there was so much ego, it neutralized ego, and ego overflowed off the stage and into the whole house. That's why they were the house band.

After the show, I ran to the liquor store and bought her an ass pocket of whiskey and a Coke.

I went up to her and said, "You sounded beautiful tonight," and presented her with the alcoholic offering.

She said, "Hey, Jim, you live in the city. I need a place to live there. Let me know if you hear of anything?"

She dug in her jacket and pulled out an old receipt and a lipstick, smushed her name and number out, and handed it to me. Then she kept listening to the rest of the worshipers posing as pals. They must have been worshiping, because anyone could see she was God.

I ran outside to brag.

"Frankie, Frankie, look what I got. Allisandra Dellacava's number in *lipstick*." Frankie smirked. Nobody was impressed. Amused at how impressed I was. After all, it wasn't like Ally was a big famous superstar. That would be wrong, anyway, as punk is the antistar machine. And being in love might be wrong too, as punk is also the anti-romance machine. I piped down and stood around staring at my paper scrap for a while. Then I folded it very carefully, so it wouldn't smudge, and put it in my front jacket pocket next to my heart.

I still have that receipt to prove what's mine.

She is the future. She ponders the magnitude of her brilliance, more awestruck by her own genius than anyone else, because only she is deep enough to see her own depth. She loves to talk about death. Says, Prepare to let go. I love her so much, obsession becomes paranoia. Strippers, they live dangerous. And dangerous men want Ally. She inspires marriage proposals from strangers on the street. It's only a matter of time before someone's driven insane by the need to possess her, as I am. I ride home at night with visions of her wide-open green eyes peering out of a Dumpster, blood everywhere. It would have to be like that, like her life, designed to shock you into reality. Slit throat and me calling *Ally*. Prayers to defuse prophecy. I don't care if we never fuck again. I just want to watch her ascent and disintegration, because anything burning that bright one day must consume itself and float away, an ash, and no one has the power to stop it. It's flirting with disaster to love someone that much, someone who's always on the brink of going away. I know she doesn't need saving, but I dream of saving her, of rolling a rock up the mountain and being flattened by it as it rolls back over me all the way to the bottom again. And then I push it right back to the top, because if it takes this much sweat it must be worth it.

Obsessed with angels, she's divinely twisted. She builds neon-winged sculptures, and in black ink she scratches out demonic, sunken-eyed, jowly, pear-shaped angels that she thinks look like her, with bat-wing claws. She doesn't see what we see when she looks at herself.

One night, before the punkrock show, we walked down the train tracks from Gilman to the industrial waste park and crawled in a cement tube. We fucked like it was the first time and the last time, and then I smoothed down her dress and said, tell me what the world looks like now. I loved to hear what she saw in her post-fuck bliss, how I was better than drugs, so she closed her eyes and described the patterns behind her eyelids.

"Well, let's see, it looks like fish-food flakes, the suspension of matter, like a relief map. There are windows of a fifties' flying saucer. It's viscosity, like no color I know, gaseous, waferlike, a frosted glass orb about a light, a cool air hollow space. I am afraid to go where things don't exist yet, there or here, and the atmosphere is cool like the breathing of the dead."

I said, "I fuckin' love you."

She said, "I'd live in a paper box with you."

JERK OF ALL TRADES

When frustrated or annoyed, ride up a hill. It's always a relief. You are so busy sweating and straining, you do not have time to be annoyed, and your own heart swoops you up like a hawk and carries you far, far from your troubles, and drops you off at the top of the hill, in a state of exhaustion which some people call relaxed. The idea is to put as much distance between you and sadness as you can.

I could take the Broadway tunnel to Polk Gulch and find Pez, but that would be the flat way. There is a flat way to everywhere in San Francisco, which is handy to know in a hilly town when you're tired, but I ain't tired. I have to work out this hurt she put on me, so I climb straight up, three vertical blocks past the cool dark mouth of the tunnel with the headlights roaring through. I stop at the top of the mountain for a smoke to catch my breath and contemplate my sins. Below, the city's candle-lit. Through my wavy wobbly eyes, it's laserlike stars throwing silver swords.

I bet she's still mad about last week too, when she said I could beat her with words. I didn't know anything about it, before she said that. I thrashed and thrashed her, without ever touching her. I watched her cower and cringe, get small. I couldn't see why. All I did was tell her in no unfucking certain terms just exactly what the hell it was that she had done to me, and how I suffered when she didn't give it up and fuck like normal girlfriends are supposed to do, and how I would just have to go out and find a girl who *would* fuck, and so what if she had been diddling herself all day for money in front of every Tom's Dick that's Hairy, so what if she was tired, if she loved me, she would have saved some for me. Nothing she could say or do would redeem her.

She just curled up like a pill bug and got littler and littler until she was nothing, and she didn't say nothing no more, and I was done. I felt better, relaxed, cooled down. I laid next to her like nothing happened, and she didn't breathe or slink under my touch, so I just rolled over on my back like a king and dreamed easy. I could feel her turn away and stare for a long time into the dark.

I felt lowdown and mean about myself the next day.

You're a fucking asshole. She never did nothing to hurt you.

Yeah, well, sometimes I just want to yell, and I'm hoping she'll yell back, but she never does. Sometimes yelling's the only way I can feel alive. Breathing. Like riding up a hill. Like speed. I like it when I can hear my blood pump, my motor roar.

But you knew you was bad. And all the times you made off with her cash and got wired and drunk, you're a jerk.

I thought she could handle herself. She don't need me.

I don't know why she stuck with you this long.

There must be something wrong with her.

She's an angel. You're just like everyone you hate.

Yeah, I'm a fuckup, but, hell, I love her. She doesn't have to be the Ice Princess. So what. I don't care. I got plenty to do and plenty of pals, and plenty of girls got crushes on me. They're no good, but at least I could get some kind of babes.

But she's the best babe there is, ever. Poet genius punkstar.

Who needs her. Not me. She thinks she's so high and mighty. High maintenance. High standards. Fine. She's just a pain in my ass anyway. I'm the president of the He-Man Woman-Haters Club.

I start rolling down the other side of the mountain. The street's starting to dry up. I flick my smoke and yell yippee. I'm picking up speed. It's nice, no streetcars, no cars at all. I'm screaming through red lights, wheels spinning so fast pedaling makes no difference, flying off plateaus at every intersection, catching major sky, landing halfway down the block. Whee. High Priest of the Asphalt. If you yell yeeha no brakes, and there's no peds to scare, does it make a sound? I zip around the corner at Polk, coast uphill a block, and there's Pez, where she always leans against the lamppost.

I like old Pez. She's a yes man. There's times you need a guy who's going to smile and be in a semi-decent mood, no matter what. She always listens like she's interested, and doesn't give you a lot of back yak about what you ought to do.

She always looks so cool. She's got that little-boy look chicks go for, not to mention men. I wish I had that look down as good as she does, because that's how I feel inside, like a fourteen-year-old boy. It'd be nice to have your insides match your outsides. Then again, I wouldn't want anyone seeing *my* insides.

She's got the scruffy crewcut that's a new color every week, and she wears the oldest vintage band shirts, like original Germs, with the sleeves cut out real low so you could see her tits if she had any, but she doesn't. She sports her tracks like she doesn't care who sees them, because she's a track star, she says, and her eyes are always pinpointy and blue and cheerfully satanic. She wears that same PSYCHOBUNNY baseball hat backwards all the time.

Usually she has a sugar mama that she talks into shooting smack with her, which sucks, because they're usually these sweet, young, immaculate things that never seen a needle before in their life, who end up all strung out, stripping or whoring to support her. It's ugly. But when she's in between babes she has to work for a living.

"Pez. My pal."

"Hey, Bub." She looks me over. "Uh-oh. What's the matter?"

"Nothing but a old Ally Cat."

"Female trouble."

"She don't love me no more. If she did, it would be forever and no matter what, but it's always *if* I don't steal her money and *if* I don't go out and get high, and *if* she doesn't catch me runnin' with no other hoes. That's . . . what is it . . . conditional love, isn't it."

"Hmm. Yep, well, they are touchy about those things."

"I love her forever and no matter what. But she doesn't give two shits about me. She's a liar. Got her nerve calling me a liar. I never lie on purpose. I always plan for what I'm sayin' to be the truth. Sometimes it just don't work out the way I planned, that's all."

Pez puts her arm around my shoulder. "That's how girls are.

They're contrary. They like to stir up excitement, to stave off boredom, see."

"Yeah, I do that. But I think if you love somebody, you should let 'em be free and do what they want and be who they are, that's real love. I don't never tell her what she can't do. I never say, 'Don't strip, I'm jealous of those skanky customers.'"

"You should tell her if you don't want her dancing."

"But I do, I think it's hot, it's her deal. Why can't she get off on me livin' my crazy life too. . . ."

"Sometimes they just want you to show 'em who's boss."

"Well, no, not Ally. She's definitely the boss. If I try to show her otherwise, I just end up sorry for livin', so there's no point, really. . . ."

Up rolls this Japanese import brand-new coupe, slow with the passenger-side window rolled down and a clean-cut creep inside.

Pez says, "Hey, this guy likes someone to watch. Ya wanna make some money?"

Shit, not this again. I'm just not in the mood. It makes my skin crawl. But what the fuck, it's not like I have a whole worthwhile evening planned, a fancy date or anything. Plus, I could use the cash. She's leaning in his window.

She saunters back over to me and says, "Now, remember, I'm a boy, so don't blow my cover and say 'she' or somethin' stupid, OK? Come on."

She climbs in the car, and I follow on my bike down the block to Cockroach Motel.

There's a green fluorescent glow in the lobby and a layer of grease and nicotine on the walls. The carpet's mildewy with piss and beer, dotted with hard black holes in the shape of smokes dropped by the fingers of a thousand dreaming junkies.

A big sign blares NO GUESTS, so we sneaky snake in the elevator and glide, noiseless, into her room, the one with the aluminum number six nailed to the door and two more sixes tagged next to it in fat black marker.

So now Sleazebag, he doesn't waste any time getting his worm out. Ally could spot 'em a mile away. *Customer,* she'd whisper, until I realized there is no social hierarchy, all men are created equal when you get them alone. They all wanna get their rocks off and get their money's worth, or more than that if they can.

Pez sets him straight about the sequence of things and gets the ducats up front. Forty skins, twenty for taking it and twenty for me watching. She jams the cash in her pocket, turns around and unbuttons her pants. Family Man grabs her from behind, one hand gripping her hipbone and the other pulling his big old greasy member the rest of the way out of his pants. It's a grower not a show-er: I'm slouched up against the wall. I catch my breath. Damn. No grease. But then Pez sticks her hand in her jacket pocket, pulls it out cupped and dripping Astroglide, and slimes the lube up her crack just in time. He pushes his naked knob right in her old brown eye. I can feel the spit start to puddle in my mouth. I can't help it.

It doesn't take him long to stop grunting and muttering about altar boys. He whips out a clean white folded hankie, wipes the shit off his dick, zips up, and slips out the door.

Pez hands me the twenty.

"Ah fuck it, you did all the work. It was my pleasure."

"No, get outta here. Keep it. I need a bodyguard anyway."

" 'Kay, fine, so what about a rubber. Still don't believe in 'em, huh?"

"I do, I just ran out. I gotta get more at the needle exchange."

"You are blowin' it so bad."

"No it's cool, he's a regular. Since when are you so health-conscious, anyway?"

"I'm not. It doesn't take a genius to figure it out. There's a plague. You get it by gettin' fucked up the ass and sharin' bloody rigs, that's all."

"Yeah, well, he's married. I'm the only one he fucks. He doesn't even touch the old lady anymore."

"LIES. Hey, lemme see your dick."

She shows me her nylon stocking stuffed with hair gel.

"Aren't you supposed to get hard when he's fuckin' you up the ass?"

"Yeah. You gotta choose. Hard all the time or soft all the time. You don't let 'em touch you anyway, it's just in case they cop a free grope."

"Izzat right."

"Why so curious, Bub? You wanna turn tricks? I told you I'd show you the ropes. Hook you up anytime."

I can't see myself letting any old guy off the street pack my peanut butter, although there is a certain attraction-revulsion thing watching it. Actually, I gotta hand it to old Pez. She's more hard-core than I'll ever be. She don't care about nothing. I mean, you never know what a guy'll do once he gets you alone in that room. I'd rather be smeared across the pavement than found naked and bloody on a bare buggy mattress.

"I'll stick to *pedalin'* my ass all over town, but thanks. You never do know when things are gonna get desperate."

"Come on, let's go see the man."

"I don't ride that horse."

"I know. Don't trip, he's got more than smack. Go-fast, weed, crack. He's the A.M. / P.M. fuckin' mini mart."

I follow her out. The sky's turning light. I'm not thinking about Ally Cat no more.

TAKIN' WHAT THEY'RE GIVIN'

I need time alone. I get my stash and go to Bernal Heights up in one of the secret garden staircases between houses, in the sweetest nook of jasmine that peers out on the brightest dawn, to do the sanguinary deed. The sky's like it is just before light, then the sun's painting windows on Noe Valley with gold leaf. It's gorgeously private.

I take in the light through wide-open pupils and superdark shades until it's time to ride my bike for money. The birds are tweeting full blast. The haze is gold, and the air still smells sweet and balmy cold. I zip through the Mission down Folsom. The old leather boys are squinting home from their one-night stands. I race traffic on automatic pilot and glory in my third consecutive sunrise without a wink of sleep.

I waltz up to the dispatch window.

Marty Repulski, a small ducklike character with bad skin, gives me his Bette Davis look. "Oh, Sixty-One," he says, "to what do we owe this honor?"

"Yeah, yeah, just gimme a radio. What." So what if he's the captain of my fate all day, deciding my fortune and whether he'll give me any rushes. So what if Repulski makes me rich, or gives me the shit tags. If he doesn't feed me, I'll drink beers behind Harvey's Liquors, living on the tab that Saint Harvey extends to those too drunk to get good runs, drowning failure till I'm too drunk to ever get good runs.

You don't know what I'm talking about do you. Rushes. Those are the fifteen-minute and thirty-minute deliveries that messengers call gravy, because they pay the most amount of commission in the shortest amount of time. Hence feeding, as in gravy, that's what the dispatcher does when he gives you good runs. A run is a whole bunch of high-paying tags along the same route, so you can make more money per hour than when he's starving you, that is, giving you only one tag at a time, or just shit tags, which the client is in no hurry to get, therefore the price is low, therefore your pay is shit.

Who cares about Repulski. You always know when he has a hangover, because he's reading that big blue AA book, and your day is about to suck.

Then I see him. The big boss. McGinnis, the kind of nerd who has phone sex instead of a girlfriend. Not to supplement his sex life, but to simulate one. And you know his dick is so small, that's why he has to lord it over you all the time.

The look on his face is always, *Smirk, smirk, I'm so relaxed and superior, I make out your checks, so grovel, submit and be mortified, lowly peasant, and work your ass off.*

He likes to make you squirm, but he just makes me want to spit. I can see the lecture brewing right now.

"Good morning, Elizabeth." He's constipated.

"Good mornin' Mr. McGinnis. But it's not Elizabeth, it's Jim, just so you know."

"Oh? We don't make your checks out to Jim. I distinctly remember making them out to—"

"Yeah, I know. The deal is, I don't feel like explainin' right this second, but take my word for it, it's JIM, OK? Hey, Repulski, can I get a radio?"

"Isn't Jim a boy's name?"

"Am I a boy?"

"No . . ."

"OK, I guess Jim ain't a boy's name then, is it? Yo, Repulski."

But McGinnis is just getting started, with how they hired me back on good faith because I promised things would be different, but they're not different and I'm STILL never here, and where was I yesterday, it's Tuesday, most people start the week with Monday, I can't wander in whenever the mood strikes, and I'm thinking, *Is that so? I thought it* was *Monday. It's Tuesday already?*

"And where's your uniform? We can't have you riding around out of uniform now, can we Elizabeth?"

Why can't we? "Jim. Please. Call me Jim."

"Do you even *have* a uniform?" he says.

"Yeah, but more importantly, I need a RADIO to actually do tags." I stare down old Marty until he forks it over. Neither of these assholes controls me, because once I'm outta here, they can't see me smoking herb, getting laid, or cussing them out while not holding down the button on the radio, their only connection to me, which *I* control. "It's been lovely chatting, but I have to go downtown now."

I bang the door extra loud on the way out of the hallway into the locker room. Empty beer bottles from Friday night, bike parts, grease rags. I open my locker and dig through a pile of moldy uniforms. I know I stashed a beer in here. There it is. Warm breakfast suds to go.

I jump on my bike and I'm gliding downtown. The crispiness of the air makes me think of my old pal, Roo Camacho, and that day when we were eight, and we cut school, and it was springtime and flowery just like today, only then it was quiet, and we rode over people's front lawns as we rounded corners, instead of mowing down drunks.

I loved Roo because she was the smokinest, cussinest, treefort-buildinest, shoplifting little fuck in the whole third grade. She had two sisters named Norma and Gisele, whom we secretly called Normaldehyde and Grizelda. They were about eight or nine years older than her. My mom said that meant Roo was a mistake. But I couldn't see anything wrong with her. I thought she was perfect.

Anyway, that day we acted like we were going to school, and then we met on the corner and rode to the vacant lot to hide out. When we figured everyone had left Roo's house to go to work and school, we snuck back there for provisions. We laid our bikes down on her weedy front lawn and busted in the door giggling, and there were her sisters and their boyfriends, sitting on the sofa with their hands in places where it ain't fitting for churchgoing folks' hands to be. We all gave out a synchronized yell, us saying "yaa" and them saying "Lucinda!," as that was her name and not Roo at all, see, although they usually called her Roo, except when they were mad, and then they called her Lucinda. Which made it handy because then you could know when it was time to leave.

As I reached for the doorknob, Roo grabbed my arm and pointed to the coffee table. There was a framed photograph of the sisters at their first communion, in white starchy petticoats and white bobby socks with lace trim, holding bunches of flowers, their faces all shined up and ready to say ten Hail Marys, and on the glass covering the picture were lines and heaps of white powder, almost but not quite blending in with their white dresses, and a stripy spoon straw from the 7-Eleven cut down to two inches.

Roo said it looked like we'd found ourselves in a helluva bargaining position and began to negotiate. She directed me to get a paper bag out of the kitchen. We put in a can of Coors, two Kool Filter Kings, a pack of matches, and four potato chip and mayo sandwiches. Then we thanked them very graciously, sailed out, and had a fabulous day in the tree fort.

That was just one of the things I learned from old Roo. You've got to keep your eye out for opportunities, and fuck them before they fuck you, because, like she always said, "It's a doggie-dog world out there."

So I'm moseying downtown and I go to the Wall. It's a three-foot-high wall around a toy store for rich grownups, full of gadgets no messenger can afford. Messengers meet there and get high, hanging out in the sun, waiting for tags, yelling "Get hot" at any passing messengers who are working, which means "Go faster." Nomads, gypsies, they need a central place to meet. Ours is the Wall, or as we affectionately call it, Wally World.

I see Luigi Con Carne and Scott and Buzz, Hugh Hefner's bastard son or so he says, passing the morning pipeload and talking about Scott's two-headed turtle that eats out of both heads.

The nice thing about messengering is, you got pals you can hang out with for a while, but you're not stuck with them. All day you're alone, riding around, thinking to yourself, and, once in a while, you can turn down the dickscratcher blabbing nonstop on the radio and have total silence. But then you get so lonesome, you appreciate seeing your buddies. You never get sick of them, like you would if you worked in an Orange Julius stand right next to them, day in, day out. And then it's really important to talk about your adventures to pals that get it, because the shit that happens out there is too much for TV, and there's no one to tell, "Whoa, did you see that shit? That was fucked up." And whenever you try to talk about it to the old lady, her eyes just glaze over and she changes the subject, not seeing it's killing you that your whole life and everything you are bores her to tears.

Whereas your buddies, they been through the same gnarly shit all day, riding alone, getting yelled at and run down by people in cages, and they know. So you're mavericks, all alone, but you belong to this fellowship, like Knights of the Round Table who come home to share the glories of ass kickings and grail hunting.

I pop the top on my breakfast.

Con Carne, he's telling us about the asshole who cut him off in a Beamer and started yelling at Con Carne like *he* was a threat on his ten-pound bike to a guy in a ton of steel, and so he loogied in the open window at the guy, right on his red power tie.

And then Scott says, "Yeah, that's nothin', I was cruisin' around the corner in North Beach onto a one-way street, and this lady comes roaring out in a red sports car, and I go flying into her windshield head first, and I'm lying there on the hood staring at her through the cracked glass and she's all 'AAAGH!'"

"Shit howdy, so then what'd ya do?"

"I pulled my Krypto outta my pocket and said ya want somethin' to scream about lady? I'll fix *all* your windows but good."

He passes me the pipe.

I eyeball it. "Hey, this is my granddaddy's pipe."

"No, it isn't. No, it isn't," says Buzz. He always says, if you can't say it twice, don't say it at all.

"Yes, it is."

"Is not. Is not."

"Is. It's his sixty-two-year-old corncob pipe. My Grandpa's, on my dad's side."

"Gimme that," says Scott, "and quit bogarting." I suck down a cloud of skunk and pass it on.

"Well it's mine now. It's mine now," says Buzz. "You gave it to me at the kegger the other night."

"Did not."

"Did too. Did too."

"I wouldn't because it's a family fuckin' heirloom, asshole."

"You did, and that's tough titty said the kitty and the milk's all dry, because I traded you a bag of speed fair and square. So shut up. Shut up with yer family heirloom." He's laughing. "I got yer heirloom hangin'."

I hear my mom in my head saying, "Possession is nine-tenths of the law." She loves to say that.

Scott passes me the pipe. I shove it in my pocket, still hot against my leg, run for my bike, jump on it, and fly off the curb yelling, "NYAH-nyah."

I wave 'bye and pump up Market Street to a phone.

IF MOMS WERE GIRLS

I can't stop thinking about Ally. She can't be over it. She's trying to break my heart. Well she can't. No lousy girl's going to break my heart, even a brainy Hollywood movie star–looking girl.

The first and last girl to break my heart was Sandy Clooney, when I was fifteen. I stood on her front lawn, yelling, "It's not over," with my fists balled up and my lip sticking out. I was determined to stand there until she came out and took it back, that she was through with me and was gonna go out with that lame disco bunny Julie Milton, the cool chick with the hip polyester clothes, who probably read *The Joy of Lesbian Sex* and cut to the chase instead of standing there staring at the unexpected vision of breasts. I would have got it, eventually. Patience is a thing Sandy didn't have though. She wanted McOrgasm. And I really couldn't blame old Julie Milton for stepping in, elbowing me out of the way, and giving it to her.

I stood on the lawn, half waiting for Sandy's asshole dad to come out and tell me to stop yelling, and then I yelled some more. "I said, it's not over. This isn't it."

The door opened and she stuck out her face with its perfect bone structure and straight teeth, her hazel eyes flashing under long lashes.

She said, "Oh yes it is," and slammed the door.

Even then, I yearned for girls who were too beautiful to love me, dorky nerd boy. I waited for the princess to point and laugh at me, and reveled in my annihilation. Drama queen of a child, I listened to *La Boheme* on the record player and cried as Mimi died of . . . what was it, consumption? I craved tragedy like a big faggot. To this day, to thrill me, all a girl has to say is "no."

My face got hot. I threw down my skateboard and skated as hard as I could all the way home. With tears blowing past my ears in the warm jasmine air, I skated up the driveway, popped the board up and caught it. I ran in the house. Mom was cooking dinner and she had on her pink chef's apron, with tits and a belly button and a fig leaf painted on it.

I was crying and blubbering, so she turned off the stove and held me and sat me down on her lap and listened to me whimper and sniff about how much I loved that girl and was in love with her too, and how could she, and I was hiccuping and wailing.

Mom flipped open the totally cool mahogany wet bar that was the centerpiece of our living room, like the TV is in others'.

She designed it and Dad built it, and I loved to impress my friends with it when Mom and Dad weren't home. Dad was a thorough guy. It took him months to build this behemoth. Not that he was much of a drinker or looked forward to using it. It's just he liked working his ass off to make something perfect, which made sense to me. And then he could stand there all proud and say, "I made that."

It was always a comfort to know that inside it were plenty of fancy alcoholic flavors to go down smooth and salve a wounded soul. A medicine chest to fit American and European tastes. Scotch, bourbon, vodka for Dad's friends and family; Rémy Martin, Pernod, Grand Marnier, Poire William for Mom and hers. Cocktails, ginger ale, five cents a glass for me and all my pals playing hooky. This eight-foot-long, four-hundred-pound chunk of furniture was the cornerstone of our lives, where the love came from, and the solace, whence flowed the glue that bonded us together.

Mom reached in and pulled out the cognac and poured us a couple of snifters, then lit a cigarette and petted me.

I quieted down, and she told me about the actor she fell in love with, the one who went to the boys' school around the corner from her girls' school. Her parents said she was too young to date, but he stole a kiss or two. He signed a photograph for her, "With love, Axel." Then he went to war. She went and got the photo album and showed me the brown-and-white picture with the fountain pen autograph.

Mom said, "See? If I had stayed with him, I wouldn't have met your father, and there would be no you."

"But me and Sandy aren't gonna make babies. . . ."

"There will be other girls."

"Not like that one."

"Someday there will be an even better one."

"I highly doubt *that*."

She pulled a Marlene Dietrich record out of its jacket, laid it on the turntable, and lowered the needle. Dietrich crooned about why would you cry when you split up, when there's another one already standing on the next corner; you say, so long, and think secretly, I'm finally rid of that ball and chain. Mom sang along in German, appropriately out of tune, sexy, and deep as Nietzsche. Nothing could make the hurt go away like Mom did, not even a good hard skate to the tree fort or a fat snifter of Courvoisier.

I had plenty of babes since Sandy Clooney, but I always watched out. Pretty soon, along comes Eurobabe. I loved her a lot because I never knew her long enough to hate her, but also because, ever since I was a kid, I wanted me a girl just like the one who married dear old Dad, so I had a thing for German girls. It doesn't make sense for a guy like me to try to get love from a German, because everyone knows Germans are hardasses, very serious, anal perfectionists with no sense of humor, unless they're Berliners, like my mom, then they're *sarcastic* hardass anal perfectionists.

And you gotta have a sense of humor to go out with *me,* know what I'm saying? So this Eurobabe, she was no Berliner. But I smashed beer cans on my head and did other Belushi impersonations. There's a certain satisfaction you can get from making sad girls laugh. She was virtuous and sweet and hurt by her dad, so of course I loved her. She was too pure for this world. She had been tyrannized; I thought she should be canonized. I loved toiling to draw her out of the cloud that she floated on above me, and when I did touch her just right, the payoff was pure Vegas. I chased and chased her ethereal ass, not-there girl, hide-and-seek girl, space baby.

"I need my space," she said.

I said to her, "Eurobabe, you are the alpha and the omega, worship, worship, worship."

She said, "Be careful you don't lose your heart."

I said, "Don't worry, it's surfer love. If you're a gnarly reckless surfer who rides a lotta waves and wipes out a lot, you don't want to go swimmin' after your board every time you wipe out. So you have a leash, which is a three-foot bungee cord looped around your ankle, and the other end's laced through a hole in the end of your board. My heart's bungeed to my ankle the same way, see.

"There's only one downer. . . . Every now and then, when you wipe out harshly, the force of the wave sucks the board way down deep and then lets go, snap, with a slingshot effect, so the board becomes a missile and shoots straight out of the water at ninety miles an hour and smacks you in the head and kills you."

So I'm riding and stopping at every phone booth but of course no phone works, and then finally I find one that works, and I call Ally Cat.

Her sexy voice answers.

So I'm all, "Hey, darlin'."

"Get away."

"Honey. Honey . . ."

"Scram. Leave me alone."

"Aw jeez, how can you be so mean. I feel bad enough."

"Do you feel bad? Poor baby. Why don't you call your mother." She hangs up.

Call my mother, I can't call my mother. It's always the same spiel: "What are you doing with your life? You're such a genius. You should be in college. You'd make such a good lawyer."

I call my mother.

"You love to argue and you're a big asshole. Why don't you go to law school?"

"Because, Mom, I don't want to be a lawyer with a two-by-four up my ass always worrying about this deadline and that case. There's no justice anyway."

"You can go into family law . . ."

"I need fresh air and sunshine. I can't deal with that fluorescent light. It warps my nervous system. Anyway I can't talk. I gotta go. I got a date."

"Oh? With whom? That Roseanne Roseanna Danna girl?"

"Allisandra Dellacava. God I hate that. You always do that. You do it on purpose. Dad always hated that too. Bet he still does."

"What. I'm bad with names. And there's no need to bring your father into it."

"Yes there is. I need backup. You deliberately say people's names wrong to indicate your disdain for them. Can you say passive aggressive? You know her name's not Roseanne Roseanna Danna."

"Well, how should I know. You've got a new one every week. I can't keep up."

"I do not. She's the love of my life."

"Hmmph. That's what you said about Randy Poontang."

"Sandy Clooney!"

"And you've had a million girls since her. Why don't you find yourself a nice lawyer? Look at Judith, she's a lawyer, civilized, secure. . . ."

"Yeah, she's a babe, and she and I would last two minutes. Look at me Mom. I'm a bike messenger. I date strippers, not lawyers."

Silence. "Is that all you ever think about? Sex? When that wears off, you're going to need some intellectual stimulation."

"Ally stimulates plenty of intellectuals. . . . It's not *about* sex. . . . That's her job, we hang out *after* work. . . . *God.* Mom."

"So. Why don't you let me take you shopping. We'll get you out of those godawful combat boots and ripped T-shirts. That all-black thing is too stark for your complexion. Makes you look much older than you are. Remember that pink dress you used to have?"

"Mom—"

"Nordie's basement had the best sale last week. . . ." I swear my mom's a drag queen.

"Mom, do I tell you how to dress, do I say Jesus Christ you look like a fuckin' Easter egg with all those ridiculous colors, I can't be seen with you, why don't you let me take you to the upper Haight and find you a little number in black latex? No. I don't care if you wrap yourself in a Chanel suit or a rainbow flag. You look like you, and I look like me, so let's leave it that way, OK?"

Silence again. "So when are you coming over again, next Christmas?"

"I'm very busy. I'll call you."

"Busy what? Drinking beer? That's all you do. Well, I have beer here." I hear her drag on a cigarette. "I'll cook you a steak."

I don't tell her I'm not eating meat these days. I just eat it when I go to Mom's. It's easier that way, and besides, she does cook a mean filet mignon in cognac and cream sauce with green peppercorns.

"Does that Ellie Mae girl cook for you?"

"No, I'm on a liquid diet, me and Karen Carpenter. Ipecac on the rocks. I gotta go."

"Fine."

"I love you."

"Bye."

I ride up to the park to have a nap in the sun. The radio's cooing, "Sixty-O-o-one . . . Oh, city-one? Are you out there?"

THE TRIP

Out of the cigarette cellophane, I pull a half-inch square of blotting paper, black and purple and red and green–jewel-star design. I hold it like a slide by the edges, so as not to sweat the LSD out of it, tear off a corner. Lightweight, you say. But this is four-way. Each quarter is a twelve-hour flight. On my four-day empty stomach, this tiny scrap will warp me nicely, oozing my reality from come-down to meltdown. Hallucinogens and THC, the only way to ease off a speed run. I scrape the resin out of my freshly liberated bowl, collect it up, roll it into a poor man's hash ball. Now all I need is a taste of hard liquor, and it's just like as "I'm surfin' on heroin, get a needle and stick it in." Great song, but I never touch the stuff. My recipe beats any death dream.

I reach in my jacket for a pack of matches. Familiar squishiness. Poke my finger through a hole in the lining, grope around. Yes. Another cellophane. I pull it out and yippee, surprise-party pack, a fat bud of skunkweed, sparkling with dew drops of clear resin, red hairs, and there's two hits of mescaline stuck to it. It could have been a *High Times* centerfold. I put one hit under my tongue and save the other one for breakfast.

I whip out the Swiss army knife and snip bits of green into the pipe. Then I lean back, the bowl lovingly cupped in resiny fingers. Auto-pilot ready to fly out of a hallucinogenic cartoon snooze and land on a THC tarmac.

I light my granddaddy's pipe and think of a man I knew only as a big cozy lap. I wonder if he used this pipe to float away too. Maybe he smelled the tobacco in the pouch before he pulled loose a moist chunk and packed it into the bowl. Then, as he sat by a river and fished, he might have struck a wooden match against his boot, held it at just the right angle in the bowl, and chomping down on the stem, sucked a sweet familiar taste into his mouth that told him he could breathe now, he was free, as he let his troubles swirl into thin air, exhaling them all in a gray cloudy stream of daydreams.

Because the ritual is it. It's the preparation of the high, the look and feel and color of drugs, the smell as you cut up weed, the taste as you breathe it in, lit or still in the baggie, the taste of powders as they run down your throat, numbing or stinging, depending on what flavor. Half the fun, the meaning of it all, is in the ceremony that precedes the trip, plowing the field of your mind, planting the seed of the herb, the powder, the pill, with love expectation placing the sapling deep in the soil, the plunge of the needle, the drop on the tongue. The highs bloom into a garden of unearthly delight. And in that garden, tied by a rope to a post in the dirt, is a hydrogen dirigible. You jump in the little basket, cut yourself loose, and soar to who knows what fiery fate.

I'm sure when the angel of death asked Grandpa on the way up to heaven, Was that riverside smoke worth a heart attack, he said Hell yeah.

When I fly, the higher I fly, the higher I ascend to the god of my perception.

All the tools and toys I use to tempt muses are precious and cured with gourmet poisons: the wooden bowl to roll seeds from the herb, seeds in their metal case that seals with a decisive click the future of hybrid highs; boxes, containers humbly designed to carefully separate out potions and pipes, papers, syringes, hermetically sealed mushrooms that wait like virgins for wedding days.

I slip off into a tentative sleep, fitful then peaceful then squirmy again. The sun lingers through trees and flies buzz lullabies, haranguing, chasing. Leave me alone. I just want to find a quiet place to jerk off, to bang speed alone. I'm running running to find a moment's peace, so I can whip myself into a comforting crescendo.

But dogs are chasing me, always chasing me, *SLAM*, I slam the big oak door. Quiet here. Dusty sunbeam slicing through the gloom, I'm in trouble. I look at myself in the shard of mirror held in place to a beam with three rusty nails. Cut my hair off. Bleach it blond. Dye it red, poppy red. I'm in my dad's abandoned farmhouse shed where the panel van is parked. It runs good. I know it does. Staring in the mirror, comb my bright red hairs back with a fat-tooth comb, oily like Valentino. I stare at myself. Do I look like me anymore? Or like my stillborn brother whose soul slipped into me, the next body that came down the chute.

At night I go into my father's room, the living room. It's dark. My father has five o'clock shadow. A white T-shirt. He slouches in front of the TV. The TV is his friend. It watches over him at night. The flicker and glare flash on his face as he dandles me on his knee. Staring at the TV, he's singing me a song about I'm his son and he loves me, Bing Crosby–like and in tune, perfect like a pro. Like he was hired to. He loves me the best he can, so I sit on his lap and wait for him to finish and don't struggle to get away.

I lay my head on his chest until I feel its sleeping rhythm, his soft snore in my ear. I don't know how many hours I sit still, not wanting to wake him, until I ride down his knee and leave him with empty bottles he calls dead soldiers around the perimeter, guarding him, empty but for a swallow of backwash in each, and the TV softly chattering electric dreams to cradle him.

I sneak back to the shed. To the panel van. The dry yellow grass is growing up around the tires and the windows are covered with dust, but I get in, turn the key, and it starts like a charm.

Well, I would drive it away, it would make a studly getaway car, but the sheriff would flag me down for sure and say, Your daddy let you use this?

So I run outside, down and alongside the boxcars as they slow down, and I jump up, gripping, clawing, grappling my way up, sweat pouring, leg up, lying on the floorboards, saying yes to the chemically fortified wine served from a shadowy corner.

It gets to be late and I jump out into the snow and the dogs and headlights are still there in the woods, and I'm tearing off through the thicket of black tree trunks, their shadows poking and pointing at the snow, bunching together to hide me from the posse of vigilantes closing in behind me. I swim through the icy creek, and the dogs lose my scent, and I run into a junkyard, and here comes the halfwit junkyard boy, so I duck behind an old Buick and slip into a ditch, hanging by my elbows from a pile of engine parts, my feet dangling, kicking. The boy's stuffing greasy plug wires in my mouth, or cow shit. I opened my eyes and it's Smash, with black watery eyes like the view into two wishing wells, and her top hat and blue paint streaks in her hair.

Smash is the unofficial head of Hags SF. Her, me, Pez, Frankie, Fuckalot, Hags are us, crazy, rocker-pervert hellions outside even dyke society, banished by lesbians to the pit, where we mosh after ingesting copious amounts of stimulants on the bathroom counter in front of regular dykes applying lipstick and otherwise grooming themselves. Hags have special anti-grooming rituals, like streaking hair with blue paint. We don't de-escalate. We're not afraid of blood. "Ha-AGS," we yell swooping up into a high-pitched growl. It's our mating call. We spray paint skull stencils everywhere. Some, like Smash, are rock geniuses, and play guitar like fucking. Hags have a no fraternizing rule, but me and Smash have the secret hots for each other.

So I say, "*What the fuck* are you putting in my mouth?"

"It's just magic mushrooms, what, ya think I'd poison ya?"

She's so smart and crazy you can't get mad at her. You're always just grateful and love her right away.

She says, "Come on, we're going on a trip. Here, shhh." She hands me a warm half-pint of Stoli.

I choke down spores, salivating, eyes watering in that prepuke overflow of facial fluids cow shit–flavored fungus always triggers. Yak.

We're lying back, watching the full moon rise through the trees and over the city. I'm pontificating and gesticulating with a green pack of matches in my hand and I wave it near her hair. Her hair turns green.

"Whoa. Did you see that?" I take the matchbook away. Her hair turns black. Touch her hair, her hair turns green again. Green black green black.

She leads me out of the forest and down to the concrete, geometric waterfalls of animation in the starry street, hash pipe floating up to my lips.

Smash says, "Let's see the old wise woman, the one who makes the potions."

I say, "O-h-h kay. . . ."

We go into the magic store through the magic door, and everything is neon blue, and hanging from the ceiling are models of heavenly bodies lit from inside, everywhere wrought-iron candelabras and animal skulls and chandeliers dripping fat candles. There's giant bird wings, and a mummified bat. Everything's lit from I can't see where, shining with its own light, including a bloodred silk cape hanging over the mirror, very Anne Rice. We climb up a ladder, up to the attic and out to the roof garden, a latticework room choked with bougainvillea, wisteria, and jasmine that fills the night up to the sky with perfume, to a ceiling of stars.

There's the old lady, she's only thirty-four, but she's had a hard life on coffee and smokes, so she has a lot of wrinkles. She's got seven swords, seven feet long, shining silver crescents, she has no legs, she rocks on these machete blades, making seven parallel slices in the roof tar under her weight.

She says, "Jim, you are trying too hard. When one looks directly into the light, it is as if there is no light at all. You are always running. You say you want love, but whenever you see love, you think it is a snake and try to kill it. Snakes are sacred. You will have to live a thousand cockroach lives every time you kill love or snakes. Don't run away. Be the snake and glide to your destiny."

"Shut up, stop lying. You're fuckin' nuts." I'm backing away, my foot slips over the edge of the roof, I fall between two buildings, hanging by fingertips to each, my mouth opens and makes no sound. Below, the slithering pit hisses with B-movie vipers.

Smash grabs me by the wrist and pulls me up. I run down the ladder into a street, not the same cartoon-starry street through a tunnel of small trees, but a crowded Manhattan avenue, bagel shop after deli, fire escapes slashing brick walls, water tanks silhouetted against the sky, the whole city your mother's skirt to hide behind. A green-eyed girl holds out her coat for me. I know she wants something in return. I don't want her to freeze, and I don't have anything to give her. She's begging me please. So I take it and keep running.

KLEPTOMANIA

I wake up on Smash's striped mattress with the blood stains on it. I really need a beer, but I'm gonna try to go straightedge. I love me some Ally. I think I can do without, for her. She says she's the wrong reason. I can't think of another, so she says that will do for now.

I drag my broken body outside, gently shovel my ass onto my sweet, forgiving bike and ride over to see Rosemary at Jack's bar.

Afternoon sun streaming in the open door. Hard hats, house-painters, and messengers start to wander in. She's in a mood. Cutting up piles of lemons.

This guy comes in and sits at the end of the bar. She walks over. "What d' ya want, then?"

"Bud."

She gives it to him. He starts talking about taking the bus for cheap, and what day is it, and he has a bit of an accent, so between his Spanish and her Irish native tongues, they're having a rough time of it. All of a sudden, I see Rosemary wielding the big lemon-cutting knife and saying, "WHATSH? WHAT DID YOU SAY?"

With terror in his eyes, in a last-ditch effort to save his life, he says, "FAST PASS, FAST PASS, TODAY I GET MY FAST PASS!"

She lowers the knife and says, "Oh." Walks back over to me. "I thought he was sayin' today he was goin' to fag bash."

Rosemary. Ya gotta love her. She don't take no shit, and she stands up for her friends. If it weren't for friends, I don't think I'd like girls much at all anymore.

She gives me a free bottle of mineral water with a chunk of lime stuffed down the neck, and I talk to her about dames and true love. Who needs a girlfriend when you have a bartender.

She says, "Whatever happens, Jim, just keep your heart open."

Well, that sounds like just about the stupidest advice I ever heard. Why would you want to do that when everyone just wails on it with a nail-studded baseball bat until it's hamburger. My heart's a knight in shining armor.

I can't stay much longer or I'll drown in a puddle of my own drool watching Rosemary tap snakebites of Red Tail Ale and Blackthorn Cider. So I thank her for the water and slither out the door.

I roll down to Treat Street by Frankie's house. Not that I'm looking for Frankie, I just like her neighborhood. Through the looking glass to My Fair Lady. Victorians, flowers and white-picket fences, birds tweeting in the middle of the afternoon. You'd never know you were three blocks from Mission Street, drunks, crack whores, balloons full of smack.

The sweetness of it all straightens me out. I'm watching this little girl across the street.

She's hoarse as if she's been screaming her whole six years.

She's saying, "Kitty kitty kitty. C'mere kitty."

She grabs the kitty and dandles it on her knee.

"Nice kitty," she says.

She's petting it and bouncing it on her lap, squishing it. The cat patiently submits, but is scouting around for a way out.

"NICE KITTY," screams the child.

I try to get her attention. "Hey. Pepe le Pieu."

She looks at me. She stops bouncing the cat and holds it possessively to her chest.

I say, "You know what?"

She starts bouncing the cat again, muttering to it, singing sweetly like a tiny Janis Joplin. "Nice kitty . . ."

"Come on, I'm not the CIA. You know what?"

"What."

"Chicken butt."

She curls her lip in a sneer, keeps dancing the cat.

The cat looks more desperate.

"You know what else?"

"Hmm-hmm hm," she hums.

"If you squish it as hard as you love it, it will die."

She's about to test this theory, but the cat picks up the vibe and escapes under a parked car. The kid's turning out to be not much of a conversationalist. That's OK. I just so happen to be a fabulous talker and don't need her help.

"Ya know, once there was this dog I used to pass on my way to work every day. It would always run out on the porch to bark at me, but when it opened its mouth, nothing would come out but this raspy cough. I guess its humans were annoyed by it always yapping its tiny dog yap at everyone who passed, so they had its vocal cords cut. Just like that. The American way. If you can't fuck it, eat it, if you can't eat it, kill it, if it makes noise, make it shut the fuck up. One day the dog didn't come out anymore. I hoped they just went ahead and finished it off. . . ." She sits with her face in her hands watching me. I can see she already knows the moral of the story.

Pretty soon the kid's mom's yelling out the window about dinner, and there goes my entertainment.

I could use a beer, but if I keep myself distracted, I can postpone it.

I need to do crimes, get a rebel thrill but not go to jail, get me something for nothing. Piss people off when they see I'm long gone and shit is fucked up.

Then again, no one has to know. Pure sneakiness is enough. Getting away with shit nobody ever finds out has hit the spot for me, I like it.

Ten feet away from my girlfriend, I once stole a kiss in a bar. I had been wanting to kiss this girl for a long time. She was there with her girlfriend too. In fact we were on a double date. Double trouble. My girlfriend caught us swapping spit and slapped the shit out of both of us. Then *her* girlfriend got mad at *my* girlfriend for slapping *her* girlfriend. . . . Much theater. You get more bang for your buck on a double date.

Did I get cocky and sloppy, or was I asking for it? I'm just a fucking masochist. That's what all the girls say. They say, You're asking for it, pal. You goaded me into it. You just get snarkier and snarkier, you don't shut up until I slap it out of you, you got a mouth that won't quit, you made me do it. I warned you.

I figure they just got frustrated because I was smarter than them, and they couldn't think of any snappy comebacks, and I told them what time it was but *good*, and they got madder and madder, because I was right and they couldn't take it. So I'll take my licks, because I still won in the end and we both know it, so there.

I got to work up a different entertainment scheme tonight though, because Ally's not around. Not that I could ever piss her off enough to hit me. She's no fun. When she's had the radish she just bails. But she wouldn't give a shit now if she walked in on me boinking thirteen girls in her bed. She's over it, darling.

Solo thrill seeking tonight.

So what's it gonna be? I head over to the Castro and find myself in the spray paint aisle at Cliff's Hardware.

I don't hang much in hardware stores. I dumpster shit I need to fix up the house. Cliff's is good though, because it's a fag hardware store, and they got ten different kinds of chain you can buy in bulk, and eye hooks, and snap-on clip-on bondage shit. And there's a big China and glassware department, and fancy wooden dish racks, very tasteful, and a big old toy section.

I like to go there and take the squish-a-Martian toy out of the box. It's a rubber thing full of air you play with in the bathtub. When you squeeze its body, its eyes and ears and nose all bug out. I can kill a lot of time doing that.

I shoplifted one once and gave it to my dad for his birthday, but he didn't get it. He laughed, like, *What the hell, you call this a birthday present, what am I supposed to do with this?* Like he laughs at all my presents. I know he's just confused, but why? He's the one who taught me about supply side economix. Being an economix teacher he ought to know why as soon as they supply squish-a-Martian toys, I demand them. The apple doesn't fall far from the horse, says Mom.

See, it's hard to snake stretchy jeans at Mervin's. Socks all the time are boring, and underwear is inappropriate, because once I gave him a pair and he looked embarrassed. I guess it's supposed to be sexy to give a guy underwear, I don't know. I thought it was practical. So he gets a squish-a-Martian toy. It's the thought that counts, that's what I always say.

Anyway, I'm in the spray paint aisle and I stuff a can of red glossy in my jacket and stroll out the door, rushing on adrenaline.

Once when I stole a Hello Kitty lipstick for Ally, she said, "I admire thieves. As long as they steal from corporations, not me."

Heterosexuals own everything in Boyz' Town, so I guess that's as good as corporate.

I jump on my bike and roll down to the corner where the Sisters of Perpetual Indulgence, the Castro's answer to the Catholic Church, are handing out condoms and fliers. I love them. I always try to drum up a conversation with them. I want to be cool and hang out. They're so big and tall, and they're wearing nuns' habits, and they're in white face with two-inch lashes and six-inch heels and glitter in their beards. I'm glad someone's revolting and stopping AIDS and being funny about it. Because I'm busy shoplifting.

I've always been a connoisseur of drag queens. When I was in school, I used to hang with boys that wore girlie haircuts. They would come over and try on all my mom's clothes and drink my dad's beer, and we'd get stoned instead of going to school. They'd come out of my parents' bedroom, parading my mom's makeup and furs and ankle-strap platforms, while I raided the bar and smoked on the couch, approving this outfit, nixing that one.

We had this one pal named Sheila. She was a real-live drag queen that worked at Finocchio's in North Beach, the oldest drag club in the world, and she was giving you realness, honey. She had padding, custom made to fit her calves and thighs under three pairs of nylons, and gel-filled titties. She had big blond hair, eyeliner, false eyelashes, and too much foundation for daytime, and we would go to the mall with her made up like that. After our shopping trip, when she got off the bus at her stop, I would kiss her good-bye. I would look out the bus window at her as she slinked down the suburban sidewalk. I could feel the eyes of everyone on the bus staring at me, and then out the window, trying to figure out if we were dykes, or a dyke and a drag queen, or two straight girls, or a straight couple.

"Keep 'em guessin', honey. They need shakin' up in this town," Sheila used to say.

I learned a lot from her about wearing your balls, your heart, your whole insides on the outside, and not giving a shit who didn't like it. She's probably dead now. Balls out, you don't last long in this world. Like bombing down Nob Hill in the rain, sooner or later you're gonna tabletop right through a taxicab's windshield, but oh, did you catch air on the way.

I remember being in love with Sheila and thinking, *No one can know this. This isn't normal. I'm supposed to like girls. I'm a fucking freak. But then, she's the biggest girl I know and I'm a boy, so everything's fine, except that she would never be caught dead loving me back, as I'm not that kind of boy. Maybe she's just like my mother. . . .*

Wouldn't Freud have a blast now, exploring why dykes kill because they're looking for a drag queen who'll love them like they wish their mothers did, only different, which ultimately frustrates them, because they are homosexuals who desire romance with homosexuals who are the opposite sex. Doomed.

So I'm hanging with the Sisters, but then I start looking around for other shit to do because I'm all tongue-tied around them and can't think of anything to say that would entertain a person who is so purely entertainment itself. I start thinking about stencils I could make to spray paint a quick, permanent message around town on the sidewalks everywhere. But I'm swimming through Jell-O. I need a speed shot jumpstart to think of the most basic concepts anymore.

Aw fuck it. What's the point of trying to do anything without the aid of modern pharmaceuticals? It's such an effort. I should find some dank, get stoned and embrace the idiot within. Thinking's only fun when it's riding a jacked-up runaway train, else it's just a headache.

I slog up the hill called Red Rock and collapse, sweating in the dust. It's a secret place that's hard to get to, and you have to push your bike straight up a dirt hill, but when you get to the top, it's a perfect patch of desert wilderness overlooking the Castro right below you, but none of the people swarming around ever look up long enough to see you. Just like when I was a kid and me and Roo had the tree fort. I'd climb the boards nailed to the eucalyptus trunk at the vacant lot, like Jack and the beanstalk, up up up to the heavens, shaking, pull myself up on the platform. Then I'd relax, invisible spy, watching cars drive by on the freeway, soothed like a country boy watching steamboats.

The city lights up and the sky washes down dark from light. It's a rare night, warm, the fog not hurrying down the hill, freezing wet.

I smoke about five cigarettes, until the shoplift rush wears off. Then I get a hankering to socialize. Cafe Hairspray is down the hill at the corner of Market and Castro. I can see it from here. It's been a year since they eighty-sixed me. They probably forgot the pool cue I broke and the good old barroom brawl I started. Yippee. Too much acid and tequila. I thought I was Paul Newman playing a pool-shark cowboy.

Sam's probably working the door. I went home drunk with her a few times. It's smart to pal around with a bouncer, because then you can stay after hours and drink for free and do lines on the bar until the sun's up and play anything you want on the jukebox without having to sit through everyone else's boring selections.

Me and Sam, we're fuckbuddies. She's a charmer, a boy, like me, and she knows how to have a good time. No drama, just good clean fun. I like fagging out once in a while, because there's no falling in love and pining away and you forgot my birthday. Yeah, it's Sam at the door, we grabass and I slide in, past all the paying outta-towners lined up outside, to the disco inferno upstairs.

I elbow up to the bar.

"Oh 'scuse me, ma'am." I nudge past this slick babe in a too-new Italian motorcycle jacket and slip her wallet out of her back pocket. That's the fucked-up thing. A black leather jacket used to mean cool, now it's like star-belly sneetches, everyone's got one. But they're not fooling me.

"Hey pal, gimme a Stoli for Sam will ya?" I walk away and swig it down, then go back and order another one. I actually make it downstairs with that one and hand it to her.

Aw shit, I went and fucking drank. Damn. I forgot. Oh well, it's just one, to loosen up. Can't play pool totally dry. I'll get the shakes. Besides, how can I get drunk? I don't even have any money.

But of course, the girls can't resist buying me beer, and I can't resist beer, and so I'm getting sloshed. I try pool, but I can't hold the table. My focus is off without skank. I mosey over to the bar and scam more beers, working the place from one end to the other.

I still need that rush, though. I reach up and snake a pile of fives off the bar some dopey broad left there, like this is a high-class place where she can trust everyone. I slip it in my pocket, slide down the stairs, and go go go. " 'Bye, Sam," I'm yelling as I hurdle onto my bike and fly off the curb. I don't turn my head to see who's screaming, "Come back here, ya little slimeball." As if.

I don't know where the hell I'm going. Where's Ally. I deserve a fucking medal for staying off crystal a whole day. If she would just hold me and say I was good, that would be enough for me. I wouldn't need no other thrill.

SO MUCH CLIT, SHE DON'T NEED NO BALLS

Someday I'll jump out of a plane, but for now, the thrill that fulfills is kleptomania. That's gonna have to tide me over while I get this jones out of my system. Beer in my veins, wind in my hair, I'm Peter Fonda, easy rider, flying down from the Castro over train tracks past the park. Outside of society. I'm a outlaw. I got a horse and none of its feet touch the ground. I'm the Sundance Kid with a long black duster flying behind me. I got the money, the heist was a success, we're going to Argentina, start a ranch. There's no real rebels left but me. I got my arms folded across my chest, clamped down on the open brew in my jacket. Good score, all in all, free money and a beer to go, and all I had to do was hang out with a few snooty lesbians.

The old 500 Club sign with the giant neon champagne glass is glowing red two blocks ahead, sucking me like a magnet, because I know who's in there. I'm Ulysses tied to the mast, and the siren inside is a snaggle-toothed dyke-hag of a fellow named Bones. Strange breed, they never go after a flatcracker for sex, just cower in her presence. This one pays for the privilege with a constant flow of meth from his horn o' plenty pocket, just waiting for a fine young snake food–eater like me to snort out of his hand.

Whenever I see him, I challenge him to pool for beers, then follow him to his no-tell motel for the big powder payoff.

One time when we closed the bar, he was the only one with any steam left, and I wanted him to share it. So I invited him to the squat. Skinny gray-headed geezer coupla-teeth-missing motherfucker, he wouldn't be any trouble, and I didn't care if he was. We grabbed a six-pack right before two. I got that timing down, the fifteen minutes between last-call-for-alcohol-last-chance-for-romance and when the liquor store closes. You can keep the romance because I'm busy scrounging up a collection and running next door to buy brewskis and vodka. I hear in certain states you can buy booze to go right out of the bar, but here they make you be an Einstein at two A.M. and run a marathon besides.

Anyway, we cab it up the hill. The guy's loaded, hawking quarter grams all night, so he pays out of this roll of bills he's always waving. Nouveau riche is what my mom would call him. She says a guy like that's got no class, always trying to show off. Bones thinks he's subtle, though. He hangs back with a glint in his eye, waiting for me to come to him. He's a fisherman. He flashes the bags and waits for me to bite. He knows he's got the only thing that'll make a guy like me look a man's way, a wad of cash and a big stash.

So that night, I slapped a tape into the boom box, singing, "My girlfriend asked me *which* one I like *better*. . . . SIX PACK. I hope the *answer* don't *upset* her. . . . SIX PACK." I cracked a beer and tossed one to Bones. Then I took the piece of mirror off the wall and put it on the table. He does rails, not shots, so I wanted him to feel at home with the proper tools. I ought to write a column on drug etiquette. I know what to do. Miss Fuckin Manners.

He was rolling up a twenty, like a one-dollar bill wouldn't do, and folded and tucked it into a corner of itself so it stayed rolled up. Then he started smashing up rocks with the butt of my blade.

Gentleman that I am, I tooted up a couple perfunctory lines. After we swilled us a half-pint, I was feeling less polite, so I said, "Hey gimme some more," and he laid out hefty rails. I scooped them up with the edge of a matchbook, toted them in the bathroom and poured them in the spoon I kept hid behind the toilet tank. I banged that shit and kept it up all night until I got bored, playing DJ in between and ignoring his puppy eyes, with which he was trying to shame me out of my vein game. But a junkie don't feel no shame, honey, all she sees is the high, and the source whence it is flowing. So we kept on until he got tired of shelling out and feebly protesting. Then he left, bleary eyed, into the dawn.

Tonight I'm scooting by, the promise is nigh, but I'm yelling Ally and don't slow down at the 500 Club sign, I just keep sailing, thinking he'll be there every night, I don't have to go tonight, tonight I find Ally. That's the mantra. Ally. Ally's just getting off work, Ally, Ally Cat won't love me if I stop here. You'd think it'd be easy choosing, Beauty or the Beast, when the Beast offers super powers and emancipation, but I've always been a slave to love.

I jump my bike up on the curb in front of the Regal. It's two. She ought to be coming out any time. So I roll over to the liquor store two doors down and grab a pack of gum. She probably wouldn't mind the liquor stank, she's had a greyhound, that's grapefruit juice and vodka, from a plastic cup, if I know her. One of the girls always brings cocktail provisions and passes them around. But I don't remember seeing a toothbrush any time recent, so I figure a roadside freshen-up won't hurt. I'm picking the scum out of my teeth with the corner of a matchbook, when this big drunk guy comes out the door of her most excellent place of work. He's yanking on his zipper. Crusty sonofabitch. I'm wondering if he was just in there wagging his dick at her.

He walks up and says, "Hey baby, ya got a light?"

"Fuck you baby, ya got a cigarette?" I says.

"Oh, tough, aren'tcha honey. I like yer attitude," says he, shakes a couple cigarettes halfway out and thrusts the package in my direction.

I see I'm going to have to deal with this asshole, since he's decided to hang out with me and I'm too tired to shake him. Miss Thang, she doesn't know I'm waiting. She's taking her time switching to street fashion.

Now get this, Freak thinks he's actually putting the moves on me. I just fix my eyes on the doorway and wait for her to waltz out of there.

Finally. There she is and she's laughing with this fine chick she works with who's got a big diamond in her dimple she probably got from that rich plastic surgeon customer of hers. Ally sees me and her eyes get cold, like, *What the fuck are you doing here,* but she doesn't miss a beat talking and carrying on until Diamonds crawls in a cab.

"Hey darlin'," I give her the old sway-vee routine, "Howza bout ridin' home in style." I pat my jacket, bundled and bungeed onto the crack rack over my rear wheel for her comfort, all inviting.

She gazes into my sleepy eyes, assesses the lack of speed, slings her arm around my neck and gives me a friendly kiss. "Well alright then, stranger."

"Aw Jesus, yer a couple of fuckin' dykes," pipes up old asshole, who's been watching the whole exchange. "Shit, whassa matter witchu, bitch, whyntcha gitcher self some DICK, that's whatcha need." He grabs himself for clarification.

All the times she made me shut up whenever riffraff said shit to us and pushed me and sneered at my skinny ass, she'd say, "No, let me handle it." She'd put them in a trance between her eyes and her cleavage. I would be dying and she knew it. But she'd get us out alive and kiss me into oblivion, smooth the shrapnel out of my pride. Even though butch pride is a buncha shit, I still want to kill assholes and save her.

So this time I'm not listening to her. I lunge for the bastard and start flailing, swing and a miss. He grabs me and spins me around, damn deft for a drunk, but he's a big guy used to fights, puts me in a headlock, flexing like a nutcracker. I'm turning purple, sputtering. I would say uncle but I can't say shit, he's crushing my larynx. I'm tippy tapping my toes trying to stomp his feet, but I'm hanging from way too high. I grab for his hair, but it's too short, everything's going red, and there's no air.

I hear Ally at the end of a tunnel say, "Hey, big guy, put that down, let's you and me have some fun," and her eyelashes go down, come-fuck-me style.

I feel him let go like a fool, air rushes into my lungs and I stumble to the comfort of her tits.

She pushes me aside, keeping her eyes on the prize. "Get on your bike."

And when I turn, I see him holding his face with both bloody hands and she punts, splattering testicles all over the place. She's a fucking ballerina. With ease and grace and not a hair out of place, she sidesaddles the bitch pad, and we weave off into the night, him groaning and writhing in spit, piss, and blood. Her hand snakes under my shirt.

MAGIC HANDS

This is the best part, the way she rides on the back, dress hiked up and tied in a knot, legs crossed, a smoke in her hand. She's a saloon girl on a bar stool. And me pumping down Market. I gotta get a Dutch rack. She's always bending the back wheel into a potato chip, she's a big girl on this flimsy rack made for fifty-pound packages. But I don't care, I just true the wheel every week. That is, straighten it out, so it doesn't rub on the brakes like a warped record. Them Amsterdam racks are what I need, heavy-duty steel for carting around healthy babes.

She starts in on me right away.

"What in the hell are you thinking, coming to get me at work? Whenever I see you it's drama. Quit it. I thought I told you to take a hike."

I'm still reeling from near death so I'm short on witty comebacks.

"You've just got to stay away from me. It's no good, Jim."

"Whaddaya mean?"

"I get enough junkie energy dripping all over me at work without you sliming it in my bed."

I figure she's talking about Ice Dream, her colleague what she fucks occasionally. Ice Dream, she ain't got no eyebrows. I don't see the attraction. But she sure does have it bad for old Ally. I guess Ally mercy fucks her. So what. Have at it.

"But honey, I been clean," I tell her.

I turn right on Kearny, breezing down the high-rise corridor ghost town, all the traffic and peds out of the way, four lanes to myself and drunken lone taillights weaving away down the road.

"Yeah, clean, right. I've got news for you, sweetums, a week clean does not a sane person make."

"Why not?"

"It takes time to clone brain cells. And you're just taking a breather, as far as I know."

"Well, it's a start. That's all it is. Just wait, you'll see, I'm straightedge, I am, 'cept for smoking and sex and a couple beers. . . . Trust me, I'm a doctor."

I'm breaking a sweat the last block up Grant to her flat. The beery speedless night, the ass kicking, it's all catching up to me now. She hops off and flings her arms around my neck. I see a chink in her heart. I could wedge a crowbar in there and open her up.

"Come on. Please baby. Lemme in."

"You are pitiful, aren't you. Alright, I'll heat you up some lasagna."

"Yippee."

"Don't get any funny ideas. Stay off that shit. Or you get none of this." She grabs her tit. "Besides, I'm busy."

"I can stay outta the way, I won't be a pest, honest. Busy doin' what? Huh? Is it fun? Is it boring, is it exciting? Can I watch?"

She says she's recording, and making cover art for the record, you know, band shit. And she can't do it when I'm always hanging on her neck, so I should back off for a while and get my shit together.

Tonight's the night. Gotta work my charms or no more chances. She's getting ready to close up shop.

We go upstairs. The blues bar downstairs is jumping. We get in the shower and she's washing off makeup and hairspray and lube, and I'm washing off beer and road sludge and stink, and we're washing it off each other, fighting over the shower stream and it's nice. I love when the mascara smudges under her eyes and she looks like the sexiest most innocent waif that I love. She looks at me and her eyes turn into half-moons, straight side down, and she looks so deep into me it's that laser beam cutting me down, right in half, I crumple to the ground, like the hero, he's been shot, he falls to his knees in the dirt, in the middle of town, his gun in his hand, he didn't even have time to shoot, and he looks at his girl on the porch of the saloon, and she's got her rifle hanging by her side, it's still smoking and so's she, cigarette hanging out of her lipstick lips, smoke curling past her beauty mark, making her squint, and she says, I had to do it, Jim, you done me wrong.

I love kissing her in the shower, everything all wet and rainy, and she dries me off with a cushy pink towel, like Mom used to do, and tucks me into clean silk sheets and brings me pasta and fuzzy water in a blue bottle. Everything's fancy. Then she slips off her bra and pulls down her G-string all slow, like she's unwrapping a big piece of candy and she wants to make it last because there's only one left. Her tits fall when she takes off her bra and I'm glad she didn't get a tit job. Hers are squishy. Fuck them *Hustler* centerfolds. So what they're perfectly round. What I want is the squish action you don't get with plastic. I mean, I tried to squish me some fake titties, and parts of them were nice and all, but Ally told me horror stories. Diamonds got a tit job and her boyfriend, the surgeon who made the damn things and should have known better, grabbed them before they were set like Jell-O, and the bags popped and all the silicone leaked into her body, and she almost died. He figured like Dr. Frank-N-Furter, I made you, I can break you as well.

She crawls in next to me and her gazongas are so soft and perfect I disappear in them. Sometimes I think of my mom's tits, only she calls them breasts, and how they're still perfect, even though she's old, and how she says they're that way because she didn't breast-feed me, and how dumb it is to have stretch marks forever when you could give a kid a bottle and it's just as satisfied.

I polish off the food and toss the plate on the floor. I roll over on Ally, push her tits together and rest my chin on them, kiss them, absentminded, listen to her tell a story, ancient dream of us, she's my mom, queen mother in a long white sheet pinned up with big blue rocks. There's love talk, death plots, gonna kill Dad, jealousy, he's in the way, hemlock, exile or execution, slipping away in silent reed boats at night, this is real and they want to kill it because real love threatens the very fabric of society.

When I wake up the next morning, I watch her sleep. I want to kiss her. She don't be a mouth breather, all slack jawed and snoring like me. No, she's perfect like lilacs, sweet, her hair draped across the pillow, an ad for bed sheets. Sun's streaming in through Italian lace curtains. When she wakes up, a gold beam of light lands in her eyes and turns them into green glass.

We get up and start amping balls on coffee.

"OK, sailor, you've got to go, I've got an action-packed day."

"Don't you want a ride? I could give you a ride."

"No, why don't you get yourself some lunch and rest up so you can look for a job?" She hands me a five spot.

I hang on until that last good-bye kiss and the look that says she's serious, she doesn't want me around for a while. I ride through North Beach Sunday morning, cafes and cathedrals and pigeons taking their time scattering. I'm dead again. See, all a cowboy's magic ain't worth shit, once his girl decides she just don't need him no more. So what's the point of doing right.

A DO-RIGHT MAN

I don't know what happened. I was all hunkered down at the squat with beer, cigarettes, and dumpster-dived pizza, had my snipe rack. Snipes. Them's cigarettes that are half smoked, or good-sized butts, snipes, and you lay them out in a row on the edge of an ashtray, that's a snipe rack. Frugality and prudence, see, I had it planned so I could survive, hole up for a while, away from the candy-store world inviting me to indulge in hedonist pleasures. If I could just stay on the hill, not mosey down to Sixteenth and Mission where Dude always mumbles, Outfits, outfits.

Ally just laughs and says, "Thanks, you're pretty style-y yourself." Not me. When he says outfits, I'm Pavlov's dog doing the impulse-shopping shimmy. I got to buy one, fill it with stardust, and bang bang, you're live.

If only I could keep my ass at the squat, I could get clean, get the girl, get everything. But I'm too brilliant.

I do stay clean for a minute. First thing, Frankie decides she's going to get us cleaned up, and she takes us up to Russian River on her motorcycle. It's nice and hot, and we stay with a friend of hers that used to go out with Melissa Etheridge, anyway, that's what she keeps saying, and I keep saying, Who? And she says, Oh she's brilliant, she's about to make it big.

I feel big just staying in a place where a future rockstar might have made sweet love down by the river.

So the chick has a real nice spread up there in the mountains with pine trees all around, and a deck, and it's hot and summery and smells good, and I just lie out on that deck, soaking in the morning sun and watching the blue jays yapping and the squirrels run up and down the tree. I miss my bike though, which I wish I was cruising through the forested lanes, where there's no traffic and rules to stop me from rolling up and down hills, sucking in tree stink, and cooling myself in the ninety-degree heat with homemade wind. But still, lying here's so peaceful, all I can think of is, I'm nice and serene. Ally's gonna love this. She's gonna love me, wait 'til I get back and she checks out the new me. The mellow me. Danger Dyke all gone.

So after two weeks of recuperation, we feel like a couple of fucking Betty Ford Clinic graduates. We roar back to the city happy joy joy, singing, "Take me down to Paradise City," at the top of our lungs into the wind.

When we roll into town, I have Frankie take me over to the office and get my paycheck. It's a fat one, considering I called in sick half the time and didn't show up the other half. I must have been wired for sound the days I did work.

We go over to Harvey's Liquors, where Frankie drops me off. Harvey's the patron saint of messengers. He fronts us all sandwiches, cigarettes, and beer until we get our checks, and then he cashes them and takes our tab off the total and never charges a fee. And he let all the guys hang out in the alley in the back, drinking beer out of paper bags after work, talking about narrow misses, Krypto revenge, and dispatcher stupidity.

I cash my shit, and Harvey says, "Where you been?"

"Took a break."

"I thought you change careers, become a stockbroker." He laughs.

"Naw man, you know I'm a lifer, Harvey."

Lifer, that's a career messenger, a guy who knows there's no other life for him, who belongs to a brotherhood, and ends up an old, toothless, slow rider with bad knees.

"Anything else?" He always says that. Anything else? He's a real business guy, came here from China and took over the world at Fifth and Shipley.

I get a pack of smokes, take my forty and my cash, and walk out back to shoot the shit with my bros.

Then here comes Smash, and she says, "I was just going over to see my man, don't you want to come along and invest that cash before you just fritter it away on a barrel of beer?"

And I says, "Why, yes, that's a capital idea. Speaking of capital, I would love to double my money, and what better business to enter but speed dealing, for if anyone knows speed, it's me, your pal Jim, even though I no longer partake, myself."

She looks at me sideways. "This guy's got the best shit around."

"No kiddin'."

"You're smart not to pass it up," she says.

And I nod, thinking that I like Smash, and trust her, and everything she says always sounds like a good idea, and that yes, I am smart and the talents that make me a good messenger probably also make me a good businessman. I choose my own path, I'm a loner, a self-starter, independent, fearless, a gambler, a thrill seeker, and I believe in the benefits of hard work. And as I have just graduated from the Betty Ford Clinic of Guerneville, I do not suspect there will be any danger of me ingesting one grain of my product. Any crack dealer is clean as a brand-new car, knowing full well that one hit leads to the smoking up of all profits.

When we get to the pusherman's, they make us sit in the living room for a half hour watching daytime TV with two teenage girls bored to a simmering, don't-fuck-with-me silence. We're waiting for Billy, that's the man. Finally, chica motions us over and closes the door behind us, all elite and important like a country club. She takes us down the hall, opens a door, and there he is.

He ignores us for a while, then gives Smash her order, jacks the rig absentmindedly, like drinking a beer. Smash slips out, unnoticed by me. I'm watching him fuss around like he's got all the time in the world, indifferent and cool with the thing dangling out of his arm, walking around. I go clammy, my palms are wet.

I hear myself say, "Hey, you mind if I try some that way?"

He says sure and tosses me an outfit.

I'm shaking, with fascinated revulsion watching the point find old faithful like a divining rod. I don't know why it's so different this time. Because I just tried to quit. I mean, I *am* quit.

So I'm booting the stuff, and I feel my status shift. The last time that happened was the day I finally learned how to do myself. For years, I always said, as long as I don't know how to fix myself, I won't lose my shit entirely. I'll keep a lid on things. I'll WANT to bang speed twenty-four hours a day, but in fact I will not be able to, because I will not have a servant with a tray full of syringes waiting for me to snap my fingers. I will have to depend on the kindness of strangers. But one day, five years ago, Carlton got tired of having to hit me first. He used to always do it that way, because if he hit himself first he'd be too wired and his hands would shake. But he wanted to go first this time. He couldn't wait 'til he found one of my invisible veins, and he wanted to get high now. So he said, "Fuck you, hit your own self." I did, and that was the moment everything changed. He handed me the controls and there was no stopping me. I did it every day, everywhere, in public bathrooms and in your mom's house. I graduated to a whole different league that day. Today's a more subtle promotion.

But making that decision is always like jumping off the high dive. Standing there endlessly waiting for balls, resisting the impatient shouts behind you of *"Go!"* And you're choking, but you just pretend you're looking at the baseball game over the fence. And you know this is really crazy, and a normal person in his right mind wouldn't do it, but you want the thrill, you ain't no chickenshit. So you say fuck it and go flying.

Anyway, Smash was right about this shit. It's good, or else that break of cleanliness and purity I took in the nature made the rush more intense, returned my blood to its virgin state and then fucked its baby freshness up like it was the first time again.

So I start coming back to see Billy twice a week. I got me a hell of a racket, thanks to my business consultant, Smash. Who knew you could stay high for free and make money too? Guess them crack dealers just aren't as slick as me.

Now let me tell you about this house where I go to score. Billy, he's a tiny Jim Jones, seventeen and king of his cult in this Edwardian flat swarming with devotees, speedy scruffy scrawny punks, outlaws with way too much eyeliner. They eye him to see what his need is, dodging his wrath and looking for love, elbowing each other out of the way, pups gauging a schizophrenic's whims. This house is a trip even if you're not tripping. I inevitably am, always doing a taste before I leave with the stash.

He makes you wait. Power tripper. Like my boss at work. He's the king, and he holds the gold, and you need it, and you'll do whatever he says to get it. That's the game, and you play by sitting there and not acting antsy. Be patient. Be polite. Always ask permission. He offers you the rig. Don't act too tweaked. Leave incognito.

One time I get too focused, and he gets mad because I climb up the side of the house and crawl into the attic and lay on a beam for two hours thinking the cops are coming. He says I'm blowing it and won't let me get high there anymore after that. Course it's his fault, he lets the doctor shoot me up with a half gram. See, because he's overseeing the whole wildly quiet party, everyone pounding speed not saying anything. The silence is loud, like big electrical wires buzzing overhead. He sees the doc, that's a guy that can hit anyone and never miss, drawing me up a freebie from the spoon, and I hear him say, Hey that's enough, but the guy has it in my arm before Billy can do anything.

I go ricocheting off the hallway walls to the porch outside and see two crows with big tits and green eyes land in the tree and chatter at me.

They say, Jim, you're blowing it.

BIG BUSINESS

I weigh up quarters every night to sell at the club. I'm doing alright, supporting myself and my habit for free. I stay jacked. There's never any downtime, unless Billy runs out for a few days, like if the Feds bust a factory. That doesn't stop him. He always comes up with another connect, and then we're rolling in skank again.

But I got it under control. I stay up for days and days in a row, but I don't go nuts. Five days is my limit. Not like those wacky guys that stay up for a month, and you're always having to yank them out of the way of diesel trucks. And I don't like mixing speed with too much hallucinogenic, aphrodisiac shit either. I'm a purist, know what I'm saying?

Then I let this nomad nutcase stay at my place. She almost blows it for me. She brings this ecstasy to sauce up the meth. It isn't like the old days with MDA that made everyone look like they were floating in stardust. This shit's main claim to fame is an emotional hallucination of paranoia and shame. I can't wait to do more, and we shoot it nonstop.

We're walking around Alamo Square where the fags go to the bushes, that's what they call it, communicating with one another in "the talk of the turning eyeballs," as Wally Whitman, an experienced cruiser, would say. The night's pitch black, but I swear I know every zombie lurking in the shadows, and I duck behind trees all night, so they won't see me so high.

Anyway, chickee babe loses her shit after four days on that trip. She steals my speed and does it up, and then lies and says she doesn't know who stole it. Well, I say, there wasn't anyone else in the house. She's cutting numbers out of the sports page and pasting them together and telling me it's an outer space alien code that actually spells words, but you just have to know the code. She says my name isn't Jim, it's J3. Severe and permanent loss of grip.

I say, I don't know what page you're on, but the book you're readin' is way too long. I tell her to leave but she won't, so I grab her by the hair and drag her out the door kicking and screaming that she's going to tell the pigs I got drugs in the house. I say, go ahead, there aren't any more, cuz you did 'em all bitch, so shut up and get the fuck out of my life.

Houseguests. It's not hard to overstay your welcome at my place. My temper gets short when the nights get long. But some people take the cake, and anything else they can get their hands on. Most of the girls hanging around are sweet though, bartenders, ladies of the night, and gutterpunx escaping bad dads.

I hang out at the bars and everyone buys me martinis and loves me and invites me to parties and shit because I'm such a witty guy. True, they love me because I got the goods, but hell, I got snappy comebacks, good looks, and right things to say, so how could they resist me even if I wasn't Doctor Feelgood. I am a mobile buffet though, plenty of meth, always 'shrooms, and doses, windowpane, or blotter with Disney characters on it, and Cali-diggity dank to take off the edge. What you want, baby I got it.

I'm in with the in crowd. I ain't dork boy no more, so there, Sandy Clooney. I do a nice shot before riding down to the bar with a half-pint of Stoli in my jacket, order a martini, and fill my glass all night in the bathroom. I'm a cult of scintillating personality.

I gave up on ol' Ally. She's high maintenance. It's always something. She's looking for perfection and that's one thing I'm not.

I got a career now, I ain't got time for babes demanding shit. Looking at their watch when I come home, checking my arms for tracks. Ally'd be going nuts right about now anyway, if she had stuck it out, wanting to beat the shit out of every fine young thang who bats her eyelashes at me to get free shit.

Sometimes I go home and put on a Blatz tape, pour down some beers, and rage around the house yelling, "You neeeed . . . HOME-MADE SPEED."

This is the fucking life.

A ROLL IN THE GLASS

I sleep a lot in between runs. Three days at a time. I dream of looking out the open door of a plane that wafts like a leaf, I step to the door and look down. Diesel trucks inch like ants down a dental-floss ribbon of highway. Underwater, guts somersault. I know I will have to look out at the sky in front of me, out to the edge of the earth curving away, ignore instinct, and defy death.

The Hags go to punk shows and shove each other around every weekend. We fling each other into boys and fuck up anyone that gives us shit, wearing our leather to cushion blows, with nails sticking out the epaulets and lapels, so everyone keeps their distance. We take the chains off our necks so they can't grab and twist and throw us down.

See, it's not that we're looking for a war. We just want to get our yayas out on each other, scream and yell and jump and pound on each other. It's the assholes that fling a fist in your eye, throw you down and jump on your kneecaps, but you can't beat the willing. We like it, smashed by sweaty bodies, bodies craving contact and black eyes, to see if any of it can get through to us, make us feel at all.

Smash says, when they push you, and keep pushing you, and knock your tooth loose with their elbows, thinking you're just a girl and they can whup you, you duck out to the back of the pit, sidle up behind them, and suckerpunch them in the side of the head when they're not looking, then duck out to the back again. Satisfaction guaranteed. Hero worship, I watch Smash do it, but I always hang back.

The other night I'm taking a break at the bar, pounding a beer, and I see this girl. She has black hair and the words FUCK UP tattooed on her neck inside a small blue heart. She's wearing big motorcycle boots up to her knees and cutoffs with a garter belt reaching down from under them holding up torn fishnets, and black lipstick. She looks like she'd rather kill you than smile. She's got those really sad eyes, black like coal. I don't know if I only notice girls that have really sad eyes, or if fine girls are just sad because the world has given them so much shit that they are over it.

She's perfect, what a dish, so I ask her what's up. She says she has to go to work, and I say where, and she says the Cinema. I should have known. I ask her a couple questions. She answers in three-word sentences. She has a motorbike outside.

The whole girl thing seems so complicated these days, so in the way. But I know I'll still be wide awake after they kick us out of here, so I say does she mind if I come and see her later at work, and she says no, it livens things up to have a girl come over, breaks up the monotony. I tell her I'll check her out. But already I can see the complications starting, as I don't have but five dollars for two more beers, and I'll have to slip her at least a ten to show respect.

So she leaves and I think about her while I watch the band from the bar, about how mean and sad and joyless and hateful and perfectly fine she was, and what the hell was her name. I do like the way she sulked and glowered and you had to use a claw hammer to get two New York words out of her.

The band gets done. I finish my beer and swipe a couple tips off the bar. This guy keeps stumbling up against me, groping and stinking like gin, so I pick his pocket while I let him slobber on me and shove his tongue down my throat. That adds up to twenty-seven bucks.

I ride over to the Cinema, lock my bike to a parking meter, wander in, and sit down in front.

A girl disguised as Barbie is jiggling around. But wait. Isn't she the pink-mohawk bass player for that dyke band I saw the other night? I can't be sure. The guys are trying hard to act disinterested. Masking their hunger. We all know why you're here, pal.

Out comes the Despondent One, swaggering to Diamanda Galas's "Baby's Insane," and my chest stutterstarts. She wraps around me, never stops slinking, grabs my hair at the back of my neck and gives it a clench. I know the Rules are I can't touch certain body parts. There's always a bonehead hovering to make sure you don't. I touch her thigh, just friendly, in a secret code I'm-your-pal way, and these jerks don't get that you just do this for the money. I tuck the cash in her garter belt. She moves on down the line, looks at me as she finishes up, caresses the bald guy's head and slaps his drunk hand away. She slips backstage. I wait outside, confused, dangling from her stare that seems dead until it connects to yours and she becomes Nastassia Kinski, snatching you out of comfort, stinging you awake. When you look at her, you know the world is shit.

We go around the corner into an alley and wrestle on someone's cardboard house, behind a Dumpster in the broken glass and disposable lighters spent on crack pipes. I throw her legs up and she jams the soles of her boots into my chest. I cut her Victoria Secrets with a knife, my fist better than dick in a maniacal trance. She straightlegs me and says, "Get off me," and leans back smiling.

I look at her. "What."

"Sometimes you just don't feel like coming, know what I mean?"

Yep.

I put my head on her chest. "Your heart's beating."

"That's not my heart. It's Satan knockin', sayin' lemme outta here." Twisted fuck.

"And don't try gettin' under my skin. I fuckin' hate that." She pulls up her pants and walks away.

I like her. She doesn't care. Nobody gives a shit, nobody gets hurt. A live body under me is all the danger I can stand anymore. I climb up the last hill to the squat, sweat and fog clinging to me. Blue lights flash down in Hunter's Point. I'm invisible, safe from cops and love. My throat is bruised where she tried to rip my jugular out with her teeth.

I don't like anybody, really.

PART TWO

DAYTIME HUSTLER

TWEAKAZOID

Pretty soon shit is starting to catch up to me, but I don't notice. I don't have to watch how much I do. Marching powder's always there in piles, so I fix what I need when I want it, which is more and more. I keep selling five or six quarter grams a night, just the quarters are getting smaller, because I'm snibbing a little out of each for-sale baggie to put in my own personal baggie. I go in the bathroom, squirt in a couple drops of water and bang it. I need more than they do. I deserve it. I don't give a fuck if it's right or wrong anymore. The voice in my head used to whisper the rules of etiquette to me, but now it only whispers, *Fuck them*.

The product is good. Nobody's going to notice if it's a little short. They're just weekend users anyway, what do they know. If they complain, I just say, Hey, if you want me to cut it, I can make it LOOK like more, but would you rather have a LOT of baby laxative, or a LITTLE high octane. Alright then. You can't get nothing this good anywhere else. I got the sole connection to godspeed, so quit whining.

Sometimes I go out and see shit that pisses me off. Then I don't even want to go out selling anymore, socializing, I just sit at home and tweak to forget. Saw Ally hanging out with some stupid fuck I seen around. I didn't say nothing to either of them. They didn't say nothing either. Just looked embarrassed. I don't give a shit. I just thought maybe she would have some respect. It's a small town though, so what she's supposed to be, a nun? I just hate them both, is all. Fuck them for feeling sorry for me too. I can't even look at them. And I'm not giving Ally the satisfaction of me being jealous. I'm not jealous, I'm just gonna puke. She would be thrilled to prove I'm human and justify her own jealousy, but she can't, because jealousy is just insecurity, which I do not have. I just would like people to have a little discretion, is all.

So what, I don't care. I got a new batch of Mr. Clean, and that is always good for escape into your work. You have to make little plastic baggies by cutting up a big plastic baggie into small pieces and clamping the edges in a cassette case and lighting them with a match, then smoothing the hot plastic over the tape case with your finger. This makes a piece-of-shit baggie that will leak if you keep it too long, but you do not have any business keeping it long anyway, the way I see it. That little bit of snakefood should be gone in twenty-four hours at the most. I don't understand people who keep it in their shoe or their wallet for weeks. It's sweaty placebo powder by then. And what's the point of little tiny dabs, spread out over days? You want it all at once, that's what a serious person does, am I right? I mean, what do you want to do, stay awake or touch the sky?

Then you have to weigh the shit out into little piles and then scoop them into the baggies with a matchbook cover and tape them up. Then you take what's left over and, bang, you are ready to do some remodeling and general housework.

My squat is old and beat up, a fixer-upper. It could be real nice. I notice stuff more when I first do a big shot, after I have been starving on little maintenance-sized shots for a week as the supply thins out.

All the details come alive, things you don't usually notice. Your universe gets very small and focused, like you are walking around with a microscope on your eye. You can see that the doorknob under those twenty coats of paint is actually this ornate, shiny, flowery work of art, like the finished sculpture visible in a lump of clay. And the door itself has antique molding and dark wood underneath the same twenty coats of paint, and your heart races fast, you're inspired, you see the veneered mahogany and yellow metal. You are not thinking long term. You have left the planet and your body's beyond pain. It's aglow, pounding molten light through your bloodstream. You have unlimited strength, and you are not bound by time. In the moment, the zen of speed.

So you tear the door down and unscrew the knob and soak it in a can of turpentine and start scraping the door inch by inch with some paint remover, until you get really wasted on fumes and you're coming down and you have no mind left. Six hours later you're getting blisters you can't feel, your muscles are stiff. It's time for another shot. That takes you out of your body and into the realm of the door again. Another six hours, another blast, a breather. You light a smoke, put it in the ashtray, and the microscope on your head screws into focus, swivels your neck and boom, the next project has seduced you to clean and arrange all the cassette tapes in alphabetical order.

Pretty soon, two, three days have gone by, and you're back down to survival stock. Party's over. Time to go to work, down to

Francine's and sell, sell, sell. Now you can't get it up for that door again, so it lies there, abandoned, a draft whipping through the space where it used to hang. The next time you score you do another big bang, but by then you don't even see the door, you've got so used to stepping over it, and the draft cools the sweat on your face, and the veins stand out on your hands, you're Marlon Brando in a Tennessee Williams hot Louisiana night, jumping off the screen. Time for a beer. Fuck that stupid door. There's a million fresh new projects to start.

So now the house is in various stages of tweak. Little junk sculptures. Construction sites with paths cleared to the vital zones: mattress, ice chest, boom box.

I sweep everything out to the backyard, even the petrified cat shit behind the couch. I dumpster some lace and put it in the window. The bike's hanging upside down from a hook in the ceiling, and I walk around it. I don't miss messengering. I'm getting my velocity fix.

Hurtling down through blue skies, I'm diving straight down at 285 mph. I catch up to Smash and Pez and the Despondent One, who are curled up in the fetal position. I pull my knees up and wrap my arms around me, to slow down. I call out: "Hey, don't you think it's about time to pull the rip cord?" They look up from a nap. "Yeah," nods Pez, and tucks her head down again. It's sad to leave them and be alone, but they're all cozy, suspended together, and I have to stay alive. I straighten out and drop past them. The ground is getting bigger.

I paint some boards black and set them up on cinder blocks to make bookshelves. This orange baby cat comes over. She watches me put the shelves together and then put the books on the shelf.

She zooms right in on my vibe, her eyes as dilated as mine. She's a very small orphan. I finally crash two days later, and she falls asleep on my head. Her name's Hat. Hat the cat.

Sometimes when I'm pushing go-fast, someone will come up and say, Hey, Jim, I saw Allisandra the other day, and I just say, Oh really, that's nice, so fuckin' what. They say, Didn't you used to go out, I thought it was the great love of all time, Tracy and Hepburn.

I just say, Bartender, gimme another martini, will ya.

SADAAM MOVES IN

In the middle of the room stands a Catholic mass candelabra, big, brass, a bludgeoning tool to fend off intruders. A cylindrical stem, wound around with vines and dead roses, holds a two-foot-long crossbar sprouting seven candles.

I'm sewing patches on my jacket, when there's a banging at the door. It's Sadaam Might, gorgeous boy with a tat around his throat that unzips and pours forth blood.

He smiles his gold-tooth smile. I slide the two-by-four back into place across the door.

My vocal cords crack from no word spoken and no drop drunk for hours. "Where ya been, pal?"

"Amsterdam, extracting money from Pops." He's got a slight Germanic accent, short blond hair. It's filthy. His black bondage pants are stiff and shiny. Combat boots, T-shirt from de Derk, a Dutch squat bar where bands play.

"Welcome homo. Sit down. Tell stories." I reach in the cooler and serve us cheap beers.

"The squat scene here is way too hot. I need some fucking rest. I can't be rousted every night by the cops. I'm sick."

"You can stay here long as you want."

"No, I'll move on in a couple of days. I don't want to disturb your peace and quiet."

"Fuck that. You're stayin' with me. Hags and fags unite."

"Yeah?"

"Too much history for bullshit."

"OK."

"I'm sayin'. We can hide out here forever without the heat showing up. I lie so low, the neighbors don't notice me. No worries."

It's good to break out of my trance and have some company, especially Sadaam. He's so fine with his skinny little ass and his eurotrash way of talking. He never breaks his party stride. Says he wants people to remember him as having fun, not buckling under the power of the plague.

I offer him a swig of whiskey and a smoke.

He takes the cigarette and looks at the whiskey.

"I traded it for jet fuel. It's pretty tasty though. Warms you right up."

The cold is rushing, misting in the window. He's shivering, so I block the draft with a chunk of particleboard.

We smoke and drink half the bottle before he starts spilling his guts. He says the Dutch system rocks, they pay for everything.

"Then why'd ya leave, fucker?"

"I'm in love."

"With an American."

"He's beautiful, there's no one like him, like me, punk as fuck.

We're the only ones. I been looking so long, Jim. He's a pervert, he's positive, and his dick's monstrous."

"Now we're gettin' to his true inner qualities."

"No, he's got a nice personality. . . ."

"A nice big personality . . ."

"Ah shut up. It's killing my mother I'm not staying in Amsterdam, but life without love . . . what's the point?"

"Oh, the glamour. You know, you don't look so hot."

"I can't shake this cough. And I'm all pukey and dizzy from these new drugs."

I suck on a cigarette. "I'll score you some herb."

"Yeah, less barfing, more eating. I'm getting fucking skinny, man."

I'm just glad he's back. Now we can have adventures. I say, Remember that caper when we went to see Nina Hagen at that SOMA disco inferno, and you were screaming like a banshee and slamdancing too rough? And he says, Yeah, everyone standing, staring, like at TV, and those pricks at the club acting like they didn't know she was Nina Fucking Hagen, unplugging her. They didn't show proper homage at all, and he was yelling, LET HER PLAY, ASSHOLES, and then they started playing techno, and we were yelling, HEY, THE RECORD'S SKIPPIN', and he was being a groupie, following her when she tried to slip in the back room. He shared a *special moment* with Nina.

"You so crazy. I loves you. Get better so we can fuck shit up," says I.

"Yeah and kick some ass. Call me a fag, het boy, c'mon. Call me a knobslobber."

"You're getting stomped by a queer. Aren't you a big man now?" We're cracking ourselves up, pretending he's not too weak to beat anyone up anymore.

Now the rain's starting to fall, soft on the window. I put on some Mozart. Reminds me of Mom. She always played old Mozart every Sunday in December before Christmas, for a Christian holiday she didn't believe in. She just liked to light candles and set out tiny wooden angels, hand-painted by children. She served butter cookies that her mom would send from East Germany (because my mom didn't bake no damn cookies), and tea with a little rum in it. That was my favorite part. I sure liked me some rum when I was six.

I put Sadaam to bed, propped up on a bunch of pillows so he can breathe and his lungs don't fill up with snot and drown him. I watch him sleep for a while. He rattles and wheezes. The rain falls harder. I wipe the steam off the window and look out. Empty city shining. Sparse traffic on the freeway goes *kssssshhh,* water ripped by tires at high speeds. Rain makes me wide awake. Another shot of whiskey. Another poem scrawled. I can't see straight no more. Double vision smears a song for Sadaam that'll be a swirly blur tomorrow.

THEY FIGHT AND FIGHT AND FIGHT AND FIGHT AND FIGHT

I'm dreaming me and Smash are big rockstars running all over a big hotel up and down the elevators like bigshots. She is beautiful again, a young heavy-metal babe with a creamy complexion, sexy mouth, black-lined eyes that seduce and laugh. Then she changes, black dready scare hair, spittle at the corners of her mouth, cold clammy sweat beading up under death-pallor makeup. We score together, Jack the Rippers, shadows lurking, stealing roses from people's gardens.

I wake up around four, grab a beer and some milk out of the cooler. I get a big mixing bowl and a serving spoon and the Cap'n Crunch with Crunchberries. I pour the cereal and milk in and sit down by Sadaam, shoveling, slurping, crunching. I watch him sleep. After a while the crunching gets to him and he opens his eyes. I pop the beer and offer him a swig. He shakes his head and sticks his tongue out.

I have a swallow. "You sure have changed."

"I shouldn't have had any of that whiskey last night either. I'm sick. Trying to tell you."

"Oh." I keep munching Crunchberries, watching him. "Whenever I feel bad, a beer makes me feel much better."

"It fucks with me. In the long run I feel shittier. I can't handle it anymore."

"Sorry. Want some cereal?"

"Don't you have any real food?"

"This is real. What am I, the Ritz-Carlton?"

He rolls over and puts his pillow over his head.

"Aw man. Here, I'll go get you some nice food. Whaddaya want me to get ya?"

"Nothing. You don't have to wait on me. I'll dumpster dinner at Veritable Vegetable later." He starts coughing and hacking and turning red.

"Damn. We gotta get you some medicine for that shit. You sound like you're gonna die." I scout around for some cough syrup.

Aw shit, I shouldn't have said that about him dying. What a jerk. Time for a wake-up call. I poke a residue-coated baggie into the top of the beer can.

Now it's Sadaam watching me.

"What."

"Nothing."

"What. Don't get all preachy on me. It's just a baggie."

He smiles with that innocent eyebrows-in-the-air look. "I didn't SAY anything."

"So now you're on some health kick? Well, that's fine for you."

"Yeah, maybe I don't feel like dying anymore. It's how to survive, don't know if I can do it. You think you're safe?"

"Well, I didn't get buttfucked by a buncha SM leatherdaddies doing bloodsports and shootin' up all night, no bleach, no latex, every night for a year, did I."

"Oh yeah? When you're in a big hurry to get the shit in your vein, you grab any rig handy."

"Do not."

"And you fuck every fucked-up girl in town, no glove, no nothing, just throw them down on a pier, in an alley."

"Lies. Besides, fuck you. Dykes are the chosen people. I studied up. We're clean. It's not even in menstrual blood."

"You believe everything you read? Who do you think cooked this shit up? You think they love you any more than me? They're not going to spare you. They may hate me because I take it up the ass like a girl. But you're worse than a girl."

I look out the window at the cars shooting flat rays of light like butter knives onto the mirrored freeway. He never shuts up.

"Not only do you NOT have a dick, not only do you refuse to TAKE dick, which makes you useless, but you want to cut it OFF. Of course they want to kill you."

"Let 'em fuckin' try." I grab my bike and storm out into the rain.

Fuck that. I'm invisible. Can't catch me. I gotta ride, clear out my head. Silly faggot, what does he know about partying or anything else.

NO FUN NO FUN

Ally's not here anymore. It doesn't bother me. I don't miss her. I don't miss her loving me forever, I don't miss her, the best fuck in the world who sees right through me. If she left, she left. I know I was good to her. So I'm a speed demon. Doesn't mean my love wasn't pure and good and true. I put my head down on her lap and cried. I grabbed her ankles and begged. I put aside my manly pride. I cut off all the parts of me that are loud and obnoxious and fourteen, duct taped them into a bundle and threw them in the corner. Shut up over there, I said.

That ain't good enough for her. Why can't she see we are bound by a string of angels? I promised her forever.

I go to the pusherman to get another front.

He says, Jim, I can't front you no more. You owe me. You're gonna have to start sucking my dick and I know you ain't that kinda girl.

You're damn right, I ain't.

He says I gotta come up with the rest of the dough and I can't come over no more cuz, like he told me before, I get too high and it bugs him out.

So OK. I go to Frankie's. She loves me so she pays off my debt and buys me an ounce of cocaine. She thinks she's doing me a favor. Since that's not my drug of choice, I'm not going to put it all in my arm. I might actually make some money off it instead.

Speed customers are not easy to switch to coke. A speed customer wants to be drinking copious amounts of booze and then go home and clean the house, on twenty dollars. A coke customer wants a nice buzz so they can keep up an entertaining conversation until the bar closes, for thirty dollars. It takes me a while to convert the speed freaks and locate the coke freaks. One night I can't sell my shit, so I go to the park and fire it up with some water I found in a bottle amongst the used condoms. All seven quarters, almost two grams, systematically, one right after the other. I would never have shot that much speed. As a result, the coke's disappearing at an even faster rate than the speed did, with an even lower return. I'm finding out I was wrong about being a great business mind. But it doesn't matter, because Frankie always fills in the blanks, just looks at me, disappointed, and hands over more product.

Every now and then I come home. I do not look at Sadaam's decay. Some days are better, some are worse, but on the whole *he's* worse.

He just lies in bed and watches the TV he dumpstered on the electricity he pirated. He's a pro squatter, you know, good at fixing the meters with a pin that keeps the needle from going around, so when the electric company comes to read the numbers, the meter always stays the same and the electricity is free. Or he can siphon electricity off a power pole so someone else pays for it. Slick Rick.

So one day I come in. He usually ignores me. Today he says, "Girl, you look like shit."

"Yeah, fuck you. What are you, my fashion consultant?"

"Your fashion's flawless, but even style can't help you now. You're beyond fashion."

I pop a beer and sit down beside him. "I didn't know it was a fuckin' beauty contest." Shit, I thought I was looking good. "Whatsa matter, PMS again?"

"If I was, at least I'd be over myself in a couple of days. If you don't stop, your face is gonna stay like that forever."

"OK, Sha Nay Nay. You can stop throwin' shade now."

I down a couple beers and pass out. Two days later I wake up and Frankie's standing over me smiling. She scored again.

Sadaam doesn't like us doing it right in his eye, so I jump on the back of Frankie's motorcycle and we jet to her house.

The thing about hag grounds is, you do it once and you are set for the next twelve hours, you don't need more all the time. But coke you got to do every fifteen minutes, or you go crazy pacing, looking for shit to do, you need something to do because you're wired, but somehow you don't quite have the energy to do it. Every time you think of something you might want to do, you go, Nah, I just wanna bang some more COKE.

And now that we got a mountain of it and no one to stop us, that's what we do for the next twenty-four hours. A shot every fifteen minutes. It's glorious, trading off, hitting each other when one of us is shaking too much to poke our own vein. Heaven. Because usually you only got enough stardust for one or two nice shots, and then you're out doing everything but five-dollar blow jobs on Capp Street so you can go cop some more. That shit is fucked up.

So there we are, the only way to fly and no landing in sight.

Pretty soon we're bugging. We start at midnight, and by morning, I can't find a vein in the bright sun. I got blood streaming down both arms from ten different places I tried to hit, where I had the motherfucking vein, but I was spazzing so hard I couldn't tell I was in and pulled the needle out like a dickwad.

She's trying to hit me behind my knees. I'm lying on the floor butt naked, demanding she shoot me up, like I'm in a position to be demanding. That's when her houseguest, this straightedge respectable girl, walks in on us. Jeez. That throws me, I got to admit. I flip out for a second, what am I doing here, ass up, face down, with a needle poking out the back of my leg.

But that only stops me for a minute. Then I get right back to the quest for rush, and damn if there's no more to get. Bankrupt. Long walk to a dry well. After a point, you can't get no higher. You're just there at the pinnacle, and you can't enjoy your amperage because in order to feel the difference you got to rush more than you already are, and you cannot, unless you overamp and die.

We're doing hits huge as humanly possible without death happening. Nothing.

I put the point in my arm above one of the swollen spongy parts where I missed, and there's a little swamp bubble of wasted coke floating around in my arm, and I shit you not, clear coke juice squirts out of another hole in my arm two inches up. I'm a pincushion. Mondo perforation. I keep poking new holes and watching it squirt out of old holes. I just stare at the liquid high spilling on the floor instead of flowing to my heart, and I'm thinking, Hey, I'm a fucking cartoon.

I roll down my sleeves and they soak up the blood, the long-sleeved white shirt I been wearing to cover up the tracks streaked with rusty rivulets screaming "fiend."

Frankie looks at me like I'm some kinda pathetic. When somebody as wasted as Frankie feels sorry for you, you know you're fucked.

She calls it quits, wraps up the baggies and outfits. I don't fight. Other times I'd be saying, Come on Frankie, one more for the road, one more bedtime story, come on baby, please.

But I ain't saying shit. I ain't crying. Don't say nothing, just get on your bad motorscooter and ride.

JOHN WAYNE WAS A NAZI

Our house is sunk down in the woodsy lap of the hillside so that only the roof pokes out like a pyramid from rain forests, all but swallowed by a snarl of vines and brambles. I duck down into the briar tunnel to the peely paint door.

Sadaam is standing by the picture window looking out to the bay and over the freeway. I sidle up to him, not talking.

The moon's rising like a big orange squeezed out of a slot in the steel-blue sky.

"It sure is big."

He says, "Yeah, it's full tonight. Magic."

"Aw, there ain't no such thing as magic."

"There is too." He's all wild eyed.

That's the end of that. Fine. I'm not arguing with a crazy queen about magic when he gets that high-pitched tone.

"Magic's real. It is. You don't know anything."

"OK, pal. It's OK, I believe in it. Magic. Yep."

"You are an asshole."

"Yep. I am." Whatever you say. I do not have the balls for a fight right now.

I go pass out.

I'm dreaming of fucking her slow up against the wall, latex dress hiked up, AK-47 strapped to her thigh, eyes streaming black, outside gunfire, pipe bombs, I'm fucking her into a soft-focus candy store, she's chewing glass in my ear, I come inside her to the sound of jackboots kicking in the door, henchmen shouting, OPEN UP, OPEN THE FUCKING DOOR. POLICE.

The door splinters off the hinges and pigs spill in yelling, GET UP ASSHOLE, GET YOUR HANDS OUT FROM UNDER THE COVERS, pointing rifles. *Click, click.* Death cocked and ready.

"Damn, chill out. You got a warrant?"

"Shut up fuckface. You'll see plenty of warrants."

Sadaam's hacking up his morning lung. They grab him and throw him on the floor, kicking him, and I'm yelling, "He's sick—"

They jump on me. I hold my ribs while they bash my knuckles with sticks.

"Fuckin' queers, you don't know when to shut up. Resisting arrest, huh?"

"I'M NOT RESISTING, I'M NOT RESISTING." That's supposed to stop them, but it never does if no one's watching or videotaping.

Handcuffs snapped on tight enough to cut. They like that shit, food for masturbation, steal your sick fantasy and make it theirs. It's not theirs. Control, domination, yeeha, humiliation. Rip the wings off the tiny fly.

Dick's too small? Nobody liked you in school? That's OK, join the police force! They'll give you a gun and a badge and you'll always get the last word from now on.

They even started making their batons cock-shaped for the schlong impaired. I would laugh thinking about it, but it makes my gut hurt.

They throw shit around, searching for what? I ain't got shit. I'm trying to think if there's drugs or rigs stashed, but my mind can't get off my ribs. Well, if they can't find anything, they can always plant it. We're cuffed, face down and naked, and they're sneering. What goes through a guy's mind when he's got a gun to your head? I can't understand how it works. Let's see. Brutalize the weaker things. Hurt, molest, kill, abuse. I try and try to wrap my brain around it. . . .

Aw fuck it, they can't be that callous. "Hey, how's about a jacket for my pal. He's got pneumonia."

"One less fag ain't gonna matter." Chuckles all around.

Sadaam's wheezing and hawking up green things.

They find some roaches, all triumphant like it's a kilo of cocaine, bag them up, official, for Evidence. Hurl us into the backseat, drive us downtown, and book us for squatting.

God, I love this country. America, right or wrong.

A BAD DAY

On the way to the cop shop, I remember the last scene I had with San Francisco's finest. I'd been up a few days without food, just speed, pot, and beer, three of the four food groups. I'd just downed a couple snakebites at the bar. I blew into the liquor store ranting, Smash was there, I stumbled into a display of Vienna sausage and Campbell's soup, and sent the whole shelf full of pseudo-food flying. I was slipsliding and grabbing at boxes of mac and cheese as I went down.

The store dude started hollering and flinging his arms around, so I said to him: "YA THINK THAT'S SUMP'M?"

Staring right at him, I swung one arm way back and swept off an entire shelf of Dinty Moore stew, sardines, and creamed corn, with a flourish.

I beamed store dude my most charming smile. "How do ya like me now?"

"I call the police, that's how I like you."

"Oh yeah? Great. They're my pals, here to serve and protect. WOO-ha."

Laughing my ass off, I ambled right into the arms of the very same pals.

I started fast talking.

"He made a pass at me, can't blame him really as I'm such a fine handsome young man." I winked at them.

They were on a sugar mission. I got away. Justice all depends on whether it's donut time or not.

Hard to stay on the earthplane when you've already been to the stratosphere, but it's just another withdrawal symptom, like from the biological response one body has to another, when magnetic fields attract, attach, separate, poison the blood, speed it up, small aircrafts spin in the sky, hearts race, drop dead. Love, lust, chemical euphoria, I inject the liquid moment when souls meet.

Much better than love.

Love, where she says she'll be constant and true and always, and you should be free, and when you believe her, she yanks your training collar.

The needle loves me. It never lets me down. I know what I want and I know how to get it. Lungs collapse, I'm atoms smashing, stars dispersing, I implode, silent, slow, one with everything, no separation anxiety. At the speed of light anxiety disappears. To be young, amped, and drunk, and to know I can't stay that way, is gorgeously tragic.

I don't care how evil the hangover. NOW is perfection worth any price. The ones who never fall under the spell of love or speed come down once and hate the high forever. Protect themselves from all pain and joy. But godhood is worth the dethroning. The game is King of the Hill, stay on top of the world as long as possible, and don't break any bones when you fall. Then climb up again, levitate.

The constabulary lets me go. They don't tell me what happened to Sadaam. He's in boy jail. I walk back to the locked-up squat, standing in front of it with nothing left. I stashed the bike in the snagglebushes behind the house, so wheels I got. That's all I need to be free. Have bike will travel. Traveling light.

The charity of friends is wearing thin. But hysteria and exhaustion are the mothers of invention, and those are my only two moods, so I'm plenty resourceful.

Frankie's balking at letting me crash there.

"What. It'd just be for a few days."

But she doesn't believe me. "I can't afford you."

"Fine, so gimme some money."

She forks over enough for an eight ball.

I hightail it over to Micky D's where I'm supposed to meet Junkie Scum to cop the shit. I'm waiting with the money in the parking lot. He wanders over, hands me the stash, I give him the cash, he bails.

I go to Frankie's and weigh it out. I lick some off my finger. Sweet. An eighth of an ounce of powdered sugar.

"Where'd you score this shit."

"Dope fiend motherfucker. I'll kill him."

She just looks at me.

I kick all the furniture. "Fuckin' prick. Cocksuckin' dicklickin' assbitin' motherfuckin' sonofabitch. Shit. Shit shit shit shit. Now what are we gonna do."

"Whattaya mean *we*, potty mouth?"

"C'mon Frankie. I'm fucked. It's not my fault the bastard stiffed me. I was gonna get a hotel room with that money."

"That's it. You gotta go. Over it."

I can't believe, my old pal Frankie putting me on the street. "That's fucked up."

"No. You know what's fucked up? You boot everything in sight. You tweak out. You take all my money and lose it. You drive me crazy. BEAT IT. I can't even deal with your bullshit one more second. Get outta here before I kill you."

"Whoa. Harsh."

I drag my pitiful ass to the park. I get a good bush to slide me and my bike under, put my leather over me and peek through the branches at the twinkly sky. It's lonely. I wish I could leave.

No matter how many times I fill up, I'm always empty.

I'm so burnt out from getting rousted, crashing off coke in jail, rustling up money to buy drugs, getting snaked by junkie mother-fuckers, I crash right out without worrying about bugs or fog or zombie fags lurching around looking for the perfect mouth.

When I wake up, the sun's burning down and the wind's rushing through the trees wet and misty. I sit up and look at the post-card view of gingerbread roof peaks sloping a blue-and-white zigzag down the sky, behind them a jagged crown of skyscrapers choked by white-fingered fog. Not a bad place to wake up with a view of my office. That's what I called it when I had work, which reminds me, I ought to be looking for some. Good thing I still got my bike, because then I can work, and then I can get money, and then I can get food.

I go to grab my bike and cruise downtown but yikes, no bike. I pat the ground where it was, snatch aside bushes. *Fuck. Where's my fucking bike.*

It's all too much. I would try to figure out if I had been really bad lately. I would cry. But I do not have time. The moment after your bike is snagged is the best time to get it back.

I squint around the park to see if anyone's stupid enough to be taking it for a joyride. They are not. What kind of sick fuck takes a guy's true love and livelihood when he's out for the count?

I'm not going to cry.

I wander down the hill, crying.

I head to Civic Center, where they're probably trying to sell my baby for twenty bucks like a cheap whore. The plaza's full of scruffy punks. Guys with carts full of stuff, garbage bags tied to the sides, saddlebags full of beer cans, funky as only Budweiser dregs rotting in the sun can be. Women ranting to themselves. Crack-heads doubled over searching, snoots to the ground, rooting like tall boars for that truffle of white rock lost on the cement, picking up pebbles, cigarette butts, broken glass, inspecting each bit like a jeweler squinting at diamonds. Poor bastards all tied up for the love of a drug.

There's a guy I never seen before riding around with no messenger bag. It's not my bike, but I know it's not his either. Uglied up with band stickers to disguise its jamming true identity, a light-weight fixed gear, one speed, no brakes, skinny tires. Only a real messenger would know how to stop on a fixie, backpedaling and skidding, except me, I just run it into a parked car. But this guy has no clue about that and keeps running into *people,* Oops sorry oops sorry.

He wobbles by me, and I grab him by the jacket and jerk him backward.

"Get off my fuckin' bike, spermbrain." I got the crazy look in my eye and the vein standing out in my neck. Whoa, I can't believe I just did that. Beat me to a bloody pulp, fine, but steal my bike, that's going too far.

"Aw shit, man, somebody just sold me this for fifty bucks. . . ."

"BULLSHIT. First you rip me off, then you got the huevos to lie about it." I push him with both hands in his chest, jump on the bike, and ride off into the sunset. "If I ever see you again, I'll cut you, maing."

It may not be my baby, but any bike is better than none at all. I figure if some messenger claims it, I'll give it up, but for now I got wheels. I'm going back to lie down in that same place in the park, and I'm gonna tie a string around my finger and the other end to my bike, and I'm gonna catch that rat bastard. Stealin' horses is a hangin' crime.

HERO WORSHIP

What a homing pigeon. I almost went back to my old job, but I don't feel down to groveling today. I'm gonna find a new outfit that doesn't know me yet, an indie joint, a new joint, where my pals are already working, where I got an in. I cruise down Market to Wally World.

I get some free caffeine from the coffee-cart babe. She's a poet I saw read once. She was pretty good. I imagine poetry doesn't pay well. But look, hell of a successful java jockey.

She's about to toss out some pastries.

"Hey. Don'tcha give those to the homeless?"

She gives me this extremely bored look.

"I'm fuckin' homeless. Gimme some, 'kay, babe?" I think she's masquerading as straight, but I flirt with her anyway because she's cute. You know straight girls are just professing to like dick. I don't believe it. What they like is penetration. Poor misguided babes. I try to help whenever I can, but it's a big job for one guy.

So I'm standing around, flirting and shoving scones in my face, and she's packing up, and I'm scouting around for messengers who can give me the 411 on jobs. The wall's empty though, because it's five o'clock, and all the secretaries are ordering rushes to get their bosses off their necks, because the dumb jerks are just sobering up from a three-martini lunch and have been procrastinating their lives away, so now it's RUSH RUSH RUSH all over the place, and the only messengers to be found are flying by at high speeds, doing America's work.

Finally Binky packs up her little cart of pleasures and pushes it away to coffee-cart headquarters, and I'm feeling low and dejected, when up rides the finest boychick that I secretly have a crush on, but I can't tell her because she'd call me a fag, and really I just want to be her. Fuckalot's hair is so big it has its own name. Its name is Herman. Inky sideburns permanently curl like paisley into the hollows of her cheeks. She's so fine, if she wasn't my bro in Hagdom we'd fuck like the Village People. She got bedroom eyes, skin that makes you shivery and want to drink her all the way down like a shot of Kahlua. Her smile's pure love, white straight teeth, one gold one in the front with a four-leaf clover carved out of the middle, and eyes that soften up to be your momma and rock you all night long. She acts sweet and mellow, until you hang with her awhile, and then you see how her kill powder-keg shit been slammed down so many times it's barely contained.

"Fuckalot, Let's get some pizza after work and you can tell me jail stories."

"How 'bout we go work on some tall bikes instead."

She's everything I want to be. She has the rage when she wants it, and the calm, sweet charm when she needs it. Not like me, smiling at the world and hurting the one I love.

"What was it like in there?"

"Someday I'll tell you all about it."

She beat up a guy in a bar who tried to take something of hers without asking. Course she wouldn't have given it to him, no matter how nice he asked. Accidentally killed him, the jury said. Her lawyer explained to the court how women who kill their beaters and rapists are America's political prisoners. Some smoke-filled back-room conversations and three years later, Fuckalot hit the streets. We wondered why such obvious and fair conclusions were still relegated to back rooms.

I look at her muscles bulging under her T-shirt. I bet she kicked the baddest asses and got all the girls to be hers.

"Hey, will you be my trainer? Teach me how to lift weights and fight? You know I got a big mouth with nothing to back it up. Which is exciting, but sometimes I could do without the excitement."

"Well, they don't fuck with me because I'm psycho. *You* know." She sounds like the most rational person in the world when she says this.

I respect her. It's weak to simper along and smile and shuffle when you're feeling mistreated. A real man takes action.

And then along come the cops to throw you in the hole for standing up for yourself. No, they'd rather have you come whining to them, even though they don't give a damn about you. It ain't a big deal unless you make it a big deal, lady.

Give me the Old West, where if someone fucked you up, you turned around and straightened it out right there, no middleman, and you felt better about it, felt like you could look at yourself in the mirror the rest of your days.

I'd rather do my own dirty work, get more satisfaction out of it and get it done right. If I was a hero with some guts like Fuckalot, maybe I would. But me, I always cross the street to avoid trouble.

Being homeless, I go into rodent mode and squirm my way into the house of the Despondent One. She's a crazy New Yorker babe. I got a thing for crazy New Yorker babes. They're dangerous. You might call it a fetish. I work my charms, and next thing you know, nice and toasty warm and roasty, a home.

She likes to string me up in front of the bay windows, so the neighbors can see. Not like I ain't a freak or nothing, it just creeps me out with her. I don't trust her. But a guy's gotta do what a guy's gotta do.

Even more perverted is the way I volunteer for indentured servitude. I can't tell which of us is sicker, me, for offering up my soul as a scam, or her, for accepting the offer from an orphan waif like me, or me, deeply wounded that she has used her superior place in society to take advantage of this offer.

She says no party action while I'm living with her. Nary a beer. She's a roof over my head and a bedwarmer though, and she looks good on my arm. God knows that's important, as I do so care about my fucking reputation.

I get obsessed with her for lack of other distractions. She's the only source of kicks since she laid down the law, and I'm going along with it. Maybe I need a girl to tell me when to quit. That's what girls are good for, reining in your craziness when it borders on the suicidal. Too bad I didn't see that quality in them before. I'd be in Ally's arms by now. But any babe's better than no babe at all. Ain't it?

Despondent One, she's hell of fine, but now and then my pals will point out that she does get this crazy look in her eye, which I think happens because she did too much acid in New York in her formative years. In New York they do acid in their formative years. Everything's faster there, so they start young. Either that or she's just plain neurotic from being raised there. I've heard the Rotten Apple's not exactly relaxing for tiny children.

I get scared when I sneak a look at her and she thinks no one's looking, when she's got this murderous look in her eye like Medusa, but she's just examining her manicure.

One good thing about her is she has this really great cat named Zoloft, he's all black with white socks and a white shirt front, and he and Hat the cat are in love and lie around together all day and purr and are happy.

Old Despondent says it's OK for her to have beers, but not me, because I can't handle it, and she can. It's a game. Sometimes she lets me drink, big-deal privilege for slave boy. I had two beers the other night and she had a bunch of tequila sunrises. We were at Lucky 13 seeing this band called the Bleedin' Fuckin' Catheads. Real flash in the pan, but I liked the name so much, I put the flier up in our bathroom. Anyway, she saw her ex there and hung all over her the whole time, putting the moves on her in front of me. Snore. We got in a fight and she said, See, you can't even handle two beers.

Hate her.

The Despondent One says she's going back to art school in New York, but I can sublet the place while she's gone. Wave goodbye as she drives away in her 1971 puke-green shoebox car. I hate that car. It's full of books and beer cans.

"Fuck you, it's a *Dodge Duster*," she always says.

There's been one beer in the fridge for months, since that night when she went out and ceremoniously presented a six-pack of Miller to me, the town lush. We drank five, and she put the last one away and said I couldn't have it. Every day I've had to look at that sad beer, and it's become like the toilet. It's there. You don't drink it. But today when I go upstairs and she drives away, I open the fridge, and there it stands, all alone, and suddenly it's its old self again. Victorious, I drain it.

I start fucking this fine young butch. I like her because we jump up and down on the bed and scream and yell and throw shit and act like we're twelve. She has her own place but stays at mine all the time. Then I fuck this other chick I been chasing for weeks, wake up in her apartment, and find my wallet gone, so I go back to the park where we fucked in the wet grass the night before, as if it's really going to be there. It's not. A weekly event, the losing of the wallet. I walk home in the rain.

I wander into my living room at seven A.M. There's Butchetta de Ville, writing me this long tweak letter about how much she loves me. I said if you can't handle your coke, don't sit around my apartment waiting, fool, when I told you I was going to be out all night. Do I look like the marrying kind? You're not even my type, your hair's too short. Get out of my life.

I'll be damned if I'm gonna let someone tell me what to do when I don't even need them for a roof over my head. She was gonna impede my freedom *and* be all up in my space. I don't think so.

So then Rosemary moves in.

Rosemary has to share my room, which she doesn't much like. I don't know why. We get along perfect, until she has to live in my room. We partied together for years, except she toots and I boot, which I never told her. Her favorite food is screwdrivers, mine is beer. See, so we got our differences. I love her like a sister you are also a little in love with. Rosemary is strictly dickly. What's to identify with in a straight girl? I don't know, but I got a thing for them. Even though I can't understand a girl loving a man. Men are so different than women, I can't figure out heterosexuality at all. You have to deny your whole being to even fuck, much less be married and have kids. Oh yeah, let's pretend we have stuff in common. OK we don't. OK, I'll just pretend I'm not me at all and that I know what you're talking about. OK great, and I'll just ignore you. Yeah, now we're having fun. Woo-hoo.

Sometimes I think me and Ally are like that. She always says we got nothing in common. But then again, at least we got the same hormones flowing through our veins.

Speaking of heterosexuality, I guess the cats have been doing the icky when we're not looking, because Hat's preggers with Zoloft's babies. Me and Rosemary are there for the whole thing, watching the kittens slip out all slimy each one, and Hat cleans them up and they look like tiny orange bears with tabs for ears, and round heads, and every last one of them is orange. We love them and call them the Keebers. We're a family.

One day Rosemary's got the ironing board out in the kitchen

and I'm trying to make a milkshake in a blender, and the counters are all loaded up with dirty dishes, so I put the blender on the ironing board and turn it on and it spews a little, and all of a sudden there's old Rosemary, hooting, "WHAT-h ARE YOU DOING?"

"What."

"Em, what d'ye mean, 'What'? You've got shit all over me work shirt." She really pronounces the "t" in shit.

"Oh. Sorry."

Like she doesn't have another white shirt.

I'm trying not to laugh. You can't laugh at Rosemary when she gets like that, even though she's hell of funny.

I guess that's when she starts looking for another place.

Then I find this cute fag boy named Walter walking down Castro one day. He's sixteen and heading to the Pendulum, the salt and pepper bar, where white guys and black guys go to pick up on each other. He says he never goes home because his uncle that molested him lives there and he can't stand it, so I say why don't you come home with me, and he does.

We spend plenty of nights in bed telling each other stories and playing with the Keebers. I tell him about girls, and he tells me about boys. I'm thinking I'm his father figure, but he sees how high I am all the time, and maybe I'm not such a great role model.

Then this other little seventeen-year-old kid I scrounge up at the crystal house starts coming over a lot, and we slam speed and play Millions of Dead Cops tapes.

One day we try to quit zip together. I explain to Walter we're helping each other clean up, and he looks at me, then says to Rosemary, "I just want to know WHO'S helping WHO."

I take long baths and get high in the tub, because it takes that much heat to make a vein come up anymore. I come out mumbling and can't look Rose in the eye, but I never avoid her, because I'm so paranoid, I figure *then* she'll *really* know I'm high, so I stand around and try to hold conversations with her, but it's always her talking and asking questions, and me mumbling yes or no and staring out the window.

She says, "Where's the Jim I used to know? The rambunctious one that's still alive?"

One night she's getting ready to go out and her leather jacket is not in the closet. She calls Esta Noche, the Latina drag bar, and asks for Walter.

"Do you have my leather?" she yells over the disco to which queens are lip synching and switching hips in large high heels on the other end.

"Ummm, yes."

"Get back here right now." She didn't count on being a mom to a teenage boy yet.

Pretty soon she moves out.

One night I come home and Walter is smoking crack in the kitchen with this older white guy he must have picked up at the bar, because I've never seen him before.

"No way, get out, both of you. No crack in the house."
"Why?"
"Cuz I'm the dad."
"You got a double standard, Miss Thang."
I say, "Don't you 'Miss Thang' me. It's my house, my rules."
A couple days later all my rent money is gone out of the rent jar.

I say, "Walter, did you see where my money went?"

He just shrugs.

That'll teach me to trust anybody.

I'm going nuts, because where am I going to get rent, where am I going to get another front, because I been selling serum to get the rent, and now I'm fucked, because I have to come up with rent for the landlord *and* money for the man who loaned me dirty water on good faith.

I call the landlord and square it away, say I had a little setback. It's all good. Walter disappears.

Then New York hoebag calls, checking up on me. I don't know what possesses me to tell her the truth, that I'm behind on the rent but I cut a deal with the landlord. I'm straight with her, you know. I laugh it off and say everything's cool as long as the cops don't raid the place. I guess she doesn't think it's funny.

Then I get a three-hundred-dollar phone bill, which is in the Despondent One's name, with two pages of 976-JERK OFF numbers. Old Walter was calling the porno line, wanking on the phone for three dollars a minute, and when you're smoking crack it takes you a long time to come, honey.

So I call the phone company and cut a deal with them too.

Two weeks later I come home from a binge. The door's open, the apartment's empty, and strangers are scrubbing it down with ammonia.

"What the fuck's going on."

They just look at me. Then the Despondent One saunters in, and now she's pissed *and* despondent. "You monster. Look at you. You're a mess. I called your parents and they're on their way."

"You what?"

She's got that crazed look in her eye.

"You called my fuckin' parents? Wha'dja do that for? You're gonna die a slow painful death, you superior little . . ."

"Damn right I'm superior."

"Why don't you grow the fuck up."

"Who are you telling to grow up, fuckup? I trusted you, left everything in my name, and you fucked it up. WHO'S THE BRAT?"

I can't believe this lunatic flew in from New York to personally screw up my life, which I was doing just fine on my own.

So then, sure enough, my goddam parents show up, the first time I've seen them together in ten years. My dad's got that intense look of disappointment, and my mom's staring in disbelief.

I'm sitting on the only piece of furniture left in the joint, looking out the bay windows on Popeye's Chicken, where I'd always get a thirty-five cent biscuit after I'd come down and that's all the money I'd have left in the world, the same bay windows I'd look out of when I used to lie in bed with the Despondent One after a good boink, and watch the fog roll in.

Now Satan whips out the evidence: rigs and baggies, ta-dahh! Great. Mom runs out crying.

"Look. You happy now? You made my mother cry. Is that your good deed for the day, scum bucket?"

I leave Dad standing there and run out after my mom, who's getting in her car. I don't know what to say, I mean, she wants me to tell her it's not true. What am I gonna do, lie to her, on top of everything? She drives away.

I run back upstairs. Dad walks out. I look at Righteously Indignant Despondent One. "What about Zoloft and Hat and the Keebers? Look."

The kittens are scattered about playing, and Zoloft and Hat are hiding in the closet.

"I'm taking Zoloft back to New York."

"Oh yeah, great, break up the family."

All my records are outside being carted away by riffraff. I'm chasing them down the street yelling, Gimme that shit, it's mine.

The scraggly retarded guy whose brother, the Hell's Angel, lives down the street, he comes weaving up the sidewalk at me. He's covered in blood, crying like a kid.

"My brother always hits me. Why? Make him stop. He's always hitting me."

I just stare at him. Fuck, stupid ugly fuck.

"Stop going over there then. He hates you. He's a jerk," I inform him. "He doesn't love you. Stop trying to get him to, cuz he's never gonna change. He's a dick."

I keep grabbing shit away from scavengers. The poor bastard keeps walking down the street, bleeding and crying.

I get a forty-ouncer and wouldn't you know it, the first day out homeless after a month of summer, it starts to rain. I go back upstairs and pack the Keebers and Hat the Cat in a cardboard box, balance them on the handlebars, and sail down the hill toward Francine's. A dyke bar is full of suckers who will adopt a kitten or two.

Maybe cats need a home but I don't. What the fuck good's a home anyway, if it's that much trouble. Awful high price on the illusion of security. Give me the open road and a couch to surf.

One of my drunk pals at Francine's insists on taking the whole fam damily. I tell her, They'll grow up and you won't want 'em anymore cuz they won't be cute, but she swears she'll keep 'em forever. I hand them over, crying like a girl.

A few months later I see her and say, How's them Keebers, and she says, Aw, I took 'em to the pound.

I'm a cold-blooded baby killer.

HOLE PUNCH

The pain never does seem to go away, no matter how many babes I date or drugs I shoot. Maybe because I see Ally around all the time. Sometimes she kisses me or I get real lucky. But it kills me. To touch her skin, it's like a salamander's, moist, it's so supple, like a baby. When her body's in my hands and I know maybe this is the last time I'll ever hold her, I feel like there's no meaning in the world if I can't possess her. And she says, Well, all you have to do is give up one ride, and you can have this one forever.

I try to imagine myself the perfect husband and it's a chasm with no me in it. I know I can never make her happy. I can never make any girl happy. Every girl I ever tried to get to love me, if I tricked her into thinking I was good and giving me her heart, I'd just throw it on the ground and stomp it. I don't really have it in me to be a straight-up guy. I don't deserve no kind of love.

I'm walking by Black and Blue Tattoo. I see Lisalotta out front. I say, Hey, why don't you pierce my lip, do it right now. And she says, Do you have any money? And I say, Naw, baby, but I'll run you some errands, and she says, Get in here then.

I never jabbed no metal through my face before. A pal shoved a safety pin through my nipple once, and I figured the pain would be about the same. I got a pretty high threshold. It doesn't scare me. I been busted in the mouth, had teeth knocked out or hanging by a bloody thread. Plenty of cars and buses knocked me off my bike, and I lived through it.

There's something about saying I want this particular kind of pain now, to decorate my face and make it more kissable, that's different from a traffic accident. It's nice. If you're dying inside, a little ink or a hole punched in your body makes it real. Marks that day so you can look in the mirror and say, I remember when that shit happened, or when I was really in love, or when Joe died. You re-create yourself. You are the act of God, not its casualty. Every day you look for the rush, taking away the shield, putting yourself in harm's way, risk being wounded to see if you can feel anything, so maybe a pleasurable sensation can infiltrate your unguarded heart. Maybe this is one step beyond that, deliberately wounding yourself to make an even more definite opening in you.

Lisalotta's sterilizing sharp metal things. I'm nervous, not about how much it's gonna hurt, but that my mom isn't gonna like it. She's just never gonna get over it, I know. She's gonna hate me and hate looking at me. Damn I need my mom to love me. Is she gonna be able to love me? Could she ever before? She has really never seen me, never wanted to. Now my guts will be even more splattered all over my face, so maybe she'll have to see, and she'll have to love me, because why? The same reason she got over my queerness, fiending, tats, because I'm the only thing she's got.

I think she'd like my tattoos better if I had one that said MOM in a heart. And since she found out about the party in my arm, she's sad, but hell, it's not like she can just focus on her other kid at Harvard. I'm it. I told her to have a baby brother when I was five. I hounded her for a couple years. But she always said, "You're plenty." Little did she know. Bet my parents wish they had listened to me now. A couple more porkfests and a few hundred thousand more dollars, and boom-ba, no more having to settle for the child that never went to grad school. They could relax and know they'd be taken care of in their old age. But nooooooo . . .

My dad is definitely not going to love me as much with the metal lip trip. He's not gonna understand and he's not gonna wanna understand and he is not gonna wanna talk about it. Cuz he's a man. He's an American man. He likes Westerns and football and he has an autographed copy of Nixon's book, *Six Crises*. I was actually there when Nixon signed it. In my stroller. Mom was getting the book signed for Dad's birthday. Whoa, that's heavy. I try not to think about that.

Because, like my Dad, when something unpleasant arises, I ignore it until it goes away. I'm sure that will be Dad's solution to the lip ring.

OK, so Mom has no choice but to love me, and Dad will change the subject.

I'm wondering, how much more of a chunk of my sneaking by as a worthwhile member of society am I giving up. I got a haircut and tattoos that warn you I'm coming from a block away. Now I jab a piece of metal through my lip. I could have slid by. See, people are offended when you don't shop at the mall. They care that you have dropped out of their normal little sorority. Then again, even though they're upset, they forgive some social defection, like patches on the back of your jacket that say BURN THE RICH. But self-inflicted FACIAL wounds, they can't get over that. They say WHAT'D YA DO THAT FOR? It scares 'em. They think you're gonna go after them with a needle and poke a hole through their dick.

Well I'm not gonna, but I'd like to.

That's cool. React. Go ahead. Weeds out the assholes. That's what I said when half my pals fell by the wayside once they found out I was fucking girls in high school. I said, 'Bye, and don't come back. Who needs your ass?

Efficiency. I don't wanna spend my whole life giving people the picture they want. Then they never show their true colors. A little metal in my face and we cut to the chase.

So I walk down the street and I'm studying the looks on people's faces. Sometimes they smile. I'm thinking, why are they being friendly, but then I realize they're laughing at me. Looking like they do, they got a lotta nerve laughing at me. Shit, howdy. Now that's funny. YOU tell ME what looks good, loser.

Can't kiss no girls with this fucked-up lip. Can't quit smokin', though I know I should. Can't eat no pussy. Too many germs. I would go ahead and kiss girls anyway, but now, with the pus all funky and shit, they're even less interested than they were before. Not like I care. Lisalotta says I ain't supposed to kiss them on any of their parts for a month, and it makes it easier now that they are disgusted, so they aren't tempting and seducing and making resistance difficult.

It would be even easier if I went somewhere where the girls were few and ugly, if such a place existed. I haven't tried geography as a means of escape yet.

Tricky Dick tried to kiss me in the illusory safety of my stroller, you know how them baby kissers are, right there in the department store, in front of all those pretty, high-heeled, silk-stockinged, perfume-smelling ladies in their Chanel suits. With his old five o'clock shadow that made him lose the election against JFK cuz of the TV debate, where JFK looked cute and Nixon looked like a child-molesting crook. Well, I bet he wouldn't wanna kiss me now, ducky.

Nobody does. 'Specially not Ally, and if anyone but her tried, I'd just straight-arm 'em anyway.

PUNKROCK MARLENE

There's a fine young Berliner hairdresser who hangs at the Firehouse. She buys me free beer, cuz I'm a friend of Rosemary. All the Mission punk girls are pals. They barhop around the neighborhood after work and visit each other drinking free Jagermeisters.

I sit and stare, pretending not to stare. She's the punkrock reincarnation of Marlene Dietrich. I gotta have a distraction to forget true love, so why not focus on some impossible dream of a straight girl with tall green hair and a deep-throat Berliner drawl. I could whip myself into a fascination. And what's more fascinating than someone you can never have?

Sometimes she brings her buzzers, sits me on a bar stool outside, and freshens up my mohawk. She pets my head. She can't shake me. She talks to tall dark strangers while I hover. I try to look at anything but her, but I can't. She's an X-rated cartoon, the ideal parts all stuck together like a teenage-boy fantasy.

Her name is Ute.

She says this "Ooo-ta."

I pass out every night pronouncing her name.

One night she gives me pink triangular pills after feeding me pints of ale all night. An hour later my knees begin to buckle.

I say, "Ute, if you do not take me home to your apartment right away, I am going to sprawl out on the floor right here in the bar."

I tell her this because it is true and think how smart and lucky I am that her apartment is right around the corner and I know she will not let me lie in the beer for long.

She says, "Just wait a minute." She's impatient with me because she's having a sexy discussion with some boy who I later find out is her stupid boyfriend.

I wait obediently and after my legs have become very watery, I say, "Um, Ute, I really do not think I can stand up for one more minute. I mean it."

She ignores me for some length of time that I can no longer measure, while I tightly grip the edge of the bar. The top half of me is holding out fine. I see just one of everything, my speech isn't slurred, and I can think clearly. It's only my legs that can't function. Surreal.

Finally she says, "OK, let's go" and walks out.

I yell, "Hey, Ute," still holding on to the edge of the bar.

She turns and looks mildly bored.

"I can't walk."

She strolls back in and offers me her elbow, and I am so happy that she is loving me like my mother used to, in a you-are-rather-pathetic-and-you-need-me-how-quaint kind of way. I am touching her, linked arm in arm like school chums. I have had the most intense romances with school chums, although they never knew it.

Her stupid boyfriend, who I still do not want to believe is her boyfriend nor how stupid he is, is walking on the other side of her. Suddenly she trips and flies sideways through the air, diving headfirst into a parked Cadillac.

I do not know if you have ever hit another car bumper with a Cadillac bumper, but I have, and the other car bumper always splinters or crumples, and there's never a scratch on the Caddy bumper because it's solid chrome-plated steel.

So I stumble over to her where she's laid out on the street between two parked cars, and I'm as concerned as I can be considering I'm on a pill that has such a calming effect. These must be the "wifey" pills to shut you up when you realize you're trapped in an ugly stucco box in a tract, surrounded by other little boxes that all look just the same.

Ute's lying there not moving. She took some of the little pink triangles too. I thought she could handle them better than I can, since I'm an avowed speed freak and she likes downers. I thought I couldn't walk because I'm not used to not being able to walk, but if you always take drugs that make you unable to walk, you will eventually learn to walk on them. But she hasn't. She musta just bought whatever was on the market that day as long as it was a pill that slowed your ass down. And boy is she going slow now, getting her money's worth.

I lift her head up and look at the baseball growing there. She opens her eyes.

I glance up at Stupido, thinking for a split second, *You are my partner in crime, we both love her, help me.*

I said, "We should take her to the hospital."

"Nah, she'll be OK, let's just get her home," he says.

God, what an idiot.

The two of us lean into each other and get her on her feet. We all have snake legs. He carries her up the stairs. Well, at least he's good for something.

I don't remember what happens after that.

I go home with her a lot, both of us drunk from the bar, whenever he's not around. One morning I wake up with the sun streaming in on a fold-out bed under a twisty sheet. I see her sleeping next to me and fall in love. I slide down the bed, pull off her tiny cotton panties, and give her some head while she's still asleep. She wakes up coming. I'll never know if she faked it to stop me because I was so bad, or if she actually came because I was so good. I do know she didn't give a fuck about getting head from a girl because she's from Berlin and nothing ruffles her.

So I follow her around the rest of the day in a rosy cloud.

And she says, "Stop trying to hold my hand. Just because I let you go down on me doesn't mean I am your girlfriend."

Oh yeah. She's a goddess, I'm tellin' ya.

One day we're walking down an alley and stop to stare at graffiti painted as tall as us.

PROSTIT UTE
DESTIT UTE
ILL REP UTE

"My boyfriend wrote that," she announces.

And I thought he and I had something in common.

PART THREE

ROCK THE NATION

A JOB OFFER

Hostile Mucous played tonight, and I went up to talk to them because Fuckalot's their new axe man, and the singer's built. Her name's Devastaysha. I go see them so I can stare at her. I wanna be like them when I grow up, except they don't get high. Can't imagine why. I guess they got rock 'n' roll, it makes 'em feel like Hole, and with that kinda buzz, who needs drugs? They fucking rock and they're hilarious too, besides just being eye candy. See, hostile mucous is a naturally occurring contraceptive made in your choch, and some doctor discovered it, and he was a man who obviously wanted to spread his progeny far and wide, so he called it hostile mucous, but to girls of course it is not hostile, it's quite friendly and helpful.

Anyway, so I'm yapping with them onstage, which is swampy with beer, and blood, and piss from Devastaysha squatting.

She says, "We're going on tour and we really need a T-shirt guy, but nobody wants to leave their five-dollar-an-hour job for a five-dollar-a-day job, and then come back to no job at all."

"I don't have a job."

She looks at me.

"I wouldn't mind, that's all. There's nothin' keepin' me here and nothin' to lose."

"Yeah well, we need someone with a sense of responsibility."

"That's me."

"You gotta count money, sell shirts, move equipment, pump gas, drive, and make coffee."

"Yep, yep, yep, and yep. With a smile."

"Clearly, you, Jim Lawless, are not a guy who will get excited about waking up after five hours of sleep, much less working."

"Yep I am. Once I'm up, I'm up."

"Yeah I bet. No speed freaks in the van."

"I can do that."

"I can't picture it."

"Look, I work hard, as long as it's fun and I don't have to dress up and be stuck in an office all day with a boss breathing down my neck. And if I get to see you guys every night for free, *and* free beer, *that's* the only paycheck *I'll* ever need."

Devastaysha says to call her in a week and if they haven't found anyone yet, then OK, as a last resort they'll take my sorry ass.

That's my ticket outta here.

Like Henry Rollins says, get in the van. Nice and cush. All the way to NYC packed like salty little fishes. Sadaam wrote me after our run-in with SF's finest, he moved there, squatter's paradise, and invited me to stay with him. We'll have a new life and I'll forget about Ally for a while, maybe even get clean and be a stand-up guy. Someday come back, get married, settle down.

What are you thinkin'.

God I need Ally, that's what.

And you're killing each other. So just go, asshole.

Maybe I'll meet some babes and see the world. Maybe I'll forget about true love. Maybe some of the Mucous coolness will rub off.

Ally is the light of the world. I can never leave her. But she hasn't looked at me for so long, why should I miss her glance. It won't be much of a stretch, living in the same town, ignored by her, to traveling around the country, ignored by her.

I pack three photos of her. Beautiful, Sensitive in Love Babe, Babe Who's Just Said Something Incredibly Witty, and Nymphet in Bondage with Duct Tape. That's plenty to pine over and jerk off to. Wonder if there will be anywhere to jerk off. With six babes in a van I doubt it. Van dykes.

TRANNY CHILD

We meet in the sunny parking lot at the practice space. I haul Killer's drum hardware, her "box of torture," down the stairs. Luscian's equally hellish big blue guitar amp. Fuckalot's Marshall, all beat up, the fabric peeling off the back, one wheel gone and the other one wiggling and turning the wrong way like on a defective shopping cart. Max's bass head and four-speaker amp, for that extra woofy sound. Devastaysha stands there waving her heavy equipment, a microphone in a small naugahyde case with a Hostile Mucous sticker on it, talking to the cute metal chick who's on her way into practice.

We pile all the stuff in the van, snax, and CDs and vinyl and T-shirts, bedrolls and duffel bags, and drive. The way to L.A.'s a desert. We pass some cows in the sun. It's hot. I bet them cows wish there was a shade tree around. Then we drive by a whole bunch of cows hanging around on dirt mounds in a cloud of stink, staying awake to stave off nightmares of slaughterhouses and Burger King.

"Cowschwitz," says Devastaysha.

I'll think about them cows next time I'm about to eat some of Mom's filet mignon.

We stop at a gas station. Fancy automated sliding-glass doors. I go in the bathroom, press the gold door handle, replicas of Greek statues. It looks like the Regal Show World. Viva Las Vegas. Inside, all mirrors, and speakers, nice ones, way up high on the wall piping in music, and a marble sink with a gold faucet.

I walk out, there's a lady who's wearing a dress with a little name tag that says Genevieve.

I tell her, "Damn. This is the nicest gas station I ever seen."

She has a German accent. "Well, we just thought there were so many ugly gas stations, we wanted to make a beautiful one."

It's hotter than fuck. Out in the parking lot, beyond air-conditioned Thunderdome, me and Max squirt each other with the hose and climb in the loft to be blow-dried by hundred-degree winds.

Max the tranny boy. I had a couple of pals start shooting testosterone and I never talked to them about it much. I didn't know what to do. But I like Max, and it isn't like I knew him before he became a "he." So, by becoming a he, I don't feel like he is kidnapping or killing my pal or stealing anything from me. He isn't turning into an asshole. He's always been one since I known him, which is not long, so I don't miss his old self. Her old self. It looks like Max is taking a road back to himself that's always been part of him, but not physically. Like going back to Ireland when you've never been there, but your parents are from there, like a promise of yourself that's always standing in the next room saying, I'm over here, until you sneak up on it and tackle it.

There's not a lot to do up in the shelf. That's the little space next to the ceiling above the equipment and the luggage. There's a piece of plywood with a moldy futon on it, and you can lie there and look at the cloth fall off the ceiling and dump powdery disintegrating particleboard into your eye, even though we tried to duct tape it. The shelf is good for naps, not for sex though, because there's no room to move, and good for secret conversations because no one can hear you up front. It's cozy like a coffin, all claustrophobic and cramped and stuffy. You can't see the scenery from up there, so I start pumping Max for information about his new boyhood.

"So, what's your deal. How's it gettin' dates. Do you take home straight girls?"

"Nah, maing. I'm a fag. Once a queer always a queer. You can take the girl outta the queer but you can't take the queer outta the boy."

We talk about being neither and both, sisterhood and abandonment, no man's land, passing, and pronouns.

Hanging with Max makes me ponder my own gender. I defy dualities of definition even if I don't shoot T. Rumbling into napville, I struggle to keep my eyes open, spying between stretches of golden, rolling, slumber-inducing landscape, a hostile world fly by. In all the malls, rest stops, and gas stations are men's rooms and ladies' rooms, and no room for us. I remember the child I was, sure of me but confusing everyone else, and lull myself to sleep with a fairy tale of my youth.

. . .

Once upon a time there was a tranny child named Jim. He knew what he was, but nobody else did. They could not see him. They thought he was a girl. Even though he demanded trucks and trains and electric guitars, they gave him dolls with pink hair. They were mortified when he grabbed his grandpa's rifle and ran around the backyard yelling, MY NAME IS JIMMY MY NAME IS JIMMY. They hated it when he called himself that. His grandpa, who loved him very much, would sit down in his big armchair and peel a pear and say, "No pears for Jimmy," and Jim would play the game and say his name was Elizabeth, so he could climb up in Grandpa's lap and have some slices of pear.

Jim had a pal named Mike Clinton. The tallest tree in the world stood in Mike Clinton's backyard. Mike could climb it, fearless and with ease, but the tranny child could only perch on the first fat limb. Mike had a Stingray, which he rode very fast. When Tranny Child tried to ride it, he flew through the air and landed face first on the curb.

One day Tranny Child watched Mike Clinton pee. He noticed Mike could do this standing up. Tranny Child was very sad. He thought he could not do the stuff Mike could do because he was missing this one thing Mike had, and that maybe Mike was born knowing how to do lots of other stuff because he had this special thing. Not that Tranny Child needed the thing, he had learned not to need. He knew he was a boy with or without the damn thing.

Out by the tetherball court in the schoolyard, he asked Jin Su to marry him. Jin Su was shy and blushed and looked down, not saying no, but all the other girls said, No, silly, you can't ask girls to marry you. He said, Why not. They said, Because. You're a girl, and girls can't marry girls, that's why. And they frowned at him.

Oh.

So he made a note never to let anyone know he was a boy again, or how he really felt, or anything about him, because everyone was crazy and couldn't see how things were the way he could, and if he let them in on it, they would just fuck it all up.

He tried to pretend to have crushes on other boys to fit in, but it felt unnatural, and really he just wanted to be them.

One day, the other boys became bigger and meaner.

Mike got in a fight with Tranny Child and put him in a head-lock in front of everybody, and then they weren't friends anymore. Tony Perelli threw a basketball into his stomach so hard it knocked the wind out of him, right in front of the guys, and told him he couldn't play basketball with them anymore. Ricky Foster finally beat him sprinting and looked relieved, as if he'd been long-ing for that day.

The party's over. Boys suck.

Hey, wait a minute, I'm a boy.

But you're banned from the country club. Exiled.

Kill 'em all?

They wanna kill you. Homicide before suicide.

But if boys suck and must die, then I must also die, since I am one of them.

Obviously you are not one of them. You're a whole different animal. Forget about them. Just do what you have to do to get love, and live happily, or if not happily, at least unabashedly, ever after.

Drive like hell, you'll get there. We hit L.A. and cruise the freeway for an hour until we get to South Central.

While we're unloading, a couple high school girls come up and announce, "Last time we played here, we got shot at."

I like tour already.

We get inside and there's four bands before Hostile Mucous. There's a skinny, punk-as-fuck fag, sweating behind drums, and two butches, drowning in liquid eyeliner and beating the shit out of their guitars. You won't catch me wearing no eyeliner. I ain't no girlie girl. But you can see the way these chicks move, they're rugged motherfuckers, they don't care. They could smash my bare face in.

Max is so happy. "Finally, Latino punx, woo-hoo."

Fuckalot raises her eyebrows. "It's been too long."

The boys mosh in that outta-control marching cartoon of a badass strut. I always know when a show is punk as fuck because I'm laughing my ass off until my face hurts.

Mucous gets on stage and incites nonstop pit.

When they get done, there's fights. Beer cans flying. Max is consternated, trying to make peace everywhere.

Outside some guy says to Max, "Hey what ARE you, a man or a woman?"

"I'm not your boyfriend, I'm in the band, I am something that you'll never understand."

"What are you, a hermaphrodite?"

I hate when people hyper-thinly veil hostility with curiosity.

What he really wants to know is not *how* Max is different, but how *dare* he be different.

But Max ain't playing. "Ooh, where'd you learn that fifty-cent word. Why don't you put on a dress and ask yourself what that makes you?"

"What did you say, maing?"

Max puts his face about an inch away from the other guy's. This boy's as balls out as Sheila, the drag queen of my childhood, was. Genderfuckers voluntarily paint a bull's eye on their forehead and then point to it, saying, "Right here, baby."

Bigotboy's pal tries to hustle him off. "Hey Homes, he's drunk, he don't know what he's saying."

"Bullshit. He knows what's up." We walk away.

Dude starts yelling, "Hey. I don't got a problem witchu, I just don't like no *pinche putos*." Spanish for "fucking faggots."

Max yells back over his shoulder, "Then stay the fuck outta the Mucous show, asshole." I don't know if he's gonna kill or cry. "And that's my fuckin' homey. I oughtta just open that boy's mind and fuck him up the ass."

I'd offer mine up, but maybe this isn't the right time.

LALA LAND

L.A., land of palm trees. You don't have to wear a lot of clothes. The chicks are tan. But I let my repressed suburban teenage standard of beauty kick in and, whoa, they're fine. I don't always have to fuck pale punkrock girls like Ally. They're trouble anyway. No more punkrock girls, at least not for true love. Just one-night stands. There's only room for one damaged fuckup in my sexual liaisons. From now on, I am going to only fuck nice normal sweet girls, not these dominatrix stripper babes that are always bitching about everything I do.

Anyway, who's gonna have time for sex when we are on tour. It's gonna be drive drive drive. Zipping all over the countryside, from one ecosystem to the next, from Texas desert to Louisiana jungle inside twenty-four hours. Do that on a bike. I'm seeing the world, who needs girls. I got a shitload right here with me everywhere I go, a harem on wheels, and I'm the eunuch. Unavailable babes, just like I like. Although they never go away either. You can't find a moment's solitude for a quick wank. Everyone is typing on Powerbooks and reading and listening to CDs on the stereo in the van and talking to their excellent babes on cellphones. Not that I'm complaining, the scenery in the van rocks. They're all flawless, so they're gonna kick ass in L.A., where looks are the deciding factor of your future.

We're playing Al's Bar tonight, an over-twenty-one dive, and the door guy's making sixteen-year-olds sit on the sidewalk.

It's smoky, I'm studying cloud formations, it smells like stale beer and puke no amount of bleach is ever gonna get up off the floors, and there's drunk guys yelling, Show us your tits, but Devastaysha loves hecklers. She don't take no shit. She just says show me your dick and I'll cut it off, and then what'll you do for brains.

Guys love her. They love them some abuse from a beautiful woman. They need the pressure taken off sometimes, as being in charge of the world is exhausting, and they need a babe like Dev to take over for an hour. Just like me, they long to be close to someone who will never let them get close. Anyway, she don't care, she gets laid all the time and has chicks lined up around the country.

Tonight I'm going easy on the beer. Maybe I won't drink until after selling the merchandise. It's really hard, cuz there's endless flowing free beer, but I got to keep my shit together for this job. It's not like messengering that I can do in my sleep. I'm hawking Hostile Mucous panties, boxers, tiny spaghetti-strap tanks for girlie girls, and T-shirts that say FUCK YOU I KILL YOU in every size from tiny to triple-XL. Not to mention a million different CDs, records, videos, and stickers.

Devastaysha gets up there and starts peeling her clothes off and screaming and yelling and kicking boys in the head when they reach for her. Guys try to get in the pit and are instantly ejected by swarms of rabid chicks, who notice when there's something in their way that does not belong there. There's something about HM that makes quiet little bookworms get completely outta hand.

After the show, Dev hollers on the mike that we need a place to stay. A gaggle of dykes forms at her feet, and she picks one. We pile in the van to go to the girl's place and Dev gets to sleep in her bed. I lie awake listening to sex noise all night.

The next day we stroll up and down the boardwalk and look at dancing poodles in tutus, chainsaw jugglers, puppies for sale, and two bull mastiffs wearing superdarks, which reminds us to buy some cheap sunglasses. Dev gets a tarot reading that says this tour is like drawing four aces in a poker game, and she's really happy. We eat dollar-a-slice greasy cardboard pizza and go swimming in our boxers. Bikini babes rollerskate to tunes blaring out of a box on the asphalt. There's a chick drummer who sucks really bad, playing in front of a big sign that says FEMALE DRUMMER. People are actually crowded around staring.

Killer's cracking up. "A female drummer was allegedly sighted on Venice Beach today. . . ." Killer could beat her with one hand tied behind her back, Def Leppard style.

I swim in the ocean for a really long time, until my hair fades to light blue. I put my jeans on over wet boxers.

Back in the van. Out of the yard, back in the cage. I can't get my velocity fix in this van, no matter how fast and how far we go. The cocoon, the sarcophagus moves across the country, while those inside don't move. Inertia within constant motion. Lie down in the space capsule to wake up light-years later in another world.

MAYHEM

Ally writes the most poetic love letters. Even if she can't love me. Can't-love letters. They are nice presents on the road waiting for me when we get to the club, bedraggled. I gave her an itinerary so she can write and send care packages of chocolate.

I have pictures of the babe, and when I miss her bad, I look at them, and then I realize she doesn't want me, so how can I comfort myself with these? But it's nice to drool over a girl, even if she don't reciprocate.

We are driving a straight line to the edge of the earth through the deserts and prairies and plains of America. The sky is big and full of tall white clouds and tall square mountains, Thelma and Louise country. One hundred degrees, no air-conditioning.

I wish I was on my bike, hanging on to the doorjamb through the open window, going seventy miles an hour. I'd be petted all over by a warm wind, outside and getting some alone time and a sense of the wide openness of the land.

I put on two wet T-shirts instead, and stay cool while we sing Eagles songs and crank up the classic rock station and drink Cokes in the van. They do not allow open containers. Very strict, straightedgers.

But only straightedge in the van, because we stop at the Happy Trails Saloon in Bumfuck, Texas, and pound a couple of Lone Stars. The locals get a good laugh at us. They need a joke to spice up their poker game, and here we are. A skinny old one-armed man, and a big woman no older than me with babies, dandled, at a table loaded with longneck bottles of beer. The bartender, she's real nice and runs down the history of the bar for us.

"Oh, we've had it about twenty years, and before that a friend of ours had it, but she died of a brain aneurysm." She points to a frame full of dollar bills with people's names on each one in thick black ink. "Them are all the folks who died who used to patronize this place."

I'd like to hang out and get drunk and familiar with folks, but we gotta jump in the traveling sauna and keep driving.

I like how the road makes you feel free, never letting the moss grow beneath your toes, so you don't die drinking at the Happy Trail Saloon and get your name put on a dollar on the wall. Tour's different than a bike trip, though. It's more like a pilgrimage, because you've got this gang with you. Or like a buncha ducks, flying around the planet. You don't get your own flight plan, you're tied to everyone's agenda, so you're not free as a bird, are you. You just get shuffled around with the rest of the flock.

I don't mind, though. I like the flock, and we always end up somewhere entertaining.

When we get to Austin, I set up the merch table.

I'm praying to Jesus for a fan that wants to trade snake food for seven-inches. I've traded records for food stamps, leather cuffs, a choke chain, beer, a bottle cap with a skull on it, some mint-flavored rubbers, girls' panties, a joint, and kisses. Actually I have snogged more babes on this tour than any member of the band. Probably because chicks are not intimidated by me, and I'm just hanging out looking subhuman and kissable while the gods they worship wank.

Tonight the second act is some boy noise band strategically placed so Hostile Mucous can come after them and blow them off the stage. The drummer for the first band is a fine young thang. This nuthouse escapee guy is the singer who flies all over the place, jumps on tables, falls on the floor, screams in faces, while the drummer girl, calm, keeps the beat, a mathematician, John Bonham on speed, looking fine like Bridgette Bardot in a red cowboy hat.

She comes up after they pack their shit and says, "Hi. I'm Johnnie Mae." Then she leans on the merch table, looks deep in my eyes, and says, "Are you for sale?" with a lazy drawl and southern smile that could melt ice, which I could suddenly use down my pants.

She's a curly-headed urban primitive child with a postage stamp for a skirt.

I say, "Hell yeah," grab my longneck, and we head for the stall in the ladies' room.

It's roomy. She slams me up against the wall and lays a sweet one on me. We're face barnacles. I'm grabbing handfuls of perfectly spherical ass and crisscrossed barbell tittaes, that's t-i-t-t-a-e-s with an umlaut, neckbiting, she pushes me down on the throne and buries my face under her skirt, grinding whisker burn, then the banging and complaining starts outside, the line's getting long, and we bust out like people almost drowned and storm past the wolf whistles outside into the parking lot. It's hot at midnight. We jump in the back of her flatbed, she puts her stick-callused fingers in my mouth 'til I can feel the slime rise, and she says, Damn, ya deepthroatin' li'l faggot, ya like that do ya, and I say, Mm-hmm. I know I gotta see this girl again.

So we climb out and wipe off the slop, head in for the show. Chix are lounging about, ready to get naked and sweaty and sing all the words into the mike in case Devastaysha shoves it in their face.

I want to be Dev, adulated and fellatio-ed and heard with the keen ears of disciples, stirred up by the chance and power of the stage. What a rush to be there, where no part of you is secret, all eyes are on all of you, one false move is total humiliation, and one great move means coronation.

A look around and I can tell, Austin is the kind of crowd that's already made Devastaysha their sovereign queen, where they get onstage and lick her boots and suck her dick and compare her to God.

If an asshole flings an elbow too high in this pit, or tries to touch her, they swallow him, giant vagina dentata, and spit him out all chewed up. It's beautiful to see. Not every town is that way but you can tell you're in a big city when you walk in and the leather dykes and the punk girls lean on the stage, smoking Pall Malls and drinking Pabst Blue Ribbon in their wife beaters and boots.

The band flips switches. Luscian turns toward the amp for a long feedback call of the wild, then starts whacking off her flying

V. The pit starts swarming, and me and Johnnie Mae, we go to it right away, slamdancing and butting heads, shaking up beers and shooting them over the crowd. In between songs she pulls down her lower lip to show me what it says there: EAT ME RAW.

Dev whips out a ten-inch from under her skirt and starts yelling, "Which one of you motherfuckers is gonna suck my dick?"

Me and Johnnie Mae and about six other chicks start pointing at this cowboy who's been throwing his weight around and grabbing ass. Motherfucker must be drunk, because he gets onstage. Ann puts him in handcuffs and they start playing a cover of "Spray paint." She's trying to push him down on his knees and he won't submit, won't go down, and he's stumbling around the stage, and then he bumps into Luscian's amp. Big mistake. Luscian don't like boys much, which is always a surprise to them because of her short dresses and long hair. Sometimes she tolerates them, but you don't want to mess with her rig. All of a sudden she stops playing, throws down her guitar, and marches over to Cowboy, who looks instantly sober, but he can't move, cuffed and worried. She grabs his shirt collar. Everyone else stops playing. It gets quiet. All the babes are watching like Romans at a coliseum full of Christians. Luscian has the mayhem look in her eye and I know it's too late for salvation. She's twisting the collar tight around his neck and her eyes are wide, murderous inches away from his. She's whispering something to him.

He chokes out, "I don't suck dick," the final act of defiance.

And she yells, "When you're on THIS stage, you DO, and that's ALL you do, motherfucker."

She picks up a beer bottle and Max and Fuckalot both start talking quiet, "Come on, now, Loosh, put it down, c'mon, it's cool. Don't do it, Loosh."

Dev says, "Aw, man, I don't wanna go to jail again."

But I'm thinking, *Knock his dick in the dirt, do it.*

Luscian puts the bottle down, still clutching his shirt collar, grabs his back belt loop and tosses him off the stage, where he lands on a pile of Texas tomboys who lift him back onstage and throw him eyeball first into the corner of a monitor.

"Next contestant," yells Loosh, and a willing victim jumps on stage, assumes the position. Deep throat. We have a WINNER.

I step up on Johnnie Mae's entwined fingers, and she catapults me over the sea of babes. I get a good view of a bloody giant slumped at the bar, ice rag on his eye. Life is good.

MORE DEAD COPS

Johnnie asks me this morning if there's room in the van for her, she thinks she'll hitch a ride to NYC, and so I ask Devastaysha, and she says, Yeah, if the girl can drive and move equipment.

We head for New Orleans.

Me and Johnnie Mae climb up in the shelf and squirm around, grabassing and reaching down each other's pants in the foot and a half of headroom until the effort wears us out and I crawl into her arms, her whispering perversions in my ear.

Never had a skirt-wearing girl switch to boy so fluid. Filthy little tart, whiskey-smelling stepdad.

All around me are brilliant, pissed-off babes. I couldn't be happier.

Halfway across Texas, I'm driving; we get pulled over by the pigs. Great. Van full of scruffy freaks. Jackpot.

"Whatcha got there, son, a fire in yer pants?"

Uh-oh. No sense in trying to sound growly and keep up his illusion that I'm a boy, because in about two seconds what I am will be very apparent.

"Howza bout some ID."

He gazes down and then up at me, smirking. I smile back, *Deliverance* banjos plinking in my ears.

They look up our butts, tear the van apart.

"What's this?"

"Vitamins."

"Mmm-hm."

Needles for temporary piercings. "What have we got HERE." All triumphant.

"You really wanna know?"

"Yep, I do."

"It's for an art project."

Tattoo equipment. He just holds it up, question mark.

Devastaysha points to the Sailor Jerry flash of Betty Page on her arm and flexes.

Then they get to the bag of rubber dicks, ten or twelve wiggling in the Wal-Mart bag. Dev really goes through them, slice and dice routine. We stare, holding our breath, waiting for sentencing. SICK BAD WRONG, gavel pounding on our heads.

The pigs just look down into the Bag o' Dicks, look at each other, back at us, back down into the bag.

"Ya know, we got plenty here to take you down, but . . ."

We play the institutionalized pervert game: Yes, I'm bottoming to you, sir, and with a smile. I love it, yessir yessir yessir.

"Seein' as yer all women . . ."

All you got to do is play the goddam game. So you will *play* right?

Oh yessir we're just tiny lambs in the woods. Please have mercy on us, our lives depend on your benevolent whim, and we'll be ever so grateful if you don't off us and throw us in a ditch.

"Just git outta Texas."

Our plan exactly.

You'd think in a van you're all safe, wrapped up in two tons of steel, and secret so nobody can see you inside, but it's not something you can whip down the sidewalk on a one-way street and escape in. It's subject to rules, like speed limits and red lights. It's highly conspicuous and unwieldy. It does not afford you the fighter-pilot control of a bike.

So the idea is to blend in. We put Max in the driver's seat, incog with a trucker hat on that says WATCH MY REAR END NOT HERS. At the next gas station, we buy a Dixie flag bumper sticker and one that says ENGLISH WAS GOOD ENOUGH FOR JESUS, IT'S GOOD ENOUGH FOR MY BOY, so cops will know we ain't no foreign commies. And farther down the road at a truck stop, we find one that says WITH GUNS TRUCKS AND BEER, WHO NEEDS WOMEN? We are now invisible to the law.

While everyone's shopping for fuzzy dice and beef jerky, I get on the pay phone to call Ally. This old drunk says, *I wanna use the phone,* so I say, Scram I'm talkin' to the love of my life long-distance that I haven't seen in two weeks and I'm gonna be a while, figuring he'd understand a universal concept like true love, but no, he says, *I wanna use the phone,* so I say, there's a million of 'em, go use that one right there, get outta here, and give him a shove. I turn around and figure that ought to settle it, him being old and drunk, and then he punches me in the back of the head. I see stars, turn around and start yelling and trying to kick him in the shins but missing just like in my dreams, swinging and missing. I'm never close enough, because just like a girl, I don't really want to hurt him, and that's making me even madder. I can't connect, but finally I kick him in the nads, and all he says is *Aw, that don't hurt a bit.*

Finally Dev and Fuckalot see me and run over, push me out of the way, punching and kicking like Bruce Lee. Then, *whoosh,* we're in the van speeding down the highway.

It's one thing when a cop kicks my ass. But I can't even beat drunken bums. They're all pounding me down, I ain't shit, I'm lower than the lowest. Something's gotta give. There's no point to being on the planet, this ineffectual punching bag, this ninety-eight-pound weakling boywhore. Living dangerous, I need an ace up my sleeve.

Must learn to kill.

FUCKALOT KNOWS BADASS

Fuckalot knows six different kinds of martial arts. She wants to go to China, to the Shaolin Temple, and be a kung fu master, and then come back and teach girls for free and cheap. She don't care too much for money, if she did, she says, she wouldn't be in the punkrock business. Which really isn't any kind of business except nonprofit.

She's not trained by monks, but she's already the master of her environment, confidence like a forcefield bouncing assholes out of her way. She's got no restrictions on her, and no one taking advantage. She don't have to do nothing she don't want to do. She decides how things are gonna be in her world, not a bunch of yahoos who think they know what's right for her.

We get to New Orleans and unload, set up, and then wait for the show to start.

She says, "Got hit in the back of the head, huh? Lesson one. Never turn your back, especially after mouthin' off to some fool. Lookee here, come up behind me and put me in a half nelson." She walks away from me and I jump her. She grabs me by the collar and pulls me over her shoulder, slams me on the ground.

I look up dazed. "I can't pull you anywhere, you outweigh me by fifty pounds."

"It's balance, not strength. Just grab their hair, ear, anything you can reach."

So we spar, and then we smoke on the curb, looking up at wrought-iron balconies, tall shutters, and peeling paint.

She's talking about Brooklyn, the projects. Riding the subway, hunched down with her Walkman, shutting out the shit talking, *Is it a boy or a girl, damn, lookadem tattoos, she gotta whole mess a metal in her face, what she think she is, some kinda punkrocka. Bitch tryina ack white 'n' shit. Dat shit is whack.*

Talking about freestyling with the big boyz in the hood, competition, dazzling them at fourteen with her fast mind, and how when the kudos come down, you know they're real, because the bullshitters get called on their shit, laughed outta town, told how bad they suck. She didn't suck. She almost got a recording contract at Death Row Records, but she got shy at the last minute. Someday, though, she says. Meantime guitar with Mucous is just fine.

Up pulls a truck, and a bunch of hard-looking chicks pile out, one with a lot of lipstick and a loud gravelly voice. Ripped up décolleté petticoat dress and jumpboots just like Ally wears.

"Whatch'all doin? Are y'all Hostile Mucous?" she yells.

Fuckalot's eyes light up and I see she's getting some tonight.

Max walks up and says, "Ya learnin' how to fight?"

"Yeah, Fuckalot showed me a whole buncha shit."

"Ya wanna know how to box?"

I look at Max. He's twice my size. "Yeah, OK." I look at my skinny punkboy arms and his big meaty ones.

"You just throw your weight into it, step into it, just keep barreling into 'em, stun 'em with the first punch, then break their nose with the second one, see?"

It's like learning a dance step. And I can't dance worth shit. But stumbling into him a few times, I'm getting smoother.

He tells me keep punching hard and fast, connect halfway through the swing, get in real close, don't be afraid to get intimate, and if you wanna fight dirty, you can turn their head with one arm while you punch 'em with the other and snap their neck, then lay 'em down with their face on the curb and stomp on their jaw.

Wow. I just want to stand up for myself, I don't have to disfigure people. Do I?

Devastaysha's watching by now. She says I'm too skinny to mow down grown men the way Max does. She shows me the soft parts, throat, eyes, dick, knees, shins, feet. Then she puts her arm around me and walks me inside.

She's something, onstage and off, kicking ass. I never knew how hot an older woman could be, with her I-know-what's-happenin' attitude. She doesn't let shit faze her. She fixes the van when it breaks, in a slip and high heels, letting old guys try to help her, and when she sees them lying under the van looking up her dress, she don't trip. Everyone else is all, Fuck that noise, I'll kill the pervert, but she says, So what, he's a man, what do you expect, you know he doesn't get any, he's so old. She surprises you with compassion for people you don't think deserve any, and then you feel low because you see everyone deserves it.

She doesn't belong to no one. She wrote this great punkrock song about you always get the best fucks from the ones who can't give you their heart, but wouldn't you rather have a pistol for a minute than a lifetime of torture?

Not that a famous babe like her would ever look twice at me. Besides, ever since Frankie cleaned up a couple months ago, they're doing the icky, and Dev's got a photobooth picture of Frankie in her wallet. So that's out.

No matter how free and easy, pals can never fuck your sweethearts, even exes, until after you die, that's the Rules.

Jack-Off Jill starts playing. The singer is fully enraged. She takes pool cues and swings them at the crowd, nice full baseball-bat arcs back and forth, clearing a space. Then she throws them like spears. Then she grabs a chair, waves it around, and chucks it directly at some guy's head. The whole time she's yelling her guts out, pouring rocks into the mike, and flinging her hair around. I love southern punk girls.

After the show we all pile over to the local bar and take over, playing twenty songs on the jukebox for a buck, and dirty dancing with each other to Madonna. Everybody's voguing to the entire Immaculate Collection album, and then "Justify My Love" comes on, and I'm singing "sodomize my butt, my butt." I bend over, Johnnie Mae simulates booty porking from behind. Everyone's dancing, drinking, pool sharking.

Devastaysha's standing at the bar ordering beers. She looks over my shoulder at Johnnie Mae playing pool, and says to me, "When you want a grown woman, call me," and walks away with an arm full of brews. . . .

I do love a die-hard flirt.

LOSERVILLE, USA

I'm getting that belonging feeling, kinda like lesbian merging but times five, then times a hundred. Tour's a traveling girl gang that deflects hostile stares at rest stops and expands into a national association as you glide into each new town, each rock show an island in a seven-hundred-mile-wide sea of fast food and hate.

We stop off in FLA to play a dyke bar. Thought it would be a good idea. We're all queer, right? They'll love us. Dev flinging her tits around. Simulating fellatio. Very queer. Except guess what. They're not dykes. They're LESBIANS! We're freaks. They DANCE! We slam. They hate us, we hate them, we can't win.

So bummed. When we first walk in, they got the brand-new leather jacket, perfectly coifed big hair lotsa products featherback fur burger to welcome us at the door. But we're nice, pleasant, who are we to judge a haircut.

The nice friendly lady says, "Can't wait to hear you play. The press packet sounds real nice."

She must have read the cover page with the hated *Rolling Stone* quote about militant amazon warrior lesbian rockers or some hokey shit.

"Yeh. Heh heh. Fuck shit up."

She has no idea what the hell we're talking about.

We haul in the equipment, they turn off the disco, and the

Night Fever crowd disperses, skeptical, to watch from the safety of the bar.

Me and Dev go get brews and pitchers of water.

She says hushed so the enemy can't hear, "This is like the East Bloc," and tells me how weird it was when Mucous toured there, how people hadn't seen any Western capitalist shit in twenty-five years. They didn't really seem to want to be rescued. They were stuck in a time warp. Everyone looked like the early seventies with attitudes to match, boys shaming her, saying tits and dick's just an easy ploy for attention, as if performers are anything but attention hogs. Girls afraid to talk to her. Meanwhile, thirty miles away in West Berlin, everyone was up-to-date and loving them, and what's their excuse here in the good ol' U.S. of A.

"Well I don't think southern guys would bother you for showin' yer tits, they'd probably shout lewd things and try to grab 'em. 'Cept these ones are gay so they'll probably just barf."

"Yeah, isn't that quaint? Every culture has its own little brand of stupidity."

So the band plugs in and starts playing and about nine barely legal kids start slamdancing in front of the stage. Some hulk with a STAFF T-shirt grabs the skinniest little boy around the neck and starts dragging him away. Dev stops singing, but the band plays on, because they can never agree on which is the best way to stop fights: stop playing and draw attention to the problem, or keep playing and ignore it. So Dev's throwing down the mike and chasing the security fuck. The band's doing an instrumental and finally finishes.

Dev's yelling at Asshole. "What the fuck."

"There ain't no moshing."

" 'There ain't no moshing.' Why?"

"It's dangerous."

"YOU'RE THE ONLY ONE HURTING ANYONE, JERKOFF. JUST LET HIM GO."

Spermbrain lets go of Pencilneck. "Well alright. Just tell 'em no moshing."

"Yeah right. Any activity by those who think is 'dangerous.' That's why disco's legal." She spits on the ground, jumps back onstage, whips out her dick, yells one two fuck you, and goes into a good old-fashion anticop anthem.

The kids can't help themselves, in a small frenzy all over the disco pit, all nine of them. Three security morons rush them and drag out as many as they can, Devastaysha jumps off the stage yelling, the song falls apart, everyone's yelling. The lady who liked the press packet is throwing our shit out the door, and refusing to pay us, the Schwarzeneggers are yelling "THRASHERS" at us like it's some kind of insult. Fuckalot, smooth talking, coaxes the money out of the angry lady, while the rest of the band loads the van and signs autographs for half-strangled fans.

Nine enlightened citizens in Miami. That's a start.

A bar bouncer's a good job to have, if you're a two-hundred-and-fifty-pound meathead that's pissed off about being too stupid to work at McDonald's, but somebody's gonna pay you to take out your frustration on people half your size, which is everybody. What a scam. That's almost as good as getting people to pay you to ride your bike.

Me and Max head for the liquor store.

He says, "Let's call the girls. You can use my phone card."

He stops at the phone booth outside while I go in for pop and beer.

When I come out he's waving one hand around wildly. "Can you understand the words that are coming out of my mouth? NON-MO-NOG-A-MY. I'm free—you said—"

I hand him a pop.

"Look we had a deal. I'm on tour. Whaddaya want, a fucking monk? Even *they* fuck each *other*. I'm dyin' here."

He takes a swig, looks at me, points at the phone, and rolls his eyes. I walk away and sit on the curb.

"Don't tell me there's something wrong with me for wanting to fuck young girls. It's hot. So what. You didn't have a problem with it when we first started goin' out five years ago and YOU were twenty . . ."

I light a cigarette. This is going to take a while.

"Nobody's fawning over me. That's your little fantasy. There are no groupies, baby, you're the only groupie for me—just kidding, babe, don't freak out. OK—no, I don't get off on having more experience, well, I got nothing against older babes, there just aren't that many at the shows. It's punk rock, baby, everyone's barely legal. Know what I'm sayin' ? I'm the oldest one out here. It's lonely being a relic—"

Damn, she's really reading this poor bastard the riot act. One good thing about being single, I gotta say, is no nagging, controlling, cracking the whip over my whimpering ass. I can do what I want. It's a trade-off: the rush of screaming into a true-love intersection, balls out, heart in your mouth, on your beloved steed that requires constant wrenching and maintenance if you wanna avoid an ugly wipeout. Or the liberty of an endless pub crawl on a beat-up beach cruiser or a BMX, every night borrowing a different ride and seeing the world. I'm all about the pub crawl right now.

"Yeah, well I am not selfish, or spoiled either. . . . You expect me to have no touch for two months? . . . That's cold, baby. Can't we talk about this when I get home? I gotta get in the van. OK yeah. I love you—aw, damn. She fucking hung up on me. Do you get that? Dames."

"That was harsh. Is she pissed or what?"

"Yeah, here's the calling card."

I dial Ally's number.

"Hi honey. I miss you. Yeah. I'm having lotsa fun though. Um, all kindsa fun. . . . I get to see a really great show every night."

I pop another beer.

"Oh, yeah, I do get to meet a lotta girls, selling the merch, ya know. No, I MISS you. Why would I do THAT? I only think about you. Every girl I meet I compare to you and they're all mediocre. No, I DIDN'T try 'em all out. Well, maybe a couple of 'em. I just kissed 'em though. I am NOT a liar. Nope, I only been drinking beer. I been really good. The band's a good influence on me."

Max smiles. What Ally doesn't know . . . besides everything's relative, and I've been relatively good.

"Yeah, write me a letter. 'Kay, I love you. 'Bye."

Max gets up off the curb. "Man, you can lie your way out of a wet paper bag."

"Well, she didn't hang up on me, did she."

ROLE MODELS FOR LOVE

My dad has a crass sense of humor.

One day he says to my mom, "Women are like statistics. Once you get 'em down, you can use 'em any way you want."

Mom didn't laugh.

He said, "You got no sense of humor."

She said, "You can tell a lot about a guy's mother by his sense of humor, and I can tell by that joke you just told, your mother is a whore."

He didn't laugh.

She said, "You got no sense of humor."

He said, "If you were a man, I'd hit you."

She said, "If you were a man, I'd hit you."

Dad in the black-and-white photos was tan with a washboard stomach, blond wavy hair, all flannel and khakis. Mom hated the flannels and washed every last one of them in hot water on purpose, shrinking his fifty-dollar Pendletons into tiny baby shirts. She wanted him in his second lieutenant's uniform forever. My arrival postponed the resulting divorce for eighteen more years.

I wanted to be Dad. He was a surfer, a handyman, a kite flyer. We'd build paper kites and he'd take me to a windy hill and fly them off a cliff overlooking the bay. He had more fun than I did.

Whenever he let me fly the kite, it took a nosedive and he'd have to go run and get it and roll up the string and start over, so I mostly stood and watched him fly it, but I didn't care because he was hanging out with me.

One day he was running to get the kite going, and since I was very small, my view of the world ended in a short stretch of tall grass at the edge of the world, a sudden drop. Dad seemed to have fallen off it.

"DAD. DAD. DA-A-AD," I squeaked.

"What. I'm right here," he said calmly, sauntering back over the horizon. I had worked myself into a hot pink frenzy of hyperventilation.

"Where WERE you," I said, annoyed.

"I was right over there," he said, annoyed.

I was being ridiculous, overreacting, everything was fine. Everything was always fine around my Dad.

He was a looker, an all-American. Girls loved him. He was surrounded by Gina Lollabrigidas. That was his type, busty Italian babes. My mom's hair was dyed black when she met him. They got married. When she went back to blond, he lost interest. Some guys get very attached to physical characteristics, and if you change anything, they don't recognize you and run away.

Like my first girl, in high school, she had the most beautiful, long, strawberry-blond curls down to her ass. I don't know if I loved her, but I sure did love her hair. One day she called and said "Come over, I have a surprise for you." I came over and she had cut off all her hair. All that was left was this little bit of brown scraggles. I turned around and walked out. There was no reason to talk about it or say good-bye, since I had no idea who she was.

Not like that with the one and only. Only true love can survive the potential devastation of physical change. Like when Ally tweezed her brows.

Because as Mom says, We DON'T PLUCK, darling, we TWEEZE. We pluck chickens.

Damn, I just about lost my mind. When I first saw Ally, I saw her eyebrows. Her brows were the frame for those emerald eyes. Big caterpillars. How could she yank them? You might as well take the Mona Lisa out of the frame and tack it on the wall like a poster. Sacrilege. We had big arguments.

She said, "You're trying to control me."

I said, "No, I just love your eyebrows. PLEASE, let them grow back."

Nope.

She also had this great gap between her teeth. Like Angela Davis, Lauren Hutton, and the Wife of Bath. One day she went to the dentist. When she came back, the gap was gone.

"Baby, what happened to you??"

"I am not the gap between my teeth. I am not my eyebrows. I am not my tits."

"Tits?! Oh no, not the tits!"

Despite my extreme satisfaction with their natural state, she went to the surgeon, who "fixed" her perfect tits. If duct tape don't fix it, it ain't broke. Well, it definitely wasn't broke. But they cut off her nipples and put them on ice like two oysters, and sliced and diced, and now the once-perfect titties are Brides of Frankenstein.

"That's OK," she said. "We'll make art. Take a picture of me licking my own bruised, oozing, bloody, post-op titty in a mock porno shot." She's so punkrock. I'm just a poser.

And then there's the other equally shut-down, twisted role model for love. Mom always says, "What this country needs is a good WAR on its soil. It's the only thing that'll straighten out these spoiled brats and teach them how to treat each other like human beings. Like that earthquake. That sure shook those bastards up. You should have seen how nice everyone was to each other all of a sudden. Free rides on the bus. Hooking up the cigarette machine to a generator at the Fairmont Hotel, because what everybody really needed was a smoke."

Tough cookie, my mom, always speaking with reverence of sensitivity, which she instantly calcifies with a Benson and Hedges menthol, deflecting potential threats.

When her cat died, the one I talked her into adopting, thinking she needed something squishy to soften her up, she lit a cigarette. "See? I told you I didn't want a cat. They always die. Better to feed the neighbor's cat occasional saucers of milk. Then when they go away, you don't care."

Back in the womb I let my mother's sandy vocal cords seduce me, train me in utero to love the Dietrich my mother studied to become. She insisted the doctor said she just had big vocal cords. I imagine her one of those small croaky frogs of a child, becoming even more huskified with the cigarettes she smoked to keep hunger and tears at bay, to become the squinty, undeceivable Dietrich. The way she used men to stave off boredom. Like the look she gave the camera up from under one raised brow, the order she gave to position the lights to create a butterfly shadow under her nose, while she applied butter to her eyelids and drew a pencil line up the back of her million-dollar legs. Wartime makes scarce such indispensable petroleum products as eye shadow and stockings, but that won't stop a dedicated and resourceful glamour girl. She does her beauty duty for God and country. But mostly for herself. Because when a girl looks good, she feels good.

Marlene was the first movie-star babe not only to get away with wearing pants, but to look pretty fucking hot doing it. That's what Mom said, who wanted so bad to be a dyke. She said I was lucky. She tried to be one, but she wasn't raised that way.

"Who the fuck's raised to be a dyke, Mom?"

"Must you always express yourself that way?"

Women her age didn't see "Dyke" on the list of career choices. Let's see, there's Homemaker, Mother, hmmm, I don't see Lesbian here. . . .

She would have liked doing everything boys can do and cuddling with strong women. In fact, she confessed to spooning with her "ugly" best friend Inge once, whom Dad hated. I know Mom's idea of "ugly" was my version of butch. According to Mom, Inge never had boyfriends. I wondered if Dad always hated Inge because he saw her as a big bulldagger threat, competition. I was fascinated with the prospect of a platonic lover at an all-girls' school madly obsessed with my hot femme aloof Mom. I loved the idea that Inge chased my Mom down and seduced her years later, luring her into her bed. I smiled at the image of a diesel dyke making my Dad nervous and possessive.

Mom, I pleaded, Are there no pictures of Inge?

She said there were none and changed the subject.

Maybe that's why Mom was upset when I came out, for her lost queer life that never took off. How I came out to her was upsetting too. It all started with her eavesdropping. She overheard me confiding to my pal on the phone. I was saying I couldn't tell my mom about our New Year's Eve plans to go to the Stud, or she would find out I was a big fat gayrod. Mom came running in from the bathroom, where she was applying makeup.

Waving a lipliner in the air, she growled, "What? What can't I know?"

I said, "None ya."

"Oh yes it is."

So I said, "Oh yeah? You wanna know? Huh? Fine. I'm GAY."

She burst into tears. "I knew that stupid child psychiatrist was wrong ten years ago, when I told him you walked like a drunken sailor and climbed trees and got kicked out of ballet school."

I hugged her. "Why are you crying?"

"Because the world is mean."

"Don't worry, we got a revolution."

"At least you'll never make me a grandmother."

"Yeah, and in return, please don't tell Dad. He'll never understand."

Then she told my dad, because she said she needed to talk to *someone,* she was about to burst. But Dad was watching the game and wanted her to wait for the commercial. If you want support, you got to have timing on your side, and she did not. One more nail in the coffin of my parents' long-dead romance.

"He told me to wait for the commercial! When here you were coming out! Can you believe it???? Typical!"

Dad never mentioned it, the gayness. I borrowed the station wagon one night and came back at ten A.M. after my first fuck, some older lady who swooped me up in a San Jose bar. Dad stood in the driveway, glaring at me, sweeping leaves in the morning sun. Wordlessly, I handed him the keys and hung my head. As I slouched into the house, I wished I could just say, *Dad! I got laid by a girl!* I know he would have been happy for me. But we weren't that way with the talking.

After they had both met First Fuck, I stood in front of my parents, all aglow, effusing about love. They stared at me in helpless horror, shaking their heads. No. No, no, they said, the first time they ever agreed on anything in years. She was ten years older than me, with bad suburban fashion, no money, no job, and no social skills. They did not like her. I couldn't see past the first taste of tang. But now at last Mom and Dad could bond over the horrors of my sexuality *and* my bad choice of women.

Anyway, my mom, who stayed "twenty-nine" for twenty years, did not want to be called "Grandma." And this was her big payoff. Now she was safe, set in youth by my queerness, like a bug in amber, forever.

Anyway, I couldn't see what the big grandma deal was. Mom took me to see Marlene Dietrich, the hottest grandmother alive, sing onstage when I was eight. Mom was Marlene's number-one fan.

After I came out, she really opened the floodgates of Dietrich trivia.

You see, she explained, Marlene had a flaming desire, as much as an iceberg can flame, for Edith Piaf. But eventually it flickered down to disdain, and she summed up Piaf as a waste, such a pity she liked dick. Marlene thereby implied her superiority, since she just encouraged the *illusion* that she liked dick, by being seen with men. Men with money, power. Directors. Men with intellect. She needed her intellect stimulated, and a buddy like Hemingway to go sailing with, and a sperm donor.

Poor Edith. Her loss. Loving men shortens life, see. They'll suck you dry, said Mom, who never let them stay the night. Piaf died in her forties, while Dietrich lived 'til her nineties in a dark Parisian art studio, mending the legs she'd broken falling off a stage. She'd had them insured for a million bucks, so that they were still paying the rent, even though they were out of commission. That's Mom all over. Always an ace in the hole.

I come from a long line of women. Marlene, Mom, and me. Crazy independent bitches who'd rather die than ask for a handout, but who will whore for food. Only no one will know it's whoring. Reputation as important as survival. Desperate starvation is not ladylike. So Marlene whored her way to Hollywood. What's the shame in that? She got there, didn't she? No one will ever know. Mom once ate a whole box of Hershey Bars, in front of the American soldier who brought them. She gave it away, the secret of her vulnerability. He looked on, surprised, as if until that moment he hadn't known she needed him.

She always put up a good front. Like the time the boys at the prom slipped a dead mouse into her long kid glove when she wasn't looking. She felt the small dead furry thing, controlled her gag reflex, pulled the glove off her hand, carefully shook it out, and put it back on without the slightest change in facial expression.

"I knew they were all watching me. I wasn't about to give those bastards the satisfaction."

But now with a serviceman watching her scarf the tenth candy bar, she smiled sheepishly.

Dishonor to show weakness. He liked her protruding hipbones. Skinny was in. She looks back at those hungry years with pride. How she had to have the tailor pad her suits at the hipbones so she looked less bony.

She made her starvation glamour. Glamour, darling, an illusion old-timey babes of yore threw around themselves like a cape, so that an old woman could look like a young tasty morsel and weasel herself into castles and seduce the enemy.

She knew he wanted her small body in his hands to make him feel strong, as if he could break her. The danger was always that he could.

And he did.

Like a lizard grows back its tail, she recovered. You know, *Diziplin*. But you can always see that little bend where the new tail grew back. Her stories were packed with Americans in uniform. My TV mind made them all into one, but she differentiated between soldiers and officers.

It was a soldier named Johnny James that held the blade to her face hissing, "You think I'm not good enough for you, don't you bitch. Well, I'm gonna cut your pretty face if you don't give it up."

A soldier. So that proved it to her, you see. That the human race starts at the rank of lieutenant. That's what her mama told her and that's what she told me, coming, like Marlene, from a long line of military Prussians. But it lost something in the translation, me being raised far from Prussia.

I figure, why discriminate, they all want to kill you. They all want to torture, maim, get into your brain and do the twist. They wanna kill and so do I. Not like Mom, swallowing it with smoke and wine. They can't hurt you if you won't feel, but I say, hurt me, go ahead. Kill drive oozing out of my pores, bazooka shoot water gun vomit launch right in their eye, I'm the genetic carrier of a dormant holy war, immune, infecting everyone but me.

One day when I was sixteen the phone rang. Mom answered it, said yes, no, good-bye. She hung up the phone, ashen. Who was that, Mom? I asked. Johnny James, she said. I held her wooden body and swore, if he didn't pay, a thousand like him would, and if I couldn't save her, I'd save every girl that was hurt the way Mom was.

NOW YOU SUCK

So I ask Dev, "What's up with that shit, torturing me."

And she says, "Can't a girl flirt without you all trying to marry her?"

"Oh. I wasn't, I just got excited for a minute."

She says, "I know you and Frankie are pals. So you and me, we will be pals. Just because we think each other is hot rockin' shit doesn't mean we have to fuck each other's brains out."

I do not have a problem being pals with a fine babe. If you have to hang out with someone, they might as well be fine, so you can stare at something nice while they're talking, unless you're in love with them, and there's no hope, and they're breaking your heart, and every moment in their presence splinters it a little more. You gotta keep the antinuclear shield up around the heart. No, you gotta strap your heart to a nuke like Dr. Strangelove, so it's whooping and yelling and waving its hat, missile whistling toward its fiery end.

I'm jonesing for pain, so Dev whips out a sewing needle and some India ink and gives me a hand-knit tattoo that says "Ally" in a little heart.

She says, "Are you still gonna want this on your arm even if you're not together?"

"What, we're not together now. But I'll always love her. I'll never cover it up with a black panther, if that's what you're askin'. If she ever stopped loving me, I'd just cut off my arm and beat myself to death with it."

We stop to play and stay at an old mill in Rhode Island that's been made into a punk palace. There are many toys hanging from the ceiling and millions of black-and-white hand-drawn comic strips wallpapered in the library, no two the same, and tiny army men Krazy Glued to the wall, and frankenbarbies, taken apart and glued back together and to other toys in nightmarish combinations. It looks like tweak art but it isn't, because the punks that live here are those militant vegan types. They don't get wired. Do they? It's cozy, so I sit there and read a book about a big art fag named Man Ray and his black-and-white photos of goth babes from the thirties.

And there are bikes, all different kinds, Stingrays with banana seats and other old Schwinns, the kind "for girls" with no crossbar so you can ride them in a dress, and mountain bikes. We all take them downstairs and ride them around the parking lot. I got no idea how much I miss my bike until I get on one, and it delivers me out of the parking lot and up a little hill, past Italian delis, coffee shops, and bookstores. My lungs hurt from lying in a rolling capsule of inertia fourteen hours a day with no bike rides to expel a pack a day and bar smoke, but my legs are happy like POWs let out of a bamboo cage. I'm sucking in the foreign Rhode Island air, yelling, *I can't drive . . . FIFTY-five . . .*

I bomb down the hill through the donut shop and into the lot where the band is riding around in circles on every kind of self-powered contraption. Killer is riding this weird homemade skateboard with giant plastic wheels in her big platform boots, and I'm thinking, that ain't no good because, look, she's gotta sloop way down to push off, she's so high up, but she's a pro skater, she can handle it. Then she hits a bump and flies through the air, right as I cut her off at thirty miles an hour, and we nail each other mid-air, spectacularly eating shit, skidding across the lot, every protruding part of us grinding asphalt. But it's OK, because Devastaysha and Johnnie Mae come over and pet us, and that's the whole point of wiping out, isn't it, besides the euphoria of adrenaline endorphin speedball rush, that total babes put Band-Aids on you and kiss you on the ouchy parts.

Of course Max and Fuckalot roll their eyes and say quit whining. They think you gotta be so butch all the time. But all that stoic business doesn't get you half the attention from a girl, and I'd rather have less respect from my bros and more loving from the hoes. Killer's a skinny sensitive boy like me, and so we sit there and get took care of and don't mind abuse from hardasses at all. We're both very proud of our massive gravity check, and girls are awed by us.

After the show we head for Charlie's in Cambridge and some circus guys are balancing chairs on their chins and salt shakers on their noses and so Fuckalot and Max do some handstands and everybody's hooting and pounding on the table.

The circus guy asks Dev, "Ya got a deck o' cards?"

And she says, "Nah, but I got one o' dese," patting her beef bologna which is poking, tantalizing, out of her skirt.

He waves it away. "Yeah, I got one o' dose."

And she says, "Yeah, but you haven't put one in yer mouth today, have ya?"

"Ah, no, but I'm about to." That's the proper attitude.

In fact he looks so enthusiastic, she has to yell, "NO BITING," because when they get that excited they want to chew it off.

So his pals start yelling, "TAKE YOUR TEETH OUT."

And sure enough, he takes his front teeth out all in a little set and holds them up for everyone to see, smiling to show a nice row of gums. Yeah. Hummers are nice but gummers are better. Devastaysha sticks it in and everyone goes crazy. He's no pro or tries to act like he isn't, and after a couple of strokes, they quit, and he jumps up smiling like a teenage gymnast and his friends all pat him on the back. He's won over even Luscian and everyone's real friendly like.

The some little asshole yells, "Dat's GROSS."

Dev says, "Yeah? You didn't think it was so bad when your girlfriend blew you last night."

Cocksucker shrugs at Asshole. "I enjoyed it, what are *you* worried about?"

Rahr rahr rahr, says Asshole.

Suddenly Cocksucker, who's a lot bigger than Asshole, realizes he's offended that Asshole is offended, and that Asshole's taking offense at a simulated queer sex act is probably offensive to us, his newfound buddies.

So he jumps up and says, "Ya wanna put yer dick in my mouth, huh? HUH? GO AHEAD. I'LL BITE IT OFF IN TWO SECONDS FLAT."

Yeah, I'm thinking, he put his teeth back in. Watch out.

Nothing to calm you down like a crazy bastard threatening to bite your dick off. Normally. But the other bastard's crazy too, so he whips out a knife and starts brandishing.

I wing a mustard jar at Asshole's head and miss by two inches, smashing the mirror behind him.

Asshole's like a mad dog on a short rope, yelling and foaming. "Who t'rew dat?!"

I stare intently at my beer. Fuckalot slaps my back.

Everybody holds everybody back so nobody has to actually fight, and the owner of the bar is shaking his finger in Asshole's face, saying, "These ladies are just entertaining themselves, no one has a problem with this shit here, why are you losin' yer shit," and Asshole keeps yelling, "Them ain't no ladies, you don't understand, my girlfriend's CATHOLIC," and Dev's yelling, "So am I. You can't keep blaming the Church for everything. Move on."

So us and the circus boys, we finish our beers and go hang out under the forty-foot Madonna by the water. It sure is good to meet some nice young gentlemen once in a while and fight injustice and bigotry together, even if it is only with a few threats and an anonymous mustard jar.

OLD CAPE COD

Provincetown is Disneyland on Gay Day. It's a giant Castro. At first I was excited, because I knew no one would be mad at me for being queer, but then I realized that same-sex boinking was the only thing I had in common with everyone. They still thought I was going to mug them. I can't blame them. I look even scarier than usual with all this bacon on my head, that's bloody scabs, from the other day when me and Killer stacked.

Everybody's gay, old ladies walking down the middle of the street holding hands and shit. Butch-femme so veiled, the only way you can tell is the femme's shaved her eyebrows and drawn them in with brown eyeliner. You can tell they try to fit in and don't hold hands back home in Idaho, where they would get their asses beat to a bloody pulp by God-fearing fag bashers looking for old ladies to abuse. The old ladies look very relieved and confident at last, like, "Yay, I get to do this and no one's gonna stop me," but I'm sad they don't feel comfy like this in Idaho.

Anyway at the show there's this one girl in a Motorhead T-shirt, with bags under her eyes like she ain't slept never in her life, and so we start shooting the shit, and I come to find out that in fact she does not sleep and why.

I'm glad to meet her because the itch is back. All I've had is beer for weeks, and my system's feeling healthy, clean, like it could stand a little dirty water.

So we head down to the breakwater and hike out about a mile into the ocean. The Milky Way's out and the moon's a jelly candy hanging low.

I start crooning, "If yer fond of sand dunes and salty air . . ."

But she just looks at me really bored and annoyed. OK, so she's heard that song too many times, even though I have never actually sung it, especially *in* Cape Cod, having never been to Cape Cod before, and so find it highly amusing to do so, but I shut up and make a mental note to sing it to myself later when I'm alone, because it's a really pretty song and Bette did an excellent rendition of it, after her hair was getting frizzy in the Baths, but before she portrayed a Joplinesque singer in a movie that implied— ohmigod—her character's bisexuality.

So anyway, death mama hag hauls out the goods and I'm getting the prerush rush. Cotton mouth, hyperventilation, booty heat, sharks biting at the cage, that's what Smash says when she really has to pinch a loaf, lay some cable, that's what you wanna do right before you bang, but once you bang you forget all about it, because you're so high, your butt pinches up tighter than a rain barrel, which is damn watertight.

Cruella sucks up some water out of a little bottle, squirts it in the baggie and squishes the batter between her fingers 'til it's clear. Pulls it up in the rig and says, "Hold off."

Now I don't even know this girl, but she looks pretty adept at the whole game so far, so I stick my arm out and wrap my fingers around it. She slides the needle in, which is easy, because there's a two-inch track pointing right to Old Faithful, but it's not all tender and fucked up anymore. She leaves the rig half full, pulls out, ties off, and shoots my blood before I can say what the fuck.

I'm rushing, and I hate to talk when I'm rushing and fuck up the sound in my head, you don't want to talk over God. She lights a smoke. I lie back on the rocks with the sound of waves slapping up on them all around and stare at the cloud of stars. If you look straight into the blackest part of the sky, you won't miss the shooting stars. There's one with a tail that stretches halfway across the sky and lands downtown.

After a while I says, "Wha'd ya do that for."

She says "What."

I says, "Wha'd ya go shoot my blood in your fuckin' vein for. You tired o' livin', or what?"

"Yeah. You could say that."

"So you just go around slamming skanky motherfuckers' plasma you don't even know, hopin' yer gonna win the fuckin' lottery someday."

"Yeah."

"Damn. You must be really depressed."

"Yeah."

We don't say nothing for a while. She says, "I noticed you didn't ask if that was a clean rig."

"Well, yeah. I kinda forgot. I just assumed . . ."

"Who you talkin' about shootin skanky motherfuckers' blood then? At least when I go out it won't be a mistake. It'll be deliberate. My decision, not some 'Whoops, I fucked up' thing."

I didn't say nothing. "You're what they call a bug chaser, aren'tcha. If you wanna die so bad, whyn'tcha just blow yer fuckin' brains out?"

"Wouldn't be half as fun, now, would it. See, this way I get to gamble and do drugs at the same time. Ain't that nice."

Hard-core. Maybe she's right. Maybe I'm a bug chaser like her and not admitting it, subliminally seeking thrills or just a rest, and I'm too chicken to slit my wrists.

I really need to be alone, but you gotta entertain fuckers that get you high. The only reason they provide is, they're lonely and everyone hates them, so they got to pay you, the drug whore, to put up with their tired spiel. Fine. We go to her little beach house and tweak all night, she shows me some chords on her electric guitar, playing "Running With the Devil" really low on pygmy amps. Sky gets light, too wired to fuck, any extra-cerebral activity is annoying, hands slapped away, physical touch is out, romance unthinkable. So she cuts me. Razor blade slashing some mystical symbol over my heart she says means transformation. She sucks the blood out, ashes her cigarette on her fingers and rubs it in the open slice. I thought I was Danger Dyke. But none of it seems dramatic, just flat and tired and done to death.

Onto the sand and into the Atlantic, boots fill with water, and me filled with this uneasy feeling that for years has been the only way I've felt easy. I pull out Grandpa's corncob pipe and stuff it full of relief, but I suck it down and no easiness comes. This is the way Grandpa breathed, and Mom too, and everyone that ever taught me how to breathe. Grandma at five o'clock sharp cocktail hour, with me, a loud bundle in her arms, dipping her finger into her martini glass and then into my toothless mouth to stop tears. Mom with the snifter of love. It always worked. I pat my jacket for smokes, light one. Take a drink from the half-pint in my back pocket. I stare at the sunrise over the wrong ocean in disbelief. Nobody told me one day everything would stop working.

I whip out the phone Dev gave me to hold at the show last night, the sell sell sell phone she calls it. There's still some juice left, so I call my mom.

"Hi Mom. I'm in P-Town."

"Where's that?"

"Massachusetts."

"Don't let any Kennedys rape you."

I look up and down the beach. "Um, I don't see any Kennedys right now."

"That's because they're busy raping."

My mom. I think I'll keep her.

PART FOUR

SEEK AND DESTROY

LULLABY ON BROADWAY

I slipped up, but I been paying for three days, sleepwalking. Now I remember the price of testing stratospheric limits. But peering through the windshield, I'm in a stealth bomber, preparing to probe even more virgin sound barriers, flying over the bridge into New York City.

The lights, everywhere you look, at every edge of the world is humanity, all-night major rager at its peak, no downswing in sight, because thinking about the end of the party only brings you down while it's still blazing, and you could be enjoying it. And then when it's starting to die down, you do another blast of carbon monoxide and anxiety, and you can never really get as high as you were an hour ago, but you got no choice, you got money, and you have a moral obligation and a brain-chemical bossman driving you to achieve the highest level of pure pleasure and glitz and maintain it forever. That's your civic duty as a citizen of the Emerald City.

I'm wired, I can feel the rush coming on like adrenaline skin popped, like the time they did that to me in the emergency room for hives. They shot it in my butt cheek and left the room to see if it would help the welts disappear. While the doc was out, I felt my blood pressure rise, flushed, happy. When he came back, he said, Oh, the adrenaline's working, and gave me a boost. I was never so high on the cleanest skank for free in my life. And you can make it yourself, just driving into NYC.

I'm not even in the city yet, just racing over the water toward a kingdom of lights, and already I'm shouting and fidgeting and chattering about anything at all, and what we'll do, and where's the squat, and when's the CBGB gig, and how all my heroes had shot up in the bathroom there, and I was gonna stand ankle deep in water and gaze at the graffiti spray-paint layer fresco so beyond reading and close my eyes and feel the collective glory.

Yeah yeah, the van mumbles from sleeping corners. No one's as awake as I am. Maybe they've all been here before, they're jaded, they don't care. This is America, Times Square, the whole world watches the New Year turn here on TV, teenage runaway movies, if you can make it there, Nina Hagen, the Divine Miss M singing to towel-wrapped fags, Sinatra, Broadway, hit songs, movies, De Niro, epic. Kill or be killed. Make your destiny.

We're driving through narrow chasms of brick, and cops are everywhere, in cars, on motorbikes, like they own the joint, like vultures, like revolution's brewing, like they can stop it.

It's been a long ride across five thousand miles in a month, more ground than I've ever covered on two wheels. So I guess cages are good for something. And I'm gonna miss being crammed in a crate with four crazy dykes and a tranny boy and all our shit, waking up sore from sleeping on a shoe or a rubber dick, finding used condoms and bloody shove-ups in the bottom of my sleeping bag. No more giant Siamese sextuplet. Now I'm gonna have some air and dispatch myself. There's something to say for being lonesome now and then, not like you could ever be lonesome in this town, but I bet it's roomy and spacious compared to the van.

We say later until the show, and me and Johnnie Mae bail out at Ninth and C.

There's a bell way high up in the doorjamb labeled Sadaam Might.

I mash it, watching the raver punx with orange and yellow jawbreakers in their hair flouncing on a sidewalk mattress, surrounded by puppies on ropes tied to the bumper of a Volkswagen bus, eyed by cops.

Finally the door opens and it's Sadaam.

I knock him over. He's still skinny but less waxy.

"Don't try to carry my duffel bag, you skinny fuck." I grab it and lug it in.

He leads us down the long plywood hall, to a door with a sticker that says PSYCHO INSIDE. Fermented cat piss on the sandy floor bowls us over.

He says, "We're getting ready to put down tiles, and it's gonna be so the Ritz." Into another room with a fan as good as air-conditioning. Outside in the tiny yard is a raccoon named Kathryn. "This is New York squatting, honey. You can just rest with that tired Cali excuse for a hovel."

The tallest blondest lingerie-draped tranny leans in a doorway like every soldier's favorite whore, like a Dietrich song, Lili Marlene against a lamppost, like come and get it if you're a real man.

She looks at me and says, "Gorgeous," in three syllables, starting high in thin air and swooping down into her surgically enhanced cleavage. "Esty," she says by way of introduction, and limps her wrist to my face to kiss. "Like ST, Sophie Tucker, you know who that was, honey?"

"Yes, ma'am I do," I spent my youth memorizing the Hollywood big mama's trashy jokes. "My boyfriend Ernie, he says to me, Soph, ya got no tits and a tight box."

Esty delivers the punchline. "So I says, Ernie," screeching out the last eeee in Ernie, "Get off my back."

Esty and me were separated at birth.

Sadaam offers me and Johnnie his room, which is fine with me. Not that it's not fun doing it in front of five people all the time, just a change of pace is nice.

Esty says, "Come down for breakfast. I have an early-morning stomach herb ritual. Takes about two hours to boil, honey. The stink will wake you up."

She has a growly way of talking that slides around slow and lazy. Bee-stung lips and eyes that gaze everywhere, but you know she's not ignoring you because her pet names wrap around you like a blow job and a baby blanket and a lullaby, and you believe you are her honey baby darling.

I ask her why she has a stomach ritual.

"Because the drugs that are supposed to be saving my life are fucking with me, darling."

Me and Sadaam run to the corner for cigarettes and beer. It's five A.M., and not only are corner stores *open*, they're peddling *beer*. This town is alright. Mom would decree it "civilized," like Berlin, open twenty-four hours, nonstop, no-plot, all-action party. Sadaam picks out some fresh melon and orange juice for breakfast. I grab a bunch of daisies for the girl.

He wants to know all about her, and my braincell-cloning project (as I was down to one and am trying to increase the number again), and what happened to Ally, so I run it all down, how me and Ally Cat, we're in love forever, but you know, we just are not cut out for each other, but I'm having fun porkin' babes, and she hates that shit, and so Sadaam calls me a whore and says if I cared about her I'd try to change, but I'm all, Hey, I haven't hardly shot any skank, except the other night, and Ally's jealous as hell, all crampin' my style, puttin' me on a leash in a cage in the closet, which, beyond the bedroom, just don't fly. If I look twice at some other babe switchin' down the street in a miniskirt, she's homicidal, and even when I'm good like a choirboy, she thinks I'm gettin' busy with my mom. Whereas, now, Johnnie Mae, ya see, FUN TIME. All smiles, no problems, grabs other girls in the pit and does male-generated lesbian love acts, never bats an eye if I take someone else out to the van, free for all, no rules, *plus* breakneck speed action adventure. She's a genius in bed. Nobody plays like her, switchin' alla time, I'm the daddy, you're the boy, you're the mom I'm the boy, I'm Harvey Keitel the bad lieutenant, you're the sixteen-year-old runaway, I'm the fag whore in the alley, you're the leatherdaddy on crank cruising me on a Harley. She's got a mind so dirty make me come with a bent story look ma no hands.

Sadaam says we won't have to go bare bones tonight. Esty's got a sugar daddy that gives them all the toys they need to play dungeon and make them some free money too.

We go upstairs, and he's got harnesses and whips and gas masks and latex cop shirts and batons and handcuffs and corsets and dicks and every other costume and implement of torture. Johnnie's in hog heaven. We play dress-up for a while. I settle for simplicity and tradition, leather harness crisscrossed around my chest, and she grabs the chrome ring and yanks me around, calling me boy, in my tighty whiteys, white T-shirt, and white socks, throws me in a small cage and smokes, while I curl up and wait, a teenage sissy waiting in the locker room for the football game to end. She straps it on and pounds me all night long, pulling me to her each stroke, hooking her fingers through the ring and doing curls. Short snap up, long release back, pressing a blade to my throat with the other hand, death threats, epithets. "Who's yer daddy."

"You, Coach."

"You're a sick fuck."

In the morning Sadaam's making tea. He got me a job driving cab, which, like anything else in this world, ain't easy to get without the right connections.

Delivering packages on a bike, people in a car, what's the difference. Either way, there's no boss telling you what to do, except a dickscratcher crackling over the radio, who doesn't know what you're doing and can't stop you from doing it. Motorized, I'll cover a town as big as a small country, making bank in a ton of steel armor, safety and efficiency all rolled into one yellow tank. Who needs bikes, with all that sweat and car doors opening and skinned knees?

I'm ready for New York City. Is New York fuckin' City ready for me, is the question.

THE TRIP FROM CBGB

Adventure World is a place for places in me I only read about in books. I'm a little guppy in a big bathtub, a kid in a Toys "Я" Us. I want to jump out the window of the van, onto the sidewalk more like a catwalk, a runway, everywhere fashion, and girls, and punks, and drag queens, and rock 'n' roll, and dogs, and pizza all night long, where I belong.

No sleep, no nothing, I'm unloading in front of the famous awning with the cowboy lettering, CBGB, where it all started, Joey Ramone in his superdarks, Talking Heads when they were too weird for TV, Blondie pre–top forty stardom. If Ally were here, she'd be so excited. We'd be anthropologists and sit back and watch the tiny punks and interview them to see if they knew their history. The great thing about history is it makes you whole. No more lonesome fragment, me.

Mucous is about to play, and I'm ready to rock, but first I gotta run downstairs into the ladies' room. I don't think any ladies have ever been in here. Stand in front of the spray-paint mirror, suck in history, close my eyes and think of P. Smith.

Eight chick bands, a marathon. Cute girl, old on the inside looking out, takes my hand, black hair, green eyes that seen the sewers of the world, you know, like I like. She takes me downstairs, shoots me up. We go outside down Bowery past the flophouses and east along Houston. And then I look at her. She's the girl I saw the day me and Smash did those 'shrooms, the one that tried to give me that coat. I didn't know where I was then, but now I recognize Katz's Deli, the Economy Foam Store, Yonah Schimmel's Knishes. I almost ran past her then, but she stopped me, standing there like now, reaching out to me, only this time no coat, just bloody works in her hand.

"What did you put in that spoon?" I ask, but no words come out, and I run.

Into the squat, the big, wide open space on the thirteenth floor.

All the walls that used to separate the rooms have been smashed down and swept away. A little rubble and debris left on the floor, the ceilings high with bas-relief angels flying from the eaves, white-plaster chipped cherubs, white eyes and white wings and white stony linen draped from their loins to hide their sex. Angels have no sex on these ceilings, our limited heavens. They do have gilt wings, gold leaf on the edges of feathers, which, amazingly, no one's chipped off to buy spoonfuls of something that could make them soar like those seraphim frozen in flight, but someone climbed something and hung there to paint the toenails of each angel red.

The east wall of my room is a fresco cracked and fading of Etruscans, women wrapped in long togas, lounging alongside sunken steaming baths, feeding each other fruit.

The north and south walls are barely still covered with thick paper peeling in sheets to show holes in the stone where treasures are stashed for short times before they're shot up or drunk up. Also, some bricks removed are a shelf place for sections of latex tubing, bent spoons, and small bottles of water.

The west wall is completely smashed out, and you can lie on your stomach and drop your chin over the precipice and look down all thirteen stories to the street, or out over the dusty yellow Roman skyline in the evening, the air and the buildings all covered in rose-colored smog. The sun sets melting between ancient basilica towers and row houses with water towers standing watch, keeping secrets of how to get the water out (no one knows how to get the water out), and laundry lines and children crying, dishes clanking, momma and poppa yelling, the fresco on the back wall lit up like a junkie who opens one eye and nods out again.

She comes up the stairs, I hear her laughing, another one laughing, two, their pheromone giggles, teenagers-in-love sounds drift up louder, louder, weaving dark nets dripping something sticky, venomous, jealous, to catch me. I roll over on my back and drop my head backward over the outside wall to watch the upside-down sun rising into a celestial city, glass digging into my back with the dust and dirt and dead flies' crunchy carcasses.

They don't see me, my girl and her, they fall in a giggling, half-naked, sweaty heap of grinding hips and long hair sticking to grimy shoulders, rolling over and over each other on MY straw tick.

The shadows fall over me and they don't see me lying there, feeling my tits as they fall to the side, my chest like a boy's, my hand down my pants, coming as they come, then I get up and stand over them.

"I'm leaving you. You hate me. I'm going to drink poison."

I leave with my fingers trailing juice and spit down my belly. She lifts Herself up on one elbow, one eye closed to focus, drunk on cunt. She falls back into the pit of desire and stink they have made of my bed, and I run to the roof, where the old lady lives. I shake her by the shoulders.

"Poison. Poison, enough to die," I shout in broken Italian.

She presses into my hand a vial and pushes me away and I fly down the stairs to the beach where it's dark, the moon rising, but hordes of zombielike ravers push me back. There's a bonfire down the strada. I want to die, alone.

I run back to the house, and inside, on the ground floor, Her happy family hosts a cocktail party, and She—small daughter in her party dress, dark hair, green eyes, She's as stiff as Her petticoats, six lace ones starched—says nothing.

"Allisandra, Allisandra," I call to Her, dropping down on my knees. "Come to me, bambina."

She comes, looking at the floor.

"Allisandra, it's you. What did he do, your poppa? What?"

Shakes Her head. "Nothing. Nothing."

"Don't protect him."

"He tells me to brush my hair, and he puts his head in my lap while I sit on the bed and brush my hair for him and he looks up and watches me. That's all."

I grab Her father by the neck, his pretty-boy neck-tied neck. He's beautiful and young and I choke him with one hand, his head turning purple, blowing up like a balloon until he pops and lies in a puddle of green on the floor, and I'm still holding his neck. I can't let go.

And She goes to Her mother who says to me, holding Her close, "Thanks for taking out the garbage."

So I drink down the hemlock. It's raw pancake mix, not strong enough to kill, only to make me queasy, light-headed. On all fours I lurch up the stairs to the room where She lay, but She's gone.

Up the ladder to the roof garden, sunrise.

I fall on my knees and cry, "Allisandra. Allisandra," out over the city, "come back," but thinking me dead, She has gone.

ST. MARK'S

I wake up at noon, head pounding, boots still on, grab the board and squint outside into the day. I have a vague memory of embarking on some epic in-through-the-out-doors-of-perception journey. Now I'm bumbling to find my way out of the squat.

I hide behind three-dollar shades and skate through gaggles of cops hanging out like hoodlums, proud in front of their rousted squat. A cyclone fence, razor wire, and rubble surround postwar ruins. Those crusties must have put up some scuffle for the polizei to still be prowling a week later, quelling revolution aftershocks.

I roll down the thrashed street, stumble into a pothole, biff on the broken asphalt, get up and hobble to Cafe 7A, board in hand. No negotiating streets on small wheels until after rocket fuel. I order coffee and eggs, flirt half-assedly with the waitress who was here yesterday. She's why I'm at 7A, because it sure ain't the coffee.

No more shooting up. Just say no. They don't have anything decent to bang here anyway, except a buncha skag. Besides, it doesn't fix anything, it just makes shit worse. Look at me. Ally wouldn't touch me with a barge pole, draped over a chair like this. I got shit to do, and I can't lift a finger, I'm a pool of protoplasm oozing down a storm drain. This is New YORK, god dammit. Gotta wake up, gotta make shit happen.

Oh yeah, it's all coming back to me, something about testing limits, not injecting them, but soaring on the sugary thirty-one flavors of godhood this town dishes out in triple scoops.

I gulp down the cold brown water. You'd think New Yorkers would know how to make coffee, they know how to do everything else, but since NYC itself is speed, they don't prioritize the caffeine angle. Now in Seattle, where the rain depresses everyone, excellent brew is necessary on every corner, but here, no, you have to skate ten blocks to a coffee joint to get coffee, you can't get it at a café. I don't have the balls to make it four more blocks, so I dish out three bucks for a crappy espresso. And another one, watching waitress babe, and drooling on the supermodels walking down the street.

Jesus Christ but New York chix are fine. No wonder all my exes aren't from Texas but mostly NYC. Now that I'm living at the source, I won't have to wait so long and look so hard for the perfect psycho chick, they wear their pants so tight and their boots so big, even though their eyebrows are so little. I fall in love every five seconds, and I don't have to move from my plastic chair on the sidewalk at Seventh and A.

Bad java oozes into cranium. Plan of Action Number One begins to formulate. I wanna be a card-carrying New Yorker. These are my people, the bad-assest motherfuckers anywhere. Must emulate. The accent alone is enough to bring me to boot licking.

First phase of the hazing, explore the hood in a hangover daze.

I slap a ten on the table and heave my carcass onto the board, cruise slow down East Eighth. There's a million little shops, vintage dresses and velvet capes hanging outside on racks guarded by bitchy shopkeepers so tough you don't dream of nicking anything, and up above there's the zigzag of fire escapes on bricks, soot blackened. There's a vegan bakery run by a guy and his ninety-year-old mom since forever. I munch down a pumpkin tart and keep rolling, peering into every storefront at shoes too outrageous to walk in, rubber dresses and other forbidden pleasures. I go in a toy store and put on finger puppets, push fire trucks with real sirens around the floor. A kitten saunters out from behind the counter, and I hug it and kiss it and pet it and call it squishy, and the lady says there are more in the back and lets me play with all of them at once. Outside ten kinds of incense fill the air. The rasta man is burning little clear rocks, wise-man gifts on coal dishes. Next to him's a table spread with books, classics and Bukowski and Winterson and Allison and art books and biographies of freaks.

Hundreds thread singular paths on secret missions, through masses, like crammed into a tour van, but separate, not of one unified mind. Everyone in his Habitrail. I'm surrounded, but there's room to think.

Brown clouds lure me into a coffee store.

A small hag behind the counter shouts, "Whaddaya want?"

I have heard that there are Hags NYC, in addition to Hags SF. I bet she is a Hag with her aggro style. I make a note to ask her later. If she isn't, she oughtta be.

I stare at big burlap bags piled on the floor, overflowing with oily beans from Mexico, Italy, and Africa.

I order an espresso and she pours it. On the house. Wants to know if I'm going to the Mucous show at Coney Island High. That's a rock club, not a high school, dummy.

"Yep. I'll put ya on the list."

"OK, it's Mario Shemeinsky, that's M-A-R-"

"I know how to spell Mario."

"You're in the band?"

"Nah. Just the roadie."

In a few days I won't be the Roadie anymore. I'll shed my skin and become new.

YOU TALKIN' A ME?

It's very Witness Protection Program. I don't even recognize myself. Better than any twenty-dollar bag of twenty-four-hour makeover. I'm new new new. Shiny disguise. I'm *really* superman, now that I kicked that kryptonite habit.

So I'm driving the cab in New York, like De Niro. I'm crazy, and everyone that gets in my cab knows it, except people that are crazier than me. I don't know, maybe they buy my spiel that I'm just like them, or that I'm just like De Niro anyway, just a cabbie.

I like to channel old Bob and say shit like, "Yunno, drivin' a cab is the most relaxin' way to earn a livin' in this piece-a-shit town." I clean my teeth with a hunting knife while I say it. It's the only way to get the point across. And fuckers just peel bills off wads of green, cuz fear is the way to cash in, in this town that makes cupid out of terror.

My favorite thing to do when I'm sitting in traffic is roll down the window, pound the side of the cab, and yell, "Yo, Jersey." That means you're stupid, you're from the suburbs, and I'm smart cuz I'm a New Yorker, and so it must be YOU fucking everything up, because if I were running this traffic jam, we'd be moving.

Mostly it's suits and ladies downtown, up and down Second Avenue, up and down all these avenues, and I can go all night, because I got the sole connection to godspeed, the little Hag at the coffee shop, to keep me going. She loads me up with free organic dark Sumatra to grind fresh at home. She even scored me a tiny espresso machine, so I can make my own tweak juice every day.

This is a heroin town. How can you keep going all night long enough to make your cab rental fee on fucking heroin? They don't do speed here because NYC itself is speed. They need to slow down, to keep from going crazy, but I'm already off my bird, so I don't care.

Every cabbie in New York City gets gas at five o'clock when all the suits are trying to get a cab. Just to whip people into more of a frenzy. The filling station is to cabbies what the Wall is to messengers back home. It's where they meet and hang out and yell at each other over the tops of their cars, while they pump twenty dollars' worth of gas into their steeds, instead of talking over their bikes and pumping two dollars of beer down their gullets. Twenty dollars, Jesus Christ, gimme a tall boy and my bike's going all day.

But these guys talk about driving around New York City, and I don't know shit about that. How am I gonna bond. They talk about their jerkoff passengers. OK, I could talk about the frat boy that puked in the backseat and then didn't pay his fare. Or the people that act like they never seen a girl drive before, if they even notice I'm a girl, which I'm happy when they don't, saves unnecessary conversation about should girls drive cabs, and ain't it dangerous, and ain't I married. But these guys can't relate to that. I try to make small talk with them with my best New York accent so they'll see I know what's up, and I'm no hayseed, and maybe they'll let me in on some hot cabbie info.

I pick subjects they'll agree with, you know, like the Knicks winning, shit like that. I'm chugging my triple espresso the other day, and I'm saying to the guy at the next pump, "Seems like anyone that would shoot scag is just plain unmotivated. I mean, I'm a guy who gets shit done. I can't be all noddin' off in some corner too wasted to even give my dick a good yank, know what I'm sayin'? I got bills to pay and ladies to charm and a big yellow car to cruise, OK? I just wanna say that right here. I got goals just like the next guy and I am not gonna be some dope-ass motherfucker talking 'bout the china white god of euphoria, dependin' on the man to bring me my world, yunno. I ain't dependin' on no one but yours truly. And how ya gonna protect yourself in that condition? Huh? All drooling on yourself."

No connection despite my best efforts.

So I'm driving, and I'm getting more and more agitated. Here I thought I got a car, I'm gonna put the pedal to the metal and go places, but no.

Welcome to gridlock. No way to jump the curb and go around traffic, stationary for hours, you can't cut down the other side of the line or split lanes like on two wheels. Hotter than hell and no wind in your hair, bound by laws and signs, and passengers' cockamamie idea of how to get somewhere. Guys don't tip you, they say you took the long way on purpose and you're a lousy bastard, or they get cute when you pull up to their apartment and tell you they got a tip for you upstairs, baby. And you get more and more steamed, but you can't go hammering down the street so two blocks later you forgot why you were pissed. It just ties your neck in a knot and you want to do bad things.

So anyway the other day I drop a suit on the outskirts at a skyscraper apartment, and then I'm out in the middle of nowhere, and I'm cruising around looking for a fare, and this dirtbag flags me down. Now, I'm not scared of anyone, and also it's not like I can be too discerning, because he's the only guy around for miles, so I pull over, and he climbs in and says, the Village, Second and Houston. I start driving down FDR, which is a fully empty highway at this hour. I'm watching him in the rearview. He's not saying anything, even though I'm trying to talk to him.

All of a sudden he pulls out a .357 magnum and starts yelling, Gimme the money, motherfucker, and I'm all, No, and he's yelling, Give it to me gimme the fuckin' money, so I slam my foot on the gas, and this is a new cab, nice and shiny, so it's got a lot of pickup, you know, and I keep it floored, and he's yelling, What are you doing, you fuck, and I just keep kicking the pedal through the floor until we're going about ninety miles an hour, God I love to go fast, and he's getting really nervous and pointing the gun at my head, and I slam on the brakes, and wham he comes flying over my shoulder and head butts the meter.

His head's on the floor and he's upside down with his feet up in the air, so I reach in his back pocket, take out his wallet, uncurl his fingers, and slip the gun out of his hand. I put them both in my jacket, lean over him, open the passenger-side front door, push him out on the side of the highway, close the door, and drive away.

As Joan Crawford says, Don't fuck with me, fellas. Who's in the driver's seat, pal. I am. I'm in the fucking driver's seat.

The next couple gets in, in the nice part of town, and they see the blood and hair on the meter, and they don't say nothing. They just give me a real big tip.

YOU BETTER WORK

The gang at the squat is always working, no middle men: There's no routine of go to job, get cash from boss, give it to landlord, who gives you a place to lay your weary head.

Nope.

Make house with hands. Very direct. Indirect economics is killing me, but I'm a navigator of new skyways, so I build stairs and hand Sadaam wrenches, while he installs the plumbing.

The thing is, squatting's like tour. You're surrounded by genius, you're honored to lend a hand, and their plan is excellent, but it is their communal plan in the end, which is a challenge for a lone-some cowboy like me.

And then the cops are always trying to ruin the plan, which, even if it's not my plan, it's my pals' plan, and don't fuck with my pals' plan, man.

The polizei put up fliers on the door saying, Please move now, leave your home that you've worked very hard to make, because we would like to make some money off it. Thank you. Love, the Police.

Nobody pays any attention to the police. No wonder they're cranky.

Mucous has been hanging in the City a couple weeks, soaking up the intensity, and they got one more show, at the local punkrock fag palace, before we part ways.

Mario Shemeinsky, the coffee guy, she's there, drunk as fuck and loud, grabbing all the girls. Hi-fashion queers, colored lights, Debbie Harry walking in the door like it's nothing, saying you look FABULOUS to Devastaysha standing there half naked with her dick hanging out. Lunachicks, heroes of hilarity and tightness, fucking shit up for the drag pit, a maelstrom of neon, glitter, wigs flying through the air, and nothing but love for local girls making good. Boss Lady, drag queen emcee to end all drag queens, sings Guns N' Roses hits with the house band in a long black rock 'n' roll wig, fishnets, and an XL Hostile Mucous T-shirt shredded down the sides and braided into a tight mini dress, muscular legs all the way up to her neck, all the way down to the floor.

Backstage she lolls in the laps of two hunks, laughing, tequila bottle in one hand, glass in the other. I'm in love. No fake padding, a flat-chested potty mouth, she's everything rolled up in one, mom, dad, femme bitch top with a dick. She's got a heart tattooed on one arm that says "mother," and on the other, one that says "fucker."

I want her. She deep throats Devastaysha onstage and the fags go nuts.

I low-crawl across the stage to drool on her spike heels.

Just as good as hard work and power tools is a real woman, man enough to make me forget about Ally for another day. Johnnie Mae's magic's wearing off. She was good for a while, made the hurt go away, but she's too easy. It's the thrill that fixes me. I can't let my heart go without a million parachutes, fluttering all different colors against the sky. I can't risk falling out of Ally's favor alone. I need a hundred arms of fifty babes lined up on either side of me, like bridesmaids, to catch my fall on scattered petals. That fall, it takes so long. I need it broken.

And now, last in a long line of bridesmaids is Boss Lady.

Diabolical, the irresistible tragedy of unrequited lust. But the chase, because maybe, just maybe . . . And even if I never catch him, it's not running to or from, but after, that's always a good workout. But then, to dream the unfuckable dream is to love her so much more for sparing you the drama. Safe. No pain, no pain. If I saw him walking down the street with a basket in his jeans, I never would have noticed him, but drag switched the way we do, it's true love, the kind that never has to be sloshed through a spermy gutter. Nothing like a nelly fag in a dress to take your mind off bio girls, even if there's nothing you can do about infernal desire but flirt.

Backstage, Devastaysha's packing her bags to leave.

I tell her I got a mean crush on a queen, and she pulls her dick out of her bag and peels the rubber off. Hands me the ten-inch. The one Boss Lady put her lips around. Dev says it's got the mojo in it to get her, but I could never, I'm too shy, she's six foot five, she's a chickboy, I'm a boychick, what would I do? Dev says dinner, drinks, dancing. Charm is charm.

I jam the dick in my jacket.

We say our good-byes. This is it. Hostile Mucous keeps rolling down the road and I stay, because there's nothing left for me back home. I dropped so many parts of Jim along the way, vestiges, rag dolls, and tin cups that cluttered up the wagon, chucking them overboard to lighten the load when the one surviving nag could only drag so much. I'll restock my heart in the new country.

"You're a good roadie. Fast learner. You keep out of trouble."

"Oh yeah. I'm slick."

"Yeah. Slick." She turns around. Nice ass. Bad too. Please let me one day kick as much of it as she does.

NOXIOUS PRIX

I don't wanna sleep because I might miss something, like how I unfold when they unbuckle the straitjacket and let me play with the other patients.

The joint's still jumping at four A.M. but I'm famished. Lucky me, it's four A.M. in NYC. I do not have to decide between Sparky's and Little Orphan Andy's in all of San Francisco. No, I can go to any of a thousand restaurants and order dinner served by G-Spot the tattooed loveboy at 7A, or by tranny babes with the tallest hair at Lulu's. The view's better at Lulu's for a tranny chaser like myself, but the chef's so wired he never tastes the food. Too chewy.

Go-go dancers writhe overhead. The DJ is spinning Iggy. She's looking fine and bottle blond, polyester tank top from Patricia

Field, drag boutique fabuloso, heavily glossed lips and false lashes keeping requests at bay. We're shy. I'm gazing at her, zoning.

My mouth's watering. I yell in the coffee guy's ear.

"Shemeinsky. Let's go."

"Yo. Can't ya see I'm busy."

"Yeah, I once got busy in a Burger King bathroom. Let's go, I'm starvin'."

She opens her eyes up wide and wags her head at the girl next to her.

"So? Bring her."

"Ah fuck it, by the time I get through eatin' I'll be too tired to fuck her."

Too bad everywhere ain't loud enough to talk about people right in front of them. Shemeinsky stops to lick dancers' boots on the way out and grabs her board from the stage.

We skate through Greenwich Village to Alphabet City. She opts for the drop-dead gorgeous waitstaff instead of fine food.

We talk around mouthfuls of dry French fries about what I'm doing here, and I tell her, I dunno, maybe I'll start a new life away from the girl of my dreams, or maybe get rich, go back and marry her, and I tell her about Ally and how she broke my heart, and how Johnnie chased me down and I just ended up here with her, which was fun for a while.

While I'm talking, I see I like to do the choosing, and I'm choosing Ally.

Something shifted between SF and NYC. In the rockin' flock of autonomy that softly shuffled me, the black sheep, down the muddy road, I melded into their mentality of Do It Yourself and do it right, and nobody does it better.

See, until now, I been lazy. Decisions are such a bother. Responsibility, yech. I remember I cried when I turned eighteen at the thought of becoming a grown-up. I soon found out that was just a number and no one could make me responsible, so there. But Dev said to me, one long drive through the night with a thermos of java between us, *Freedom is responsibility.* I nodded like I knew what she was talking about, but I had no idea. That phrase kept rolling around my cranium like a marble in a drum, though. And I think I'm starting to get it. If you don't choose your life, someone else will, and that means you have to do what *They* say, which is slavery. Hmmmm. Use your freedom of choice.

I thought Ally wasn't a choice, that she wouldn't let me have her. But I was the one that wouldn't let her have me. She's been right there the whole time, waiting for me to pick her. But I couldn't pick her, because I couldn't move, I always just let life happen, except at the point when I'd put the point in my vein, and then I still just let the wave wash over me.

Every night on tour, we kicked the door down and foisted our will on whatever sleepy town we woke up. Every night the band used the power of the mike to yell our version of how things would be. They gave me a voice and I got used to it.

Shemeinsky looks at the drunk guy at the next table. "Whadda YOU lookin' at."

I'm too tired. "Aw man, why you like to start shit."

"I ain't startin' shit, he started it."

I look at the guy. "Just ignore her."

I wipe my mouth and wave over the girl with something extra. "Check please."

Shemeinsky keeps at it. "I *tole* you not to *look* at me."

I'm not in the mood. "Look ya li'l hagmeister, will ya shut up already. . . ."

The guy gets up. Left tackle for the Green Bay Packers. I grab Shemeinsky's arm, push him backward over his chair, and drag her out the door. I like this kid. More rush than a gram. She brings out the choosy mother in me, making me choose my battles.

YA GOT TO HAVE FRIENDS

Friends for life, I never had none of them. The kind you select out of a crowd because of a magnet tug, not because they got the skank, the dank, or the wang-dang sweet poontang.

Friends like I always had, they come and go. Drunk fights over drugs. You fade away, to whoever has more drugs, and then you do even more drugs and move outta their league, until you're living in a cave because you can't stand to touch anybody or be touched. You put a shark-infested moat around you. If you allow anyone near you, you're always thinking, is this motherfucker gonna kick down another line and roll a joint or what? How long do I have to put up with this boring song and dance before I get my propers?

But all that's changed.

My new friends and me, we feed each other, not *on* each other. I never knew I even wanted that. Supply-side economics. I'm fresh off a desert island with a high-limit credit card, running loose at the Love Depot.

Everyone that lives at the squat is real. They're like the Mucous babes, a bunch of hard fighting, hard thinking, no-shit-taking dirty bastards. Like Esty, they call her the transsexual Courtney Love of the Lower East Side, but she's not.

"I love women," she says. "I don't beat 'em up. I'm a man hater."

No one hates men worse than someone who's been one.

Esty, she's a string of paradox pearls, morphing from fag, to junkie, to HIV positive, to clean and slobber, to woman, to big femme dyke. She's everything at once, glam junkie in Mae West drag, and all the hipster directors want her in their movies.

She's no cliché. She's never been done before. Onstage naked with hormone titties and her little dick hanging out, truly balls-out tranny, sexy beat-up child singing fairy tale incest songs like "Carolina Vagina," her band shocks fucks out of their comfy lifestyle. So cool, they're not. Cool isn't for sale at the bondage store. You make it up yourself, pull it outta your asshole, your own unique brand that starts when you're born, and when you die, it's gone.

So not cool, it's cool.

She's not cool. She was in a heroin haze while punk was being born and growing into a juvenile delinquent. I had to give her an update on the last couple of decades. She didn't even know who the Dead Kennedys were, even though she sounds just like Biafra. She's original because she's got no reference point but her pure gold heart. Most people that don't study their roots, I got no respect for them, but Esty's busy making history, so I take time out to tutor her in insignificant details like who graced the CBGB stage before she did.

I'm her man, protecting her when she's walking down the street.

Me and her, we shout snappy comebacks. "More man than you'll ever be and more woman than you'll ever get."

That cracks up the old perverts and makes them sad at the same time, because they know it's true.

Except the other night when they didn't laugh, and I had to grab a bottle out of the trash and break it.

I'm standing there waving it around at three Neanderthals and she's yelling, "You better watch out, honey, she's crazy. She's gonna cut your motherfuckin' balls OFF."

Good thing they don't call her on it. So she struts on down the street and I back on down it, right behind her, sticking my beer bottle out at them until we round the corner, and then I hiss "RUN."

But she just keeps swishing slow. "Relax baby, you scared the shit out of 'em."

Nobody ever had that kind of confidence in me.

"You and me, we're in love," she says, "we're two sides of the same coin. Gender's a box you turn inside out, tear up, and sew a gown out of." She says most people are bored and hateful because they can't fuck with the box. They think prison's protection. They take what they're served and think they like it, but deep down they want to be something else, and they'll kill anyone sewing gowns they're afraid to wear.

Esty can't stay up talking every night. I'd like to, wringing stories from her. She's had pneumonia and every other famous complication, like Sadaam, and we all know that's the death knell, the countdown. *Oh you've had thrush? Everyone's had that, honey, how about* this *obscure disease?* They compete, one-up each other, and laugh their asses off. The three of us, we're always poised to say good-bye. We don't have time for dour conversations.

I try to push the "so longs" out of my head. Paying attention to everything when we're together is Very Important, and I save every word she says, because she's dropping those wisdom pearls like the maharishi, and we all know it will be like losing Jesus when she goes. There's something about a person who knows each moment could be her last, she is that much more alive, and with one foot in heaven, she's got a whole different view of the world. I've tried to get a glimpse from my bike or the crest of a coke wave, but the view from Esty is quiet, like the top of a Himalayan peak.

She's so alive, we don't think of death, unless we're talking about the new meds the white man in the white coat is offering. Doctors masquerading as pied pipers. They don't fool her and never did. She swallows poison because they won't give her the cure.

When she goes to the hospital, she educates the nurses about how to treat a tranny with proper homage and respect and not make comments or ask stupid questions like, "Are you a boy or a girl, are those breast implants, sir? I'm not working on THIS patient, he's a freak she's a freak it's a FREEEEEEK." At least ACT like it's all normal and like you see such people every day, even if you don't yet.

"Damn it's hard enough livin' in this sick town, sick with no money. What's a welfare queen to do?" Be a champeen squatter, that's what. I help her with paperwork and phone calls to the tax-man and the bank and the electric company, so the squatters will have a paper trail that leads to legitimate ownership. It's a scream-ing bore, but she keeps me entertained, the two of us sprawled in front of the window that lets in a tiny square of sky.

She tells me about when she was Davey and he used to party. She tells me about the bathhouses and the glory holes with cocks slipping through for him to suck, anonymous, and I can just smell the close air, steam, and jiz, and the sweat of slimy muscles in the dark, big hard dicks disembodied, and your asshole taking it soft and easy with all the poppers you sniffed in a handful of his chem-soaked red bandana.

See, the Hankie Code, that's how you said what you wanted and who you were, and you looked for the right hankie attached to the love of your night.

A red bandana in the right back pocket, oh yeah, that meant he was into fisting a hard-core biker bastard, or dark blue, a fucker, Davey's fave. Pale green if he liked to pay for it. Dark green, army games. Yessir. Yellow, watersports. Dave giggled to watch boys like baby birds, mouths open, waiting to take the stream arching through the air from burly leather fags who had to "talk to a man about a horse." Brown, he was definitely not going there, honey. I would have sported gold lamé on the right, as I am a drag racer, tranny chaser. Dave wore pale blue on the left, party in your mouth, everyone's coming. And he was the hostess with the mostest.

But in the baths there were no colored hankies, only white towels, and steam heat whisping, and oily mustached muscle men, and doors that closed. You sat in your own cell on a wooden bench waiting for Mr. Right, and when he came in, you let him take you. Then you wandered blind through a pitch-dark maze of narrow spaces, black walls, touching naked invisible bodies. Thrills, not danger.

Youth and innocence, death racing through our veins and us not even knowing. We thought we were supermen. It was our world. We created it. So what, no fear. She says, "We were fierce, honey." Shooting up or getting fucked, we were in control.

The whole time, all we ever wanted was to feel things. It took extreme deeds. OK, so we had no visions of the future, we didn't think of getting old, but we never thought we'd die young. We had shit to do and a right to do it, a whole world waiting to be civilized by us. Or maybe they weren't waiting. We'd spring it on them anyway, our perfect gift.

All I know is, when Esty dies, the world dies. There's no light, no nothing without her, because after her, the rest of us go, and without all of us hated, the world's a puritanical putrescent bore drowning in their own shit, no clowning scapegoats to scoop it up and make art out of it.

Thing is, everyone's already sitting with the lights off, so how will they know when the power goes out?

I can't have Esty on the street, dumpster dining, because I've never loved a girl this much I didn't want to fuck, except my mom. She needs this house with her family in it.

Still, it's not my house.

ROAD DOG

It's not that I'm not grateful, I am, I'm lucky, I'm a debutante, about to be groomed for the graduate program of New York's prestigious School for Bad Boys.

I'm driving cab and I roll over to the coffee store where Shemeinsky's working and will kick me down some jet fuel. I pull up outside and yell "Ha-AG."

"What the fock you want." She pokes her hairless little head out the door.

"What the fock you think I want. Grab me a coffee and let's go."

She throws her apron in the corner, taps me a depth charge, and comes flying out.

"What, you want me a drive around wit' you all fuckin' night? I thought you was jus' gettin' off."

"Nah. Come on, I'll drive you home in a while."

"Let's go to the bar and pick up girls."

"Fuck girls."

"Yeah we can do that too."

"Are you on Viagra or what."

"I'm hot blooded, check it and see."

The car behind us taps the bumper. Shems yells out the car window. "Whaddaya fuckin' thinkin', ya jerk?"

The guy jumps out of the car, Shemeinsky jumps out of the car. Great, she's half his size again. They're standing there waving their arms around.

She juts her jaw up at the six-footer. "I'll kill ya, ya dirty bastard."

Here we go. I climb out of the cab, open the trunk, and get out the tire iron.

"Just never mind, will ya? Both o' youse." If you don't talk like a New Yorker in this town, no one listens to you.

She spits on the guy's shoe, he lunges at her. I raise the tire iron, bigger than a Krypto. Is a more lethal weapon why my balls are getting bigger? Or is it just practice makes perfect, like Mom said, overseeing my five-year-old ballet moves at the kitchen sink. ONE and two and THREE and four . . .

He backs off.

I'm mad dogging him. "That's right, just get in the fuckin' car, pal."

We get back in the cab and drive. "Thanks a lot. Could you maybe start a fight with a short person once in a while?"

"I'm just tryin' a help ya."

Ain't afraid of dyin' cuz we're fuckin' Hags.

BLANKET PARTY

It's been a long time no getting high off powders, but yet higher and higher like Jack in the Love Hate Beanstalk. I never thought I could get this high like a love-fest hippie, or a Beserker on red mushrooms, dreaming giant perspectives of everyone small and vulnerable at your red furry feet. Even though they're looking you in the eye, you think you're a giant, so you are.

I call Ally and tell her again how I changed, because she doesn't believe me, though she wants to.

"You should come here," I tell her. "You always wanted to go to grad school on the East Coast. And I can protect you from all the roughnecks."

She says, "Yeah, I don't need your protection, stud."

I get a long lonesome train feeling when she talks to me. Like the only thing I ever wanted I'll never have. I'll never be what she wants, because a freedom fighter joy rider and a ruthless serial killer is what she hates.

I tried not to want. I tied myself up with duct tape, because there's no comfort like bondage, and threw myself in the corner. Then I tried to make myself want twenty other girls. Tried to pretend those rides were like the sheer gonzo ride of Ally, the most treacherous cliff, but they were just primrose paths meandering through the park, they were sweetness and light and always there and easy. I lied and said I was in love with this easy-chair life. I lied and said really I was bombing down Lombard carving brick curves, just like when I was with Ally. But I wasn't. In fact I was trying to relive love with a stand-in. I tried to be satisfied with freedom to do whatever I wanted with no mistress to chastise me, and no drama, I tried to ease back on that Barcalounger love. But in the end all I wanted was her and the never knowing if I would land in her arms every time I dove off a precipice. All in-love may be is fear of annihilation. I can't trade that for a snooze in a hammock swinging in a tropical breeze.

Everything but her is just a lie.

She says she don't know if we can be together. How can that be when we are Romeo and Juliet, Tracy and Hepburn. Fuck that. Can't she see everything but me is just a lie?

It's been a year since we broke up. A million years since I looked at those green glass eyes in the morning and begged her never to leave me. Baby please don't go. She promised she never would. Since I cried in her cleavage and knew if ever I lost her I would die. Now I'm just an old empty inner tube drying in the gutter.

I quit that stupid cab job.

I thought it would be cush and easy, traveling three hundred miles a day in a big yellow car. But I can't trade thrills for comfort, because what looks like comfort ends up being hell. I get antsy. When I get pissed, I just get more pissed. I smoke a pack a day, bang the side of the car and yell, yo Jersey, but after a while, even that doesn't work. All that steel wrapped around you makes killing too much trouble. No ride-by Krypto-vandalism vigilante, you get lazy. You're not in the world making it happen, no, you're insulated, cut off, drowning in your own sweat with your shoulders around your ears. Where's the rapture of being alive? You're nervous, chewing your arm off to get out of gridlock, and then you see all you had to do was get out of the cab, throw the board on the street, and start skating.

So I do.

I don't know how long it took them to find that cab, but I figured it wouldn't be hard with five hundred honking cars snarled behind it.

I get a job riding a bike for money again.

I buy an old beat-up bike, no substitute for my true love, but here if you got a nice bike, you gotta triple chain it, and they steal it anyway. So I get a heavy, older babe, devoted to me, that's all you need in this flat town. No looker, like my girl back home, delivering a rush with fast tires and no brakes. But she serves me, fixes me up plenty, makes the mad go away, comforts me, runs the wind through my hair, and on a triple espresso I can make her take me on a wild ride. Sometimes you just gotta get any old kinda dame for the interim, and if you keep her lubed up, she'll put out.

Today I'm riding and I see this bastard kicking the shit out of his girlfriend. He's spitting in her face, and she tries to run, and he grabs her arm like he's gonna yank it right out of the socket and spins her around and punches her, and she slumps to the ground. Something snaps in me. I don't do the usual, stare to see if she is really getting her ass kicked, size up the guy, see how much bigger he is than me and how many teeth I'm going to have to swallow if I jump in. I just get hot all over, like meth in my veins, and I can't think. Everything goes blank, and I feel my mouth fill with drool, and I think I'm gonna get sick.

I pull my Krypto out of my back pocket and, pedaling by at

high speeds, I smack him in the head. I stop, and everything rushes in, the people standing around yelling "STOP." I guess I been beating on the brat for a long time, because nobody yells STOP in New York, and he's not moving, and I'm really tired. But it's a good tired.

What's happening to me, maybe it shouldn't feel good, but it makes sense to me. It doesn't make sense to most people, that's why they're telling me to stop. They think it's wrong. My way of seeing things is upside down from their way, and if I was in their world, with a regular job, married to a regular guy, I would see things their way, but I'm not, so I don't.

There's a small vulnerable man at my feet, and my head's swimming. I pick up my bike, wondering is he dead, and weave off down the street.

Outside of society's been home since I was a tot. That's where the naked truth is, stripped of all the old-school new-school poser rules.

Self-destructo spike to the vein was a sweet way to get there once. But I'm riding through Tompkins Square Park, and I see shit that's like a steel injection in my spine, every day new resolve to get outside the system and inside me, any which way but through that helter-skelter bloody handprint door.

School me, don't mind the maggots.

I go in the public toilet. Ten stalls in a row, all closed but one. I go in, sit down. It's so quiet for a full house. I drop my head between my knees for a look. All nine stalls full, all right, eighteen boots. A jar with a point in it. Another rig stabbing a calf. Blood trickling. People just sitting, waiting. Shooting the dream, fucked by the dream, dreaming awake, dreaming the drool. You're soaking in it.

Outside in the sunny dog run, life is happening, and you're all lined up, nodding separate in dark boxes. Ten years ago you were so cool with a neck tattoo, and now you're a toothless shell, a void behind nightshade eyes. Outside in the glare, that girl next to you, bleach blonde straw head, both of you fidget and stagger, darting glances, no connecting gaze, dance around the pusherman, excited children in old folks' bodies, senile and wired, you wanna be sedated. I ride by, stunned beyond mourning the death of love in this world.

Shems, Fuckalot, and me, Hags unite, triple trouble. On fenced-off squares of green, three musketeers spar.

Tour's over and Fuckalot has come to the squat to cure home-sickness and ride with me. I could see where you go through with-drawals, when you're languishing far from the crank of culture intensity and the hum of seventeen million heartbeats at dawn on Sunday, petting and soothing, like a machine-shop sonata. So you come back for another fix. After a few years frozen in a permanent position of straining at the end of a leash, teeth bared, beating someone's head in with a ratchet starts to sound like a good idea, and you have to escape to San Francisco or Portland for another year, cool down. I get the cycle. Full-throttle forever burns out the engine.

Someday I'll idle down, but for now I like hanging with misfits. They see things my way. Upside down go go go way. We're on the fringe looking in. Me and the gang and some raw dykes from next door, we sit around drinking forties, yapping.

They say, Sadie over at C squat, her stupid boyfriend's beating her kid up. Makes the kid tell the school she fell off the swing.

Can't get away because he says he'll kill them both. She thinks he's doing other shit to the kid. Any ideas?

I got a couple.

We ride in the van. I call him over. "Hey whassup."

"Nut'n. Whassup witchu, baby?"

"You wanna get high? We're gettin' fucked up, man, we got the rolling party fulla babes goin' on here." I hold up a forty. The tunes are blasting. "Get in man, we're goin' down by the river, smoke some herb."

He's all smiles.

We pass joints, brews, one specially spiked for him. Smack Water Jack feeling no pain. Head all lolling to the side, drooling on his shirt. We roll him up in a blanket and fuck him up.

We're makin' love now, honey. Whaddaya mean, no? Bitch. You wanna get fucked? Yeah you do, if you don't, why you dress that way? I wanna hear you say 'Thank you, sir.' Come to Daddy. Maybe we're being too nice with the ten inches. No? What you want? You want us to let you out? OK fucker, here ya go. See ya never, loser.

Everyone's fighting my war today, following my plan.

A flock is good as long as I'm herding it.

Sometimes when I'm swinging, I remember Mike Clinton with his arm around my throat on the front lawn of the school, and Tony Perelli and the basketball in my gut and the wind knocked out of me, and the sting of salty surprise in my eye, and I wonder if I'm any better than them.

But I don't care because I gotta fight back, I gotta feel the power they were born with so I can give it up, I gotta get high, because you know, it was never, I will dive one day tumbling at thirteen-thousand feet, sky, ground, sky, farms, sky, little squares of parceled-out earth rushing at me from two miles up, rushing at me at a hundred and twenty miles an hour. I'm my own wind tunnel staring death down, straight down, my own pusherman dealing crack out of my brain, no commute, one-stop shopping. It was never, I will be a movie star, or race a car.

No, it was always what gritty little thrill can I devise from this moment.

Maybe on Mike Clinton's Stingray I will fly right off this curb and over the handlebars, knowing that everyone has a scar under their chin and is here to tell the story, so when I faceplant on the curb, I'll be living then. I'll have me some memoirs.

The first hit of acid was orange barrel. Cliff had a pocketful.

I said, "What's that."

He said, "You'll like it," so I told the voices to shut up, the people-have-jumped-off-roofs-on-this-shit voices, and put it in my mouth to show them I meant it, and it was too late to try to convince me.

I ain't scared to put it in my vein, up my ass, or in my eye. My dad would be proud, I thought, but then he wasn't. He wanted a brave son, but he didn't see the bravery in what I done.

When I was a freshly out kid, me and my suburban gay pals went to the City, which was what we called SF because we didn't know about NYC, and we partied all night. We snorted six-inch rails in a cockroach-infested bare-bulb hotel room. We smoked PCP and moonwalked on Twin Peaks in the whipping fog wind above the twinkly earth. In the morning we ended up in a SOMA apartment, a hydroponic pot jungle. Outside, skyscrapers carved out of graphite shone in the breaking day, while someone dropped acid in my eye from a dropper. That's the best way, they said. Everyone else did it, so I shut up the voices that said, Acid? In your eye? You'll go blind.

Funny how fearlessness, flying naked into battle, red beards flying and axes held high, devolves, cowering in a dark closet in armor that no love can pervade.

Here in NYC, party capital of the world, I put my party youth to shame. We hit the rockinest disco, with the finest of urban queers, fashion gods dancing on pedestals for the rest of us to covet. A who's who of the city's art fag and drag scene, Boss Lady is out of the dress and still fine as fuck enough to make me put boyspells on myself. There's no one to beat up here, just glitz and foxes in the pacifying strobe.

Boss Lady shoves my face in her lap, writes my name in the blank banner across his flat chesty tattooed heart, and yells, "That's right, honey, you better not mess with me cuz I'm Jim's bitch."

Everyone thinks that's a scream, but I'm proud, thinking maybe he wishes it was true too. Esty says I shouldn't get excited, Lady loves bio boys way too much to ever love me.

I look sideways at the Lady reclining in the laps of perfect boys, laughing and looking satisfied.

Queens, man, they give me that sexy mother-dom fix, punch someone out with one hand and pet you with the other, all the backflips of romance with none of the hassles. And don't they love them some perfect gentlemen dykes with boyish looks that never break your heart.

Me and Fuckalot and Shemeinsky head over to Coney Island High. I'm meeting Johnnie Mae over there.

I picked up a set of brass knuckles in a Montana truck stop, and I been carrying them around in my back pocket. Never had any call to use them, because if you're gonna use them you oughtta be serious about it. Anyway, I let Johnnie hide them in her bra, because the door guy's patting everyone down, but they don't pat down no lace-bra titty giving you cleavage all up in your eye.

L7's playing and the guys are all fired up in the pit, like they are at L7 shows, because they can't deal with a buncha fine badass straight girls fucking shit up on guitar. Dee and Donita drive them into a frenzy, outta hand, and L7 don't do no crowd control. They like it outta hand. I leap up on the stage and mosey over to the edge for a backward fling into the crowd on "Shit List." I'm surfing nicely when some guy grabs my tit. Johnnie Mae sees it, comes up behind him and taps him on the shoulder, he turns around, and she clocks him. With the knuckle-dusters. Dude runs crying to security, who takes my shit away from her, them being illegal and all.

She puts up a fight. "You ain't got no right, you big ox."

"Look, lady," he says, "you're just lucky I don't call the cops."

So I pipe up, jumping down out of the loving arms of the pit. "Aren't we always just lucky YOU don't call the COPS? I thank my lucky stars every day I ain't in jail for wiping my ass wrong. THANK YOU, oh thank you, Mr. Nobody with a STAFF T-SHIRT, Mr. Public SERVANT Mr. Fucking Bureaucrat Mr. FUCK ALLA YOUS for even looking at me. Much less laying hands on me and my shit and my girl and telling me anything at all about luck, because YOU'RE the one that's lucky I don't RIP YOUR TONSILS OUT YOUR ASSHOLE. One day I am going to think it's worth my whole life in jail to do it, SO THANK YOUR OWN FUCKIN' LUCKY STARS, PAL."

We get to listen to the rest of the show from the sidewalk out front.

I do not have the brains to fight the system. I should just get the hell away from it.

NO REMORSE, NO REGRET

But I don't run away, I live to defy, and so find comfort in the defiant lives of squatters. One night we go hang out at the punkrock show at the squat down the street from us, Dos Blockos.

Green double-mohawk mirror wraparound shades man, so tall and skinny in his tight tight bondage pants, spikes, pretty, standing out among the crusty punks. His blackness would be what makes him stand out in SF, but here the gang comes in more colors than just white, just like Fuckalot and Max said it would.

Soleil's quiet and shy, statuesque, but I know what he's doing. Mom told me, when I asked her why all her glasses were tinted, they're to hide behind. You don't want people to be able to see every emotion on your face. That makes you human, and humanity makes you vulnerable. That's why cops wear shades, so they can lord it over you like robots, so you can't see the fear in their eyes. If you could, you might feel connected to each other, cop and citizen, and then you might sit down and cry together, and then cops couldn't do their job, which is to control you by instilling fear, not admitting it.

Everyone's a Crusty and I'm not as dirty as them, so not as hard as them. They're shadows. The whites of their clothes are brown

and the blacks of their clothes are browner, shiny with dirt, thread-
bare, saying I don't have time to wash, I'm busy breaking things, or
maybe I'm too drunk to care.

Soleil is arguing with the fine babe in black patent-leather pants
with the cockrings dangling off her belt. Those two were made for
each other, all fineness and attitude and star quality, postcard punx.
They fight, he walks away, and I consider climbing in that sweet
window of opportunity when straight girl hates boyfriend and
kisses girls vengefully, but what would be the point of her. She'd
shred me in five minutes, instead of drawing out torture over
months.

Everyone's drunk. The young girls with almond-shaped eyes
and full lips, finally I get it, it's alcohol bloatation. It looks sexy on
them now, but in ten years, when they're twenty-five, it's all bags
and sags. You see them fade from happy to sad, to brain cells pop-
ping loud and clear. Annihilate, dissipate, desiccate. Useless,
whored out to self-destruction; nothing left to fight with, forgot
what we was fighting. What fight? Why was I so mad? Have
another shot. No use talking change, they always win anyway. Talk
through the night, plan it out, and in the morning crawl to the
liquor store to feed the beast. You're tired since that fight with the
birth canal.

There's some asshole Jersey boy, two-hundred-and-fifty-pound
mullet head standing in front of the squat talking shit. He won't
shut up. About ten punx are gathering around, and then he starts
spouting off about niggers and fags, and me and Shems and Fuckalot just look at each other, like that's it, Jack.

I grab my skateboard, line drive to the back of his head. It
doesn't faze him. He spins around, and I'm saying "GodDAM,

FALL, motherfucker," and he grabs the board mid arc and whacks me in the ribs with it, and all the air leaves my body.

But I can't feel a thing because I'm dazed, too high to hurt, even before the slaughter. Whether I'm running from Mom's wooden-spoon whupping, or staring down pierce queens who aim at soft tissue, or looking up the flared nostrils of no-neck hulks, I'm always making the flight-or-fight juice that doubles as anesthetic.

I guess the gang jumped in and saved me, because when I come to, Shems is handing me a beer, saying, "C'ma-a-a-n, Boss Lady's singin' with the house band, and then Joan Jett's playin'. Oh you look great, come on let's go." I got no shirt on and I say OK, grab my board and the three of us ride, Fuckalot on one side and Shems on the other, me half naked with a beaten-in skull, and the cops all ganged up on a sidewalk staring at my tits like they wanna do something about it, and us yelling "IT'S LEGAL," and their little blue heads all turning in unison as we disappear down St. Mark's.

All this life's blood to forget Ally, and it's backfired. I feel more for her every day, not the control jones that drove me to be in her, driving like an astronaut savior in a robot suit. Now I'm outside her. I see her and love every twist and turn of her driving circles around me.

Standing on the corner, phone calling. Rats fighting and chasing each other out from under cars, cockroaches big as potbelly pigs waddling across the street. Me promising love and saying Don't worry, and she promising me No worries, how she never stopped loving me, it's just that I'm such a whore and that's alright with her, but I'm not even there, and she needs someone who'll be there for her right now. But there will never be a love like ours, she says. We're just too crazy in love to be together. But I like crazy.

I wanna fly down an extreme cliff on my back wheel, chunder into a parked car and lie there happy, with my heart and all my guts laid out like a yard sale.

She says, What's all that yelling. And I say that's New York City at three in the morning. Yelling never stops. Nothing does. Oh, and you can get beer all night, honey. As long as you can find a store open, there is beer.

It's getting cold now. The leaves in Tompkins Square are turning to blood. I tell my pals, Wow, look at those TREES, and they're all just Oh, the West Coast kid is having autumn.

The Long Island poser punx with Dad's credit card have all gone back to school, abandoning pups to stray, the ones they kept around to score more sympathy change, and the doggie gestapo scoops up the rejects. I found one, with big paws, a spaz with a face like a deer. All the girls like him. Soleil named him Mingus. I said is that after Charles Mingus? He said no. Mingus runs down the street after Soleil's Harley, and whenever he sees a motorcycle that's not a Harley, he runs around and around it in tight circles, barking so they can't ride away. Or sometimes he just stands there and barks into the tailpipe. You can't stop him. Or he's lying there all calm and then *snap* he bites your shoe. He has an eating disorder too. He never gets enough, slurping up his dinner in one gulp, no chewing, and rooting on the ground for rotten pizza all day. And if he finds one of those high-powered rotating sprinklers at the park, he runs over and bites the water until his mouth bleeds and you drag him away, both of you soaking wet. I like a dog with some obsessive-compulsive disorder, who makes me feel like a dad, not alone in my craziness.

We go to the dog run so he can sniff other dogs' butts. But

when it snows, they put snow-melting chemicals on the ground. Sadaam says it burns dog paws, and Mingus will hop around like he's walking on hot coals. Mingus the frog. Hop hop. We gotta get outta here. It ain't gonna be friendly in the winter.

I like the squat family though. Charming dogs, they inspire friendliness. I like the huddling warmth of the pack, hiding in the middle, smelling soft fur, dropping off to safe dreams, and solace.

GIRLS GIRLS GIRLS

Once upon a time, when Ally was a little girl in a short flower-print dress with a seven-year-old hip chuck and a hand behind her head, she had a small stuffed Piglet. She grew up and bequeathed it to me, and I slept with it every night and woke up every morning still clutching it in my hand. One day Piglet disappeared. I think it was stolen from its hiding place under the pillow by some one-night stand who thought it would be a nice souvenir to remember "that *special* night."

I said, "Isn't it very sad, when there is just one of something in the whole world, and it goes away forever?" And I squinked out a fat tear for all things loved and lost.

For five bucks I get a copy of the stolen credit-card number from the guy hanging out in front of the liquor store. I'm a pirate, a cutthroat.

I call Ally with the magic number, give her the daily self promo, with tales of girl gangs, fistfights. She suspicions right away.

"Yeah that's what I like. Why are you calling, tough guy."

Should have known better than to try to score points being a badass. "Because I wanna marry you and have your baby and satisfy you every night forever," is what I *want* to tell her. Nah, she'll run away in disbelief.

So instead I steer her off on squat the world and smash the state, trannies, and New York's so great. We're laughing like old times in no time.

My feet are walking up high on a trampoline air pillow, every step bounding high in the starry sky like in flying dreams, and me yelling yippee down the street, because she is my girl, and we both know we cannot break away from THE AWESOME FACT OF TRUE LOVE.

Even drinking Drano every day and hanging ourselves with nylon pantyhose, we only bungee up and down, and clean out the clog of soggy Cheerios.

You can't kill Rhett and Scarlet. They're legends.

Winter's coming to New York. The leaves fall off. It's too cold for Johnnie Mae. She's from Austin where it stays warm. I put the make on other girls, and though she used to talk a good game, Johnnie's just like everyone else, the marrying kind. I don't have the heart to tell her my only true love will ever be Ally, don't wait for that to change.

"I'm damaged," I tell her. "Don't love the crazy bastards, they'll only drive you crazy, onetwothreefour," I sing her the old Hostile Mucous song. Not like she cares or hears me, or could do anything about it, if she could. And not like I want her to hear me because she's my private RN, I'm on a health retreat at the love spa, I'm here to put the bits back together and hope no one sees the cracks. She's the salve that's gonna make those scars tell no tales.

And it's good fucking, and she's easy, taking care of details. Makes the breakfast and the coffee, pets me when things go bad, laughs off troubles, never complains, or constrains me to do what I don't want. There's nothing wrong. Just she's not Ally. And that drunken proclamation is always inscribed on my body to remind her.

I wish I could feel what she's feeling when I fuck her and she cries so hard like her cat died. But I can't. I just hold her and kiss away tears. Because I need the patience and the deliverance and the luxury of lambies, just for one more day.

I say to myself, *Look, water is coming out of its eye.*

Sometimes you gotta have any kinda ride for the interim. And sometimes you find a brilliant hybrid so shiny, it's almost as good as yours from home, and you just gotta have it.

Esty is a diva Jean Harlow, heart of gold, genius millionaire. When she sings torch, I stare, hoping no one sees the need in me, it's so illegal. But then it's just puppy love, a schoolboy crush, another secret face to paste over the centerfold in my brain, to retrain myself when wanking.

One night Esty comes home after a show, some guy follows her in pretending he lives there, blocks her way. Maybe he says, *I'm gonna cut your pretty face if you don't give it up.* She starts screaming.

We jump up out of beds, tackle him on the empty street. Here, by the projects, no cops wailing to stop justice. Wrong girl, motherfucker.

That first punch I always wanna take back because they look so surprised, hurt, betrayed, as if they trusted me all their life. They think I'm a girl, I'm supposed to pet and protect them, why am I hitting them, and then I'm all, WAIT, do I have the right guy? Does he deserve this? Whose god am I, dealing out punishment? Whose inquisition?

Why have punches become like reflex, like going out for morning coffee, like doing rails used to be, no contemplation? Because I don't like being second-guessed. After my initial moment of compassion, I kinda like that they are surprised by a girl whom they expected to run, just a fuckhole, doubled over all soft when they punch me because a dyke gives them the best of both worlds, fuck 'em like a chick and sock 'em like a guy. I'm not that predictable.

It's an answer to a relentless head smack. GOOD MORNING, THIS IS THE WORLD NEWS DJ WITH YOUR DAILY DOSE OF BULLSHIT: They're doing it to you again, they're doing bad things. They're hurting you again.

Whose god am I? Mine, parting the red sea. Because no, I don't like the news, and I'm making some of my own. Reflex evolves from flinch to knee jerk to calculated punch landed on a selected target. Choice makes me human. Freedom is responsibility. Because we take responsibility for our asses, we are free to walk the streets intact.

I hold a raw steak on Esty's eye, then I go to the pier, the Meatpacking District where the drag queens stack their cardboard condos side by side. I float my heart out over the water in a toy boat to Ally.

So fine, needless makeup, wake-up gorgeous, drop-dead gorgeous, eyelashes black like caterpillars, supermodels covet the curves you got, hoping Calvin Klein's next decree will be flesh is sexy, bones are not, so they can eat and strive to look like you, healthy, the new look, glam girl next door, no more junkie waif dark circles.

When Calvin sees you walking in Chelsea, he's gonna point out of the darkened windows and whisper to his chauffeur: "That's the look."

He'll invite us in and we'll crawl in the backseat, you sprawling, I'm on my knees before you, mumbling answers to his fashion questions. You gaze, bored, at the city gliding by. I'm running my hands up under your skirt, adoring thigh-high nine-inch-heel boots. Calvin tries to look away. Pussy's not his cup of tea. I drag you to the floor kicking champagne out of the way, backhand you, fuck you up to my shoulder, you kick me off you, pounding on me, calling me all kinds of sons of bitches until we fall together sweat and breath.

Calvin lights a cigarette. Invites us up for dinner, into his Soho loft.

We say no, drop us in the Meatpacking District by the piers where the tranny hoes strut.

We find us an alley where you can fuck me up against the wall, dead fish and cow ghosts, pants around my ankles, long shirt all but covering my nakedness, grab my hair push my face into the brick, beat me with my own belt, you'll teach me to fuck you in front of rich faggots. An intimate crowd of queens and trannies gathers, sportscasting while you slam up the ass what they think's a boy.

They holler, "You're giving 'em girl realness, honey," even though your dick is formidable; it hardly hides under that tiny skirt.

Sometimes when I'm nailing Johnnie Mae, I close my eyes and let myself think of Ally. Just for a second, I pretend she loves me and lets me touch her that way. It's OK. I'm the only one who knows what a dirty dog I really am.

But wouldn't it be dirtier to do her? Or even try? Or maybe

like Jimmy Carter said, committing adultery in your heart is as great a sin.

Main thing is, don't be there when it's happening, whatever it is. I gotta allow myself a vice. Better to grope one girl while thinking of another than to grope my arm and shoot my heart sky high. I know it's wrong to dream of Ally, crying, when I'm with Johnnie. But it's better to dream of a girl who don't dream back, a girl you never had and never will. Safe that way, sinking into hot baths with forty-ouncers, private pleasure.

Surrounded by sweet dreams of girls, I curl in beds of sleeping flocks.

Leaning on the railing at the piers. Lost and found. The perfect place to run away and secretly become you. Up on a bridge over Manhattan, you can spin around and see only buildings, no tree-studded hill on any edge of the world, of a soup bowl with the crust of last night's serving cemented to the sides, every morning another ladle of ominous überdirt on a circular skyline, calling you like a featherbed at four A.M. "Come, nestle in this humanity." This is the breath of seven million people. They don't go away. They thrive in their own filth and make it into superfood. Like cockroaches, their destiny is survival. You can't kill a New Yorker. They're dedicated, lifers.

People say New York is a hateful place, but it isn't. New Yorkers have hidden charms, they're just well hidden. They've evolved into self-preservationists whose sense of mercy's a vestigial organ. Makes sense. No use sacrificing yourself to save someone else. That ain't love. That's crazy.

Of course, if you got the killer instinct, there ain't no sacrificing going on, is there.

I got the instinct. There's no love in this world, all that's left in me is a smolder, a stupid rage I can't articulate and don't want to. I just want to feel my foot in the enemy's ass, because when I'm putting someone's tender in a blender, I'm something out of nothing and everything they said I couldn't be, I'm throwing bottles at every anonymous car that yelled, queer dyke bitch cunt, can't stand up for nothing, don't deserve no pretty girl's love. Gangs whupping ass is homoerotic hockey bonding, boys in love who can't kiss, and so there, you ain't the boss of us.

Rage is cheap and makes your insides throb and your blood thunder louder than even the mob alongside you, to drown out the broken promise of a never girl.

Me, Shemeinsky, and Fuckalot, mini mob, we stay out all night and come home bruised and happy. Johnnie Mae's neglected.

And although I love the agency of a fight, ignoring Johnnie is too much like letting the high wash over me. Fuck passive, gimme aggressive anyday. I have to make a clean break. A successful sadist has to be numb, hard, and I'm too awake to stay with a girl I don't love.

Even though I almost do. Love her. Metal on her lip, straight-forward brown eyes, lips curved like an angel's, full like a child's, dark lashes. She looks down, soft corkscrews hanging around her face, the kind straight-haired girls torture themselves to get. They never can. You can only be born with it. When I pull on it, and silent, it springs back into a perfect swirling cylinder, it makes it impossible to go. It's hair like grapevines. When I kiss her, softness and metal fill my mouth with extremes. All-American masochist, all-American cheerleader, dad next door. Innocent child. Quick learner. Unconditional pain. She gives me all my lost parts back, and a kiss from her feels like home. But a kiss from me must feel like a punch.

I find myself praying please God please . . . then I realize I got no right to ask. I want to promise, but there's no future. The most mournful thing is wanting to cry but you can't.

Please WHAT. Please let me have some more. Please, no consequences. Don't let me break no more hearts. Let me walk the tightwire to the stars, one slipper in front of the other boot, always a step up to another sensation, heaven through body, risking everything. Gambler win big.

I know I don't deserve this. I don't deserve no love. But I do whatever I want, and still there's love staring me in the face. It don't LEAVE. I close my eyes, and when I open them, that Texas tart is always there with open arms. If I can't chase her away, I'll have to run.

I try to talk to her. I don't know how to sugarcoat it. I thank her for starting that rumor in my brain that I was lovable. I thank her for her one-woman cult of blood, cum, spit, and razors that called me exquisite and shunned all the winners, cheerleaders, cops, and clear-skinned Hollywood movie stars. I ask her, Johnnie Fuckin' Mae, what am I supposed to do with that kind of devotion? Give me knuckles crunching five o'clock stubble any day.

I thank her for loving me. And then I tell her that we're through. She grins with her mouth. Just how I like my girls, crunchy on the outside, squishy on the inside. Hurt buried under a mountain of smile.

It's a bad plea, I try to push it out of my heart, that she not sleep, but vow silence and chastity, drink her tears, call my name, the only thing between her and death, the hope that she'll see me again.

Then I can forget her and go, knowing she's chained to that window, waiting. I tell her all this, dry eyed, while she packs her bag. She doesn't even tell me to shut up, not once.

The driver stands against the black shiny private car, smoking, motor running, watching me kiss her good-bye over mufflers and turned-up collars.

That's his fucking tip, I whisper to her before she climbs in the backseat and closes the door.

PART FIVE

I'M SO BAD, BABY, I DON'T CARE

LEGS

I would throw everything away for her, because she's the kind of girl who would never ask me to.

I'm fondling Ally's brain through the phone. She's deconstructing gender and I have to struggle to keep up. It's agony, security, like being lashed to a mast in a harpy hurricane. She tells me what books to read. She uses theory words like "performativity" to describe boyness, and gives me a woody through the telephone wire.

She says, "Tell me about your favorite color without telling me what it is."

I say it's deep and warm and cold like a desert night, like the buttery caress of a summer wind, like the wide-strip wallops of a suede flogger. It's inside your belly on the first night with the girl of your dreams, the one you've chased down for years. It's your heart when she leaves you, desolate, desperate, exquisite silence of so alone, death. It's the night when you realize you can keep as many snowflakes as you can catch. It's the smell of the basement where you keep knocking around, looking for her in musty sea chests, listening for rats.

She says, "Honey, I need to talk to you about something. You're the only one who would understand. . . ."

"Yeah but wait, whaddaya think the color is," I ask her.

"Indigo."

"No fair cheating. You know everything about me."

"That's true. And why do you think that is?"

"Because you pay attention?"

"Jimbo, how did you get off speed?"

"Uh, everyone got tired of me being an asshole. It wasn't fun anymore."

"But you did it for a while after it wasn't fun. . . ."

"Yep. I tried to stop a buncha times, but it never worked. I guess I finally was just ready, and then it was easy. I did backslide a couple times."

"You failed to mention that."

"Yeah, I know. Didn't wanna upset ya."

"Oh, I was just . . ."

"Isn't it great? I did it. . . . I did it, uh-huh, oh yeah . . ." I chant a little song for her. "Oh sorry, what? I didn't mean to interrupt."

"It's OK. I have to go now."

" 'Kay, baby, hey mail me some dirty underwear, will ya?"

I used to be a speed punk, generally pissed. But annoyances become more distinct every day, because I'm such a good guy on the good guys' side. Superior in my Underdog long underwear.

So I'm out here pedaling my ass all over town, and I run into another lobby guard thinking he's something and looking at me like I'm a second-class skanky ass. He sneers and sends me in the freight elevator.

"What, don't think I can keep my Sharpie to myself?"

He thinks I smell bad. The last elevator I was in, a choice one, was full of posh secretaries, the kind that spend their whole paychecks on deluxe downtown outfits so they can make more money so they can buy fancier outfits. Kinda like speed. Buy more speed so you can work harder so you can buy more speed. Endless loop syndrome. Anyway, damned if these dames didn't give me the dirtiest looks and wrinkle their noses at me. Well hell, maybe I think your Chanel Number Fuckin' Five stinks. It just so happens I don't, because it's my mom's favorite, and none of you got enough class to wear anything French anyway, but trust me, you ain't so hot. Besides, I been around this great big world and I seen all kindsa girls, and I bet you ain't even left the state. And the chicks who love me, you should see 'em, they are babes you would die to look like, and your old man would dump you for them in a hot second. You think I stink? At least I work for a living, delivering to your foofy asses. Why don't you try breaking a sweat sometime, besides when you're giving your boss a blow job under the desk.

So I go to drop a package. I'm about to have a bladderburst, and I depend on the kindness of strangers, you know, I'm a regular Blanche DuBois, so I ask the receptionist Where's the bathroom, and she raises her eyebrows, smiles kind of sheepish like, and crosses her arms in front of her, pointing in opposite directions. Well, that's cute. She does seem apologetic instead of hating me because she doesn't know if I'm a boy or a girl. How about when they say, no, they don't have a bathroom. Oh yeah? Where do YOU piss, in the fucking corner? I doubt it, pal. But they'll be damned if they let my sweaty butt on the same commode where they perch their lily-white asses. And then they try to add all kinds of little excuses, like um, you need a badge, or we have to use that public one down the hall too, so don't feel like we are ostracizing you, or it's outta order, as if they would go one day without every last luxury available. Outta order. Fuck you, YOU'RE outta order.

I step over the crazy lady on the sidewalk outside, with paper-bag shoes tied to her ankles with rubber bands, outside the forty-foot ceilings and the little man in the blue polyester suit that makes sure she never comes inside.

Whenever I think I'm a one-man band, I break down. I'm no island. Maybe the squat fight's mine after all, and I'm dying for the same thing they are.

I'm careening through town, cutting in and out of the parking lot formerly known as Fifth Avenue, and this cab sideswipes me, I go down, captain crash, down with the bike because there's nowhere to fly off and throw it away, in between tight rows of traffic. I'm lying on the dotted yellow line, tangled up in the frame. He keeps going, changes lanes, and then stops again, trapped on all sides by more cabs. So I extricate myself from the bike, examine bloody knees and elbows, nothing broken, pull up next to him, yank my Krypto out, smash his side mirror, and keep riding while he sits there, helpless, where once I sat trapped in my yellow cage too.

I've rode a mile in his chair and I still I got no pity for him, because he's never rode in mine. I'm free on my bicicleta. Like stealing tips off a bar. Butch Cassidy, the Artful Dodger strikes again, unstoppable. I'm tilting along unencumbered, leaving vexation far behind, with every spin of the pedal forgetting, whistling, smiling in the breeze.

Contempt means never having to look at yourself in the mirror.

Shit, I got to get this package off. It's burning up, hot hot hot, I'm having a barbecue in my bag. I'm shredding, jump up on the curb, slam the crossbar and the parking meter through my Krypto, twist the key and run in just in time for the forty-fourth floor elevator bank. It's closing. I jam it open with my shoe and slide in between a bridge-and-tunnel babe and a lawyer. They're all wearing sandpaper jumpsuits sandy side in, but not me. I'm relaxed except for the fact that the door's opening on every fucking floor. One by one, the androids slither out, until finally on the thirty-second floor, I get the cage to myself. It shoots me to the top for a decent headrush. I jump out and push the down button so the elevator's back by the time I grab the package off the receptionist's desk, and I get there and THERE'S NO FREAKING PACKAGE. GOD, I hate that.

"Where's the freakin' package?"

"Charming," she says, looking hot like Lisa Bonet.

"Um, excuse me, I'm sorry. I mean, do you have a package going to Cheeters, Scammim, and Graft?"

She wants to know what company I'm with. I say Daredevil Delivery and I'm in a big rush. She says something snooty, like "Do tell," and walks away. I look over her desk and poke around for the package.

"UM, if you DON'T mind . . ."

"What, you mighta missed it, I'm just tryin' a help. . . ."

I ain't gonna steal nothin' off your lousy desk. Like I love office supplies. But now I am in a considerable smaller hurry, seeing that tightly wrapped tail switching down the hall. She is aces.

Reminds me of that joke, about what you get when you cross a donkey and an onion. Well, most of the time you get an onion with really long ears, but every once in a while you get a piece of ass that brings tears to your eyes.

She walks back in and sits at the desk, hands me the package. She's ignoring me, like, I'm done with you now. She's got the look. Sex kitten in black lace and tweed vintage dug up from Village thrift stores, she looks like she just popped off the *Casablanca* set. She's so fancy you know the lawyers don't say nothing to her about a dress code. They just twitch and sweat from across the room, watching her over their reading glasses, and keep her around to jack off to in the bathroom, remembering the curve of her black-seamed stocking calf, crossed and beckoning from a thigh-high slit in a tight, silk skirt.

She looks like a party girl, fashion like candy, good shallow fun, so I invite her out Friday for drag hijinks at the Pyramid.

She looks at me and smiles like she's amused at my huevos, being as I'm just a lowly messenger, and she's supreme on her receptionist's throne.

She says, "Hmmm, I don't know," meaning, *Let's see if something better comes up.* Then she says, "Maybe I'll see you there," meaning, *I'm definitely not going, loser, so don't hold your breath.*

I don't care. Flirting with the working girls, scoping out the downtown-disguise dolls, that's just something to do. Doesn't mean I could fall in love. It's just like Hank Williams. After his divorce he put on a smile and married Billie Jo What's-Her-Name.

But his heart always belonged to Audrey, until they put him in his grave.

When you dangle a kitten up out of my reach, I gotta jump up and try to bite it. I'm starving, like a pit bull in a closet. Because I don't know how to love, just kill. I just dumped Johnnie to get Ally, but hell, I need a snack to tide me over in the meantime. I waited until Johnnie's grip got too tight, but if you jump into a girl's arms, there's that moment right before she gets a hold on you that's thrills and comfort, the best of both worlds. And then you run.

Lisa Bonet tells me come over on Monday, and scribbles her address on a Post-it note. I do like a girl that keeps me guessing.

On Monday I pick up a package going over the Williamsburg Bridge, yippee.

I'm rumbling and jumping over the painted wooden slats, swoop down the Brooklyn side of the bridge, drop off the package, and pull the note out of my pocket. Through the warehouse district, past the C&H Sugar refinery. I slow down and stare into the gloom at old machines, giant vats of glaze dripping out the still mixed with soot, oozing out the chicken-wire windowsill. I pull up in front of the storefront and bang on her door.

She opens it and swishes into the kitchen. Comes back with a couple beers. She sits on the couch next to me. Crosses her legs. Smooth.

I hear my mom: "Close your mouth, flies'll go in."

She looks down. "You've got some pretty nice calf muscles goin' on there."

She puts one hand on my knee and the other on my face, pulls me to her, and Smoochville, U.S.A. Damn.

What happened to keeping me guessing? That was too easy. If you don't put any sweat into it, is it worth anything at all?

I would rather spend my life chasing down a girl whose disinterest hopelessly fascinates me.

BOMBS

See, I never get anywhere because I can't ignore a glove slap, and then I gotta stop and face down duelists under the high-noon sun.

Everything's perfect, me and Ally getting back together any second now, make way for the queen of the scene, and voilà. Just when it gets good, Ally drops a bomb on me.

She says it in an off-the-cuff way. "Oh, my brother told me he saw it."

"Saw what."

"He says my dad took him in my room when I was six months old."

I hold the smoldering phone away from my ear.

"He says Dad told him, 'Babies like to put things in their mouths. It's easy. Watch.' And then he . . ."

I watch people eat in the gold light of cafes. Nothing's wrong, see?

"But my brother's crazy. He could be making it up. He has to be. I don't remember anyway, if it did happen, so who cares. I don't care."

The air raid siren's going off, oh no, not this again, not this, that happens to all the girls I love. Sandy Clooney. Eurobabe. Esty. Is it me? Am I fucked up? Am I their dad? Is that why they always pick me? Is dad's whore a girl's life? That makes her soft and vulnerable with an edge, and that's every Hollywood movie girl, so of course I like it, I'm conditioned. I'm a hero who can't save shit.

The alarm's wailing, but I'm not diving into the shelter yet. She's not freaking out, just act natural.

"Oh yeah yer brother's crazy yeah that's it," change the subject, steer her away.

We could keep sailing on ignorant bliss for years before the shit hits the fan, before she figures it out, before the day she wakes up screaming to my touch and climbs in the closet and stays there for a year. It could be decades of innocent angelhood, of laughing naked and no tears and no going crazy and no me being Dad, not your dad, mommy, therapist, the rapist, god, exile because I'm the enemy.

"Help, get away, don't touch me, don't come near, don't go away. Stay. Go. Fuck you I hate you. I love you I'm gonna kill myself."

"No baby don't do it, don't go, we're here not there, not then, it's me, not him, petting, calm, see . . ."

We get through. Every girl I been with, we get through just fine.

I call my dad, the duelist, not a soldier. I call him when I'm having emergencies of the heart. He helps me break it down. He says to me, "All women are crazy."

Why's he telling me this? He doesn't see me as a woman, see. Raised me like a son. Let me in on all the guy secrets. If Dad had raised a girl, I'd probably be crazy too. I must be, for fucking women. They'll drive you crazy. How'd they get that way? I'll tell you. From being told they're crazy. That must fuck with your reality, knowing you're a genius and a god, but everyone's telling you the way to live is act stupid, lie down, and don't fight. I'd go crazy too. I don't tell Dad it's all his fault women are crazy.

Because I'm grateful for all the hikes in the woods and one-on-one hoops he shot with me at the schoolyard, slaughtering all the boys who joined in. He'd taunt them, whatsa matter, can't beat an old man and a girl? I lucked out. Slipped through the cracks. He let me get the notion I actually was hot shit.

So why do I hate girls? Because all the girls that didn't win the parent lottery and had to fight off evil stepdad or stupid rape date every night, I love them, and dammit, they can't love me back. Broken hearts breaking my heart.

The girl who's always there for you, like, say, Johnnie Mae, all smiles and well adjusted, issue free and content, who only cries when you give it to her right, what good is she? Devotion's just comfort, no challenge. Who wants the easy life, milk and honey, when you could drink hot sauce and get euphoric? Who cares if you die of a bleeding ulcer? At least you go down in flames.

I says to myself, what are you, a wimp? Can't take it? Be a man. It takes heart to give up light for darkness. Any boy can run to Mother, whose touch makes him smile. When he's grown, he'll choose the girl who demands he stretch out on highway lines to prove his love, while she disappears, two taillights in the night. A guy like me don't take the easy way out. Give me a girl about to run me over and back up again, and the skill to roll outta the way.

But I do just want to know, from a morbid sense of curiosity, what was going through her stepdad's head when he was fucking Ally. That's one guy secret my dad never let me in on. My dad being a real man, knew he could kill me with his bare hands but was not a sociopath.

Well, he forgot to teach me that kinda self-restraint. What drives me buck wild crazy is folks waylaying the tiny children. Like my dad, I'm a gladiator, not an infantryman. An assassin, a sniper, a vigilante. But not a gun for hire, I'm dedicated. Motivated. I gotta save the girl, and I'm genuinely interested in the motives of monsters.

Ally's stepdad, good ole Pops. What was he thinking, huh? Was he envisioning her fabulous future as a junkie, a whore, a lap dancer?

Maybe he was justifying it, wrapping it up all nice. "That wouldn't be so bad. She'll probably make $300 a night stripping after I get done training her into a porno love object. Train her real good."

Or was he hoping she'd become the five-dollar blow job on Capp Street who got it over the head with a hammer when she refused to kiss her slobbering john and got thrown in the bay for dead wrapped in a garbage bag. I bet old Dad was coming with every blow of that hammer. He wasn't even there when he was doing the deed, he was way off, daydreaming about how fun it is to ruin something that can't defend itself, and Ally wasn't there either. She was off playing in her magic forest where five-year-olds go when life gets stupid.

I wanna know what that guy was thinking when he put his dick in his little girl's mouth on the beach while Mom was collecting seashells, trusting Dad with her kid like a stupid bitch. Never trust a man alone with a kid, said Sandy and Eurobabe, watching fathers hold their little girls' hands walking down to the corner store. Mm-mm-mm, they'd shake their heads. Every day somebody soiling something pure. If you can't fuck it, eat it, if you can't eat it, kill it, if it has any spirit, give it a fucking lobotomy. . . .

What was he thinking?

Was he thinking: "She'll grow up to be a dyke, but her girlfriend won't even be able to soul kiss her, cuz every time she does, all MY kid will be able to think of is my dick in her mouth, and she'll wanna puke."

Or was he actually thinking, "Maybe she's gonna forget. It's not gonna affect her. She's not gonna kill herself over this." Well those kind of people only understand one thing. You can't talk nice and reasonable to them.

It's always a personal one-on-one battle for honor.

I want to know what that guy's gonna say when I slip into his backseat and wait for him after his cushy little office day is over, and he's driving home in the dark, and I slither up behind him and put my Glock to his temple and say, "Whip that dick out and tell me what you were thinking when you fucked your kid. STROKE, bastard. WAX that pole."

I want to hear him tell it.

I want to see him cry before I shoot his dick out of his hand and say, "I'll give you something to cry about, motherfucker."

NEW YORK'S FINEST

I dream I'm a prince disguised as a peasant, sent by God. I've come to save her. Only I can wake up her body, put memories to sleep, and make her forget his face. The walls are stone and clammy. Red lips, green eyes, black hair, blue blood. Capes and white horses, bloodstains on cobblestone streets. She searches the dead and corpses in carts, a linen cloth over her mouth. There's no refuge from the plague. She finds me among the dead, saves me from mass graves, wipes the blood from my face and says, Remember, you're forgiven one sin for every man you kill.

I'm consumed by a desire as easily fulfilled by slaughter as love.

We keep getting eviction notices. I ask Legal Babe, Lisa Bonet, LB, and she says, just ignore them and start collecting proof that you been here for ten years, because possession is nine tenths of the law.

And one hundred percent of the heart.

One day me and Boss Lady are hammering and sawing, and she's telling me about the time she threw Wetback night as the guest emcee at Tranny Shack in San Francisco, and how a gaggle of Latino fags picketed the place and called her a racist, and she was trying to explain to them that she WAS Latina, honey, and had as much right to joke about it as the next Mexican faggot, and this was camp, girl, didn't they get it, when the doorbell rings. Mingus runs to the door and sniffs. I look out the peephole. It's a couple of lady sheriffs.

"Whaddaya want," I yell.

"We just want to talk to you."

When's the last time a cop stopped by for a friendly chat. I hold Mingus by the collar to make him look like he's straining to chomp, and I open the door.

"What."

"Have you received any of the notices to vacate that have been left on your door, sir, uh, ma'am?"

"Yep, and that's MISTER Dyke to you."

"Well, we need you to respond. Can you give us an answer?"

"We ain't budgin'.'"

"We'll have no choice then but to forcibly remove you from the premises."

"Why?"

"The city needs to make room for low-income housing."

"Lady, we're about as low-income as they come, and this is free, which is pretty fuckin' affordable. There. See, we helped ya. All done. Affordable housing and ya didn't have to spend a cent."

"Look, we don't make the law, we—"

"—just enforce it, I know. But don't you think it's wrong?"

"We're just doing what they're telling us to do."

Best German accent: "I vuss chust follo-vink orders."

"If you don't leave voluntarily, they're going to send in riot police. It'll get ugly."

"Oh, police, ugly, yeah that's a new tactic. . . . Listen, don't you think it's wrong?" I look up into their faces, and check my expression in their mirrored sunglasses for friendliness and irresistibility.

"They're going to get you out of here one way or another, ma'am. We're warning you now, for your own good—"

"How do you live with yourselves?"

They stare blankly at me. Fucking automatons.

They're killing me. "I mean really. Don't you think for yourselves? At all? Maybe at home in private when you're sitting on the can?"

"You have a good afternoon, ma'am."

I watch them walk away and get in the squad car. No emotion. No nothing.

They sent women because they thought that would be a nice touch. Soften me up. Get me to see things their way. I don't see nothing the way no uniform sees it, pal, and I never will. You could send Jesus Christ in a fucking cop uniform, and I would not believe him.

I close the door and walk down the hall. "Hey, Lady. Shit's about to hit the fan."

Mingus is still sniffing the crack under the door. Tomorrow is rushing up at me like a floor to a drunk.

UGLY STICK

She smashes me into pieces and I make mosaics.

Standing in the phone booth, looking at graffiti I can't read.

I tag Ally and Jim True Love Forever next to secret code messages. I print mine clear. I want everyone to know, especially her.

"Yunno, I miss you. I love you."

"I love you too, baby. You're getting a New York accent. You sound like Sylvester Stallone."

"Yeah. Thanks. I was thinking I could come home soon, and we could be together. . . ."

"Um, you know, I've been wanting to bring this up, but I didn't want you to take it too hard. . . . I'm going out with someone. It's pretty serious."

Whoa. Ally Double-Standard Dellacava.

So she's in love with Pez. It's not like I got a problem with it. Fuck those Butch Club rules.

I mean me and Ally, we broke up right? She's fair game. Who am I to stand in the way of true love, and it must be true love if they're gonna break Butch Club Rules to be together. Not like I give a fuck about them rules, or like me and Pez were ever that tight. I mean we're Hags, but hell, face it, she's a junkie. I'm a speed freak. It could only go so far.

So what. It's only a big deal if you make it a big deal. And although it's true babes go for her little-boy style, with that green tint jealousy's casting on her, I'm just now noticing that Pez is uglier than a cold bowl of oatmeal. Course, there's a few ways of looking at that.

You could say, (a) so what, all I gotta do is go over there and turn on the charm and get her back cuz she's just feeling low about herself, that's why she ain't got no standards now, and she thinks, "Well at least I can get THIS loser to love me," but given the choice, she'll pick me, the handsome guy.

Or, (b) damn, if she picked the ugly guy, he must be really superior on the inside, so I'm rotten to the core and only superficially superior, and she prefers inner qualities to outer ones.

Or, (c) if she picked the ugly guy, I must be a lot uglier than I thought.

Or (d) she needs glasses, and, not having seen me for a while, she forgot how cute I was.

So only self-loathing or truly deep or legally blind girls with Alzheimer's can love me. Maybe I want me a beautiful shallow normal girl for a change, who loves herself enough to only treat herself to gorgeous hunks, handsome and smooth, but makes an exception for me. I want her because everyone does. I'm just everyman, once in a while. I want to be normal. Act natural. I salivate for absolute perfection, the perfect girl whose glory blesses me.

I'm good, because I'm loved by a good girl.

I'm perfect, because I'm loved by a perfect girl.

No matter how a girl tells me I'm fine, I do not believe. I look at other guys she dates and say, See, she ain't got no taste. Look at the shmucks she goes for. She just dates ugly motherfuckers.

So it isn't enough to date a fine girl. No. You must date a fine girl who has dated only fine guys. Because it's not her, but her aesthetic that really marks you good or bad.

And if that don't work, and you're still shit, you got only one choice. Kick everyone's fucking head in, because when you let a girl in, you better get ready to hurt or hurt someone else.

STEALTH

Easy street's a dead end.

Esty and me, we're hanging in the squat. Bundled up in sweaters next to the space heater listening to *A Chorus Line*. "Dance ten, looks three . . ." Singing all the words. She really gets into it. Dancing around.

Esty's a secret frilly thing to add to my collection of female trouble. I know there's only one thing worse than a dame, and that is two dames, and three is a sheer cliff front wheelie. But Esty, when she tells tales of her youth, is beautiful, soft, safe, and quiet, she must be a limousine, and so I sit with her and she carries me away.

When she tells me of the boy she was, she swings her hair around and talks like a southern belle, and her hands flutter like birds, like all the girls I love. She treats me like the boy next door, bats her lashes and smiles pretty, her voice like honeyed sandpaper. She tells me stories about military school. Wardrobe abuse, she says. Davey flirted with all his teachers, she says, and wrapped them around his finger. He did whatever he wanted and got straight As. Of course, some teachers were tough. At first they resisted, but he broke 'em down. No one can resist for long the deliciousness of Davey's mouth. She stirs her cocktail with her finger, puts it delicately between her perfectly lined lips, and sucks.

In his uniform, all skinny, daydreaming out the window, Davey knows he doesn't have to pay attention to the strategies on the blackboard. He's got plenty of his own. I sit behind him in class, hypnotized by his hair shining in the afternoon light. I'm his bad boy. After class I carry his books, talk him into stealing beers from the faculty refrigerator. We go to the stables and fall down in the hay. I tear off his gray wool pants. We run up the ladder to the loft, smooth boy bodies, fingers through each other's hair, his hand on my dick, he falls on his knees. We nap naked in a patch of sun, smooth green snakes curling over us, my dick languishing on his thigh, my belly against his ass, his long, piano-playing fingers in mine.

"Hey handsome, you aren't even listening to my tired schoolboy adventures, are you," she says.

"Yes, I am," says I.

One morning I'm piling on clothes to slide around in the ice and Fuckalot comes down, pours herself a cup of joe.

She says, Never mind that bike shit today, we got work to do, and I say, What kinda work, and she says, Important kind. Anything sounds better than riding a bike in the freezing dark. Fuck this ice-patch black slush.

She says, We gotta get ready for the crackdown, and I say, How, and she says, We gotta job down south. Nice and warm. Miami. I'm digging my swimming trunks outta the closet, but she says, Leave the bikini behind, we ain't got time for swimming, we're getting some gats.

"We're gonna be GUN RUNNERS? KILLER, dude."

"You don't have to wake the whole house. Chill, damn." She's rummaging through the fridge, throwing stuff in a bag, coffee, food, singing to herself, "'My first name must be He Ain't Shit . . .'" She chugs her coffee and slams the mug down. "Come on, bro, be ready in ten or I'm leavin withoutcha white ass."

The squat's depending on me, and I'm here for them. I can do it for short periods. Road trips are virtual freedom, even though I'm leashed to the bumper, and I'm always up for felonious adventures, as high illegality is an adrenaline bonus.

So she's driving over the bridge out of town through the downy sky, windshield wipers slapping time.

I got shades on. It's an old Cali habit from eternally dilated pupils that make rainy days painful and bright. I'm looking out the window at Brooklyn brownstones with big advertisements painted on the sides of them.

Fuckalot says, "What's up with Lisa Bonet, ain't seen her around."

"She's cryin' over me."

"Oh yeah? What's she cryin' about?"

"Well, I guess she's pissed because I don't spend enough time with her anymore."

She chugs some paper-cup espresso. "Who you spendin' time with, then?"

"No one. Esty."

"Hm. You got a way with chicks, don't you? They're always cryin' over you."

"Yeah."

"What do you do to 'em?"

"I don't do nothin'. Babes just cry. I dunno why."

"Maybe it's because you act all sweet on 'em and when they fall for your ass, you're all, ka-zing . . . buh-bye."

"Do not. . . ."

"Yeah, you do. Why'd Johnnie Mae leave?"

"*You* know, she wanted to be my girlfriend or sump'm. . . ."

"Mm-hmm. So you drop-kicked her, just like you did the other one."

"Well, what was I supposed to do? They all know I'm still in love with Ally."

"So why you wanna mess with them?"

"They're here and Ally's not. Sometimes you just gotta make do 'til the real thing comes along."

"You a harsh motherfucker. . . ."

OK so I'm an asshole. I admit it. I been using totally sweet girls to put a Band-Aid on the ouchy parts. I don't need to hear about it first thing in the morning.

"Johnnie and Lisa Bonet, they say I know what to *do*. You know a guy needs to hear that. Feels good."

"Feels good. Then why you wanna leave 'em? Because you know what? Where's Ally? Do you see her?" Fuckalot looks in the back-seat. "I don't see her. Ally? Where you IS, bitch? I don't see no fuckin' Ally, so why don't you just relax, and fall in love with some-one who wants to give you some actual action."

It's flat and snowy, flat and snowy, flat and snowy. Then the moun-tains start to happen, but let's call them hills, shall we, because they do not approach anything like what we got in the Sierras.

Driving through the snow Fuckalot's swooping around the road and slides into a big fat four-by-four wooden signpost, and then we get out in the snow flurry and push the Chevy, and then we drive real slow to the truck stop, and I eat pork and more pork and talk about the new Babe movie.

Fuckalot says, "Oh yeah what kinda babes?"

I'm all, "No dude, the pig."

And then I eat more bacon and sausage and grits and gravy and liquid Velveeta and other unidentifiable things, which I eat because it's an all you can eat buffet. And there's a big, Virginian buffet restocker, who's so glad we're there, instead of just the usual burly truckers, and she comes over every five minutes and jokes with us and calls us boys.

Poor li'l queers stuck out in the hinterland, separated from their people, and if there are any of their people around, they're in disguise, and it's a big game of truth or consequence. Do you ask your best friend if she wants to sleep like spoons, and risk losing her forever? But if you win, you win big, and finally get a respite from having to give it up to the hairy drunk bouncing on you for five minutes, three times a week. It's all or nothing out here. Most likely nothing.

Seeing what the have-nots don't have is an essential part of gratitude.

SATURDAY NIGHT SPECIAL

Mom says you can't do strenuous work without a good breakfast.

I'm sleeping like a baby when we roll into Miami. Fuckalot nudges me awake. We pull up to a loud dark seedy dive with a neon Pabst Blue Ribbon sign out front.

We walk in. I head for the pisser. There are skinheads all sitting on each other's laps in stalls with the doors cut to waist level so you can't shoot up in private. They're all staring at me.

The tall one, Leader of the Pack, he says, "Hey faggot."

Here comes the hot rush, up my ankles, up my legs, up my heart into my face. So I say, "Yeah, that's right, I'm a flamin' queen and I'm gonna fuck you in the ass, right now."

So he comes booming out, and I jump way up high, and I come down on his body in a skinhead dance of joy, jumping up on one foot and kicking with the other like I'm after a soccer ball. It's like drinking raw eggs and running up steps to my own private anthem, this time no turning my back, or swinging and missing, because this time I do want to hurt him, and like no kinda girl I've been before, I connect, and thrash and thrash, like the same kinda girl I've been before, watching him cower and cringe and get small.

When I feel like I sprinted a mile, I stop, and lean down with my hands on my knees and look around, breathing. Everyone looks sullen, but no one comes out of the stalls. I walk out and use the ladies' room.

"Damn, child, whatcha doin' in there?" Fuckalot's chugging a Coke.

"Wrong bathroom."

"You're all sweaty."

"Someone called me a fag."

I try to get a beer, but she ain't got time for bullshit and introduces me to the gun monger. He has shades on, in the bar, at night, greasy black hair receding and falling in his ragged face. Skinny pants and a trench coat.

"Hey. Sid Vicious much?"

Strong silent type. Shoots the whiskey in front of him and walks out. We follow. Nobody talks to us and we don't care.

Driving down the pitted road, street lights shot out, every other yellow bulb shining haphazard on us, everything silent but for the Chevy chugging and Gunmonger grunting directions. We pull up to a cyclone fence. He jumps out, unlocks five padlocks, and pushes open the gate. We drive in. He relocks everything. Car doors chunk closed and the sound bounces off brick walls.

Inside the warehouse, he shows us an armory. AK-47s, Uzis, Glocks, AB-10s, grenades, bazookas. Our eyes are bigger than our wallets. We want it all but shell out a stack of cash for four pieces, some bulletproof vests, and ammo. Wrap the goods in granny quilts. Heft them out to the car, pop the trunk, lay them in like sleeping children.

The two of them shake hands. She slides in the back for a nap, and I climb in the driver's seat.

I'm paranoid. The dashlight doesn't work and I got to keep lighting my Zippo to see if I'm going the speed limit. It would be a rush, except I'm not breathing. I pull over for gas and camp coffee. The cashier's fiftyish, career pump jockey, coveralls. I get a shotglass that says Everglades on it and put it on the counter.

"Can I get some hot water?"

"Nope, cold's all we got."

I look at the pot on the burner, point to it, and look at him.

"Cold," he says.

"Can I heat it in the microwave?'

"Yep."

These gas station guys don't understand about the hot water. And they wouldn't know an espresso bean if it came up and bit them on the ass. They think the brown water they're pushing is passing as coffee. They're wondering, "What in tha hell is that Yankee flatcracker doin' with that hot water? Prob'ly drugs."

Damn right.

I make my coffee and get the hell out of there. I don't need him calling his cousin down at the sheriff's office to tail me down some lonesome road.

The sky's blue as a cornflower behind Dr. Seuss trees, Spanish moss hanging down like skin off a napalm baby, wisping in the hot wind. Florida's a strange world to find in the ol' U.S. of A. in the middle of winter. No black slush here. The electric windows go down, heat lightning opens your eyes on a postnuke jungle, clouds silver veined and tall as God, lighting up white and blue every five seconds. The air fills the car with flowers and rain, and boom comes the thunder over your head like a two-by-four, crash it comes rumbling, a Mac truck mowing you down on a red carpet to announce the new day shining finery.

I'm thinking about how good it feels to beat up assholes, you are the enemy, die, fucker, ha, and how my dad still wouldn't be proud of me, he only got in one fight in his whole life, and it was between rival basketball teams on the school lawn, and he got a bloody lip. He never said he felt strong or badass about that. He said he thought it was dumb. Course he only got drunk one time too, and was bouncing off the walls down a cobblestone alley in Germany where he was stationed, and he had a big headache the next day, and so he said that was dumb. And he smoked one cigarette, and he coughed and his eyes watered, and he never took that as a sign to just tough it out, and put on some shades so your pals can't see you cry, and practice in the mirror 'til you get good at it. He's built different than me. He's a normal guy. Much as I tried to be like him, I guess I'm just never gonna be a normal guy. I'm not on the basketball team, and I'm not an army lieutenant, and I'm not a family man.

I pump up the radio and sing along at the top of my lungs, "I been drivin' all night, my hands wet on tha wheel . . ."

Fuckalot smells coffee and pops her head up into the rearview. Her hair's living large.

"Whoa. Down, Herman, down boy."

She tries to smooth it down, not having much effect, and reaches for the travel cup. Swigs the grounds.

"I did good at the bar. I fucked shit up. Did ya proud."

She squints sideways at me, like she's created a monster, like all monsters, made of good intentions.

WILD IN THE STREETS

I'm so settled in, I forget I ever had another home.

Things are good and calm for a long while, except for the occasional notice on the door, and the guns stay stashed in the basement, and we start to see we never needed them at all.

One day we're jamming together, loud, we got guitars cranked, Esty growling over the top, fuzzboxes roaring and drums ripping everyone a new ear hole. I'm jumping up and down on top of a four-foot speaker, screaming into a beat-up Shure 58 that's so full of beer and spit and dents, no one knows I'm yelling, "There ain't no love," except Esty, screaming, "Let's have a war."

Sadaam walks in and waits until we notice him standing there. We stop the noise, and he says, they're coming, they've put the Dumpsters out to block Fourteenth Street.

Soleil kicks a beer bottle.

Silence. Then everybody starts yelling.

"SHUT UP. Damn, y'all." Fuckalot grabs her jacket and sends everyone out to round up all the squatters.

Within ten minutes there's fifty of us in Fuckalot's room, as ordered. Sadaam stands on a milk crate barking like a general for welders, torches, gasoline, glass bottles, rags, cylinder blocks, barricade materials, shoe polish, tourniquets, razor blades, syringes, painkillers, guns, and food.

Esty runs in the kitchen and starts throwing everything from the fridge in a giant pot for the last supper.

Boss Lady runs into her bedroom and starts getting strapped in. In no time she's giving stubbly flat chest décolleté to the navel in black leather, miniskirt, thigh-high lace-up boots, jacket. "Mess with the best, die like the rest," she tells the mirror. "Viva Zapata."

Sadaam's standing on tiptoes behind them, bobbing his head back and forth trying to check out his apocalyptic duds, very Mad Max. I look at me. Same ripped-up black jeans, sleeveless T-shirt, scraggly head. I never do get dressed up for a fight.

Boss Lady heads for the sound system. She thumbs through crates of records, picking out a stack of "something provocative." We drag a Marshall stack to the window. That ought to do it.

Outside Shemeinsky and Soleil are piling up tires, car bumpers, mattresses, and fifty-pound chunks of cement from the demolition site of the last invasion, while Mingus bounds around, sniffing for scraps.

"JIM." Fuckalot points to empty liquor bottles, a pile of rags, and some cans of gasoline, and we start pouring it in the bottles, stuffing rags down the necks, and packing them in crates.

Clang goes the dinner bell.

We eat quiet.

Then I get up and watch Fuckalot and Sadaam weld the doors closed. Now there's only two ways out. The basement and the labyrinth of subway tunnels, or the end of life as we know it.

It's the Fourth of July. Sweat trickling down my face. Through open windows, the rumble of Russian tanks, the crackle of cop radios.

Then megaphones. "You are illegally inhabiting this building. Leave peacefully, and you will not be arrested."

Lady spins Bob Marley. "Get up, Stand up." "Armageddon." "I Shot the Sheriff."

Everyone's smearing shoe polish, strapping on bulletproof vests and layers of chain mail spray-painted flat black. They're rushing around passing molotovs and cinder blocks upstairs to the roof.

Ten or eleven cops start dismantling barricades.

Lady pumps up the volume. Patti Smith holds court.

". . . in heart i am an american artist and i have no guilt . . ."

Riot cop phalanx marches down the street, helmets, face shields, body shields, batons ready. Rags lit, bottles tossed, bricks dropped. Sirens, searchlights, fireworks, sound of choppers far away.

Lady keeps spinning the hits. "MY WAR . . . you say that you're my friend. . . ."

Everyone's yelling, the night sky streaked with light and lasers, smoke and sonic booms, rubber bullets bouncing off steel, apocalypse now, surfboards, Wagner.

"Father? I want to kill you. . . ."

"More cocktails." It's Lady, eyeliner still perfect in a sea of black, the Virgin of Guadelupe inked above LA RAZA in gangster letters on her flat belly, gleaming with sweat and gas and charcoal under the tatter of her half shirt.

Sadaam's cackling. "Get your own cocktail, bitch. This ain't my table." Flings another fiery bottle down on the cops and ducks down again.

I think of saffron-robbed monks in flames and have to remind myself, them ain't no damn monks.

Hot wind, a hurricane, blows us against the wall, we crouch down under the *fwop fwop fwop*, blades spinning decapitation threat. Helicopters, muttering death. Crack of automatics cutting through the shrill. Esty picks up the olive-drab aluminum tube at her feet, loads a grenade into the end, flips up the little square plastic sight on top. She cradles it in her arms, light as a pool cue.

Lady is so fine when she's mad. "Jim get off your fuckin' ass and get some more cocktails."

I run downstairs and tuck bottles under my arm.

"FREEZE, MOTHERFUCKER." *There ain't no moshing.*

Two big ugly-ass SWAT team bastards. *Just git outta Texas.*

I gently put down the bottles, duck around the corner. "Esty. SADAAM."

Fucking queers don't know when to shut up.

I grab my board, throw open the hatch to the basement, and jump down. Mingus follows me, and I slam the trapdoor shut and slip the lock through it.

Fuck, how are THEY gonna get out.

They'll figure it out, they'll blow a hole in it or something. I don't want to think about it.

One less fag ain't gonna matter.

I'm a traitor among mutineers.

Bullets raining on the door. I hear Sadaam yelling, more shots, something heavy slam against the trapdoor. Then silence.

I hear a little voice come out of me. "Sadaam?" And I think I hear him say, Get the fuck out of here, asshole, what are you waiting for.

I'm a duelist, a one-man show.

I jump down to the second hatch and slip down the metal stairs. Mingus doesn't want to jump. The older I get, the more I cry like a baby.

Come ON.

I don't wanna go.

What are we gonna do?

You want me to captain crash? Go down with the ship, when we could save at least us?

I climb down the metal ladder into the dark and dank. I gotta go.

War, what is it good for.

You see, no matter how hard you fight, no matter how you pinky swear and smear your blood into the blood of each other's sliced-up fingers and pledge dedication and drift into dreams of refuge, in the end there's nothing holding you together. Maybe belonging don't strangle you, maybe asylum don't have you running the length of the deck with cabin fever, yearning for horizons and the limitless world. Eventually pirates swing aboard anyway, and you see you'll do anything to preserve the tribe, draw swords and fight to the death, and you're bloodthirsty, driven to dismember.

The sad thing is, that won't save your love, because someone always has a bigger gun, and cannonballs land topside, and if you're lucky, you grab a piece of what you had and float off, free. Every man for himself. The ship sinks, and bobbing alone on your plank, you can't tell the salty sea you swallow from your tears.

Maybe it would have been better to land on that balmy island you passed and live out your lives in peace, with naked babes pouring coconut milk down your throats. But a swashbuckler's life is everything lost in the fray.

Stumbling deeper into the abandoned subway maze, through stale train stink that hangs off clammy walls. Everything's black, rats hanging out like sheep on a hillside. I got a dim light shining a short beam through cables and pipes, the ultimate basement, lighting me away from love and murder, to love that will murder me sweetly at last.

After about an hour I pitch into a huge room from lost decades, with mirrors, gold veined, and a grand piano in the middle of the train platform with a crystal chandelier hanging over it. It's the old Opera Station.

I sprawl huffing on the tile floor.

When I wake up, I crawl up on the bench, remembering fourteen years old, when I sang Bette's signature tune, all alone. I pound out Barry Manilow's riff, singing, "You got to have friends."

Mom always said someday I'd thank her for those piano lessons.

I get lost a few times, take some wrong turns. I ask around. Run into encampments, garbage-can fires warming hands and smudged faces of men in overcoats. They're suspicious. They don't like us that live in the light. I sit down with some unwashed types passing a bottle of Night Train. They warm up to me and tell me shortcuts, and I wonder if they're just trying to get me more lost. I skate platforms and hike train tracks, over the ties and the cinders clanking like glass under my feet. Then, just before dawn, I see a shaft of orange light shining down into the tomb and feel a draft instead of the usual rush of warm air whenever trains thunder by.

An escape ravine, choked with weeds whose roots, like oak trees, crack cement. I climb out into the homicidal world.

I'm skating across the concrete upheaval of sidewalks broke by subterranean monsters with brute shoulders. I fly off curbs, over potholes, pushing through the Meatpacking District, where one sleepy tranny is turning ankles on her jungle shoes, leaning against a metal roll-up door, nodding.

There's the PATH station. I skip down the stairs and run up to the fishbowl.

"One, please," I say to the fish.

A token clatters into the smooth curve of metal under the window. I slide it out, and slip it in the slot, push through the turnstile, skate down the halls, away from the fish yelling "NO DOGS ALLOWED," into more catacombs. I'm glad for the light even if it is fluorescent. At least it's too early for suit swarms, pre-coffee, with the *Times* under their arms.

Mingus crawls under a bench. I balance my board upright, sideways on its wheels, boxing him into his hiding place. With my messenger bag under my head, I lie down and pass out until the train comes, then I take it to the outermost limits of New Jersey, until the conductor comes around and nudges me awake.

"Is that your dog?"

We scramble out the door and stand on the platform, bustled by everyone in a hurry to get into the steamy day.

When I find out where the turnpike is, I skate toward it, then alongside it, until I get to the truck stop. Go west, young man.

I can't think about what I left behind. No time to grieve sledgehammers smashing toilets, or wet cement filling sinks where I washed Esty's breakfast dishes. No wondering if anyone's left to tell our side. I gotta keep moving.

Back home, to Ally, mom, and steak dinner.

I cruise up to the truck stop. Swing my bag around, rummage for a Yankees cap to cover up a haircut that would prevent trucker rides. I duck into the store, big and light and cool, air-conditioned. Suddenly I feel like shopping. Everything says buy me. A big glass case with ten shelves of tiny blown-glass swans, bears, deer, cats, dolphins, cubic Zirconium and garnet encrusted. What would a trucker want with this shit? Maybe they want to pick something up for dear old mom back home, or for the ball and chain. Truckers probably love their wives, since they never see them. Past the aisles of big-rig accessories. Giant mudflaps inlaid with chrome chickee-babe silhouettes, or with twin rubber likenesses of Yosemite Sam pointing six shooters, saying "BACK OFF."

I go in the ladies' room. A lady pops out of a stall. Her crumb-snatcher's all, "Mommy, why is that man in the girls' bathroom?"

She hustles the kid past me. Jeez, we're not that far from New York. Mental note: Use men's room until back in the city.

I splash some cold water on my face, soap up, wash out my shirt, and put it on wet. I'll just hang out in the parking lot and dry out, and if no one picks me up by then, I'll get a cup of joe in the freezing-cold coffee shop. Maybe some Key lime pie.

I pass out in the shade on the side of the building.

"Need a ride?"

I look up at a moonscape complexion with a big Adam's apple and a nylon baseball hat that says "Chicken Haulers Association."

"Sure do."

Jersey's pretty once you get out of the cesspool-smelling part with all the smokestacks and factories. Kind of sleepy and flowery with clapboard houses painted white with blue trim. We're rolling down the pike. I fall asleep to the bedtime stories of a man I have nothing in common with except the open road.

So I'm sleeping sweaty dreams, can't find a vein, into my hand the needle slides, pictures of useless claws where errant spikes hit nerves and crippled. The vein blows up, a purple balloon, no, stop, stop, pull it out, try this vein, foot, ankle, behind the knee, not the neck, can't do the neck, girl on the floor with the chicken hauler hitting her up in the jugular. She gets up, sweet sixteen, starts waiting tables in a roadside diner, truck drivers leering over hash browns. She palms tips off the tables and wipes the counters down. Cowboy invites her out for a smoke. She steps out the glass swinging door, her ass swinging before him, which he can't resist and Sweet Sixteen's too raw and tiny to know it's all she has in the world to defend. All she knows is she's gotta get outta here, and this is her ticket to freedom, metropoli, success, the movies, the

271

lights, and she's gonna be a big star. He steps up into the cab, smells like leather and Marlboros and cheap cologne, opens her door, leans over to pull her up by her miniature hand, the summer wind ruffling her skirt, and she puts her head on his shoulder. But that's not the price of the ticket to the World. Giving carnies head for free rides, that's the price, child. And she takes in her mouth the ticket, and she doesn't mind bitterness, the payoff is Love and that makes it all worthwhile.

I open my eyes and Chicken Boy's offering me a choice. "You can keep riding and make yourself some lunch money too, or you can get out here. Whaddaya say, son."

Have things got that desperate?

I'm standing on the roadside looking at some train tracks.

I AM THE PASSENGER

I hike a really long time, maybe two days. Shredded feet. Some water, Fritos, and a can of tuna. Boots crunch and thunk on ties and gravel. Mingus panting.

Finally heavy metal cars, rust, black, Golden West, Union Pacific, hissing of hydraulic couplers, hoses, lugs, pistons, big wide flat shiny smooth wheels like blades that took her legs, that girl up north whose story meandered down the coast, steel wheels flattening munching tissue. Before the train's done with its severance, she misses beloved feet, crying for long walks long gone.

Danger Dyke, sly, looks for an open car.

At the end of the train, a boarded-up station peels in the sun, where soldier boys came home. When people rode the trains, not just hobos and cargo, everyone wore suits and hats, wrapped in steam like a Gary Cooper movie.

My grandma took the train from New York to San Francisco. Her eyes saw Orville in a small field headed for a cliff, lemming-like. She had to sneak, her aunt having said she couldn't go looking at the endeavors of crazy people. Half a century later, the plane rushes up, floats up like a sky ladder, lifts her up in a Ferris wheel rocket ship, red tide, tsunami in her brain, lifted into sky-vein air tunnels, corpuscle swept up, exhilarated, time loses linearity, it's all there at once, blue light runways and paper biplanes, from crazy to civilized in sixty seconds, the future vowing airplanes packed in, flying wing to wing, computer chips navigating clouds, laughing at test patterns, hover, shooting straight up liftoff, swooping, soaring, swimming, flying underwater, diving like seagulls sucked downward on drafts, below Concordes dodging asteroids.

But I take the slow ride, hopping a crazy train cutting across the flat old ocean floor. All around on the edges of earth, crags hunch black against the blaze or light up pink, like the REGAL: WHERE YOU ARE KING sign back home. Home that I almost forgot drawing me closer, reeling me in by a string of boxcars.

Next train has a rack of brand-new jeeps on it. Me and Mingus jump in, and I turn the key in the ignition, turn on the country station, and look up at the stars in the warm wind. I fall asleep, thinking about how there ain't no warm wind where I'm going.

Along about the third day, I'm starting to feel like I'm not even me, like who is me anyway, I could be anyone, I can change shape, I can say my name's Bill or Bob or Joe or I could say I'm Mary Sue and wear a dress, and nobody'd be the wiser. Nobody'd think anything was weird, except I got a funny gait for a girl, because they don't know me and I don't know me, I'm just a product of history that's gone now with the ones that wrote it. I could just start from nothing like a Ministry of Truth typist, fresh, like a secret agent in a foreign land.

I'm floating through space they call the States, mountains, desert sage blowing, me remembering when this sky was full up with fish and sea anemones. Meeting up with other folks who give me tips, tell me not to ride in boxcars, that the doors slam shut in train yards and you're locked in for days drinking your own piss. You gotta climb up into the shiny silver gravel cars with no ceilings and slanty sides.

Maybe I drink some wine, maybe a little malt liquor, sour, warm, and flat. The emptiness is always long and dark, or long and hot, and there's always a duffel bag sliding down with a thud that announces company with crass tales and libations to share.

It's usually men, but one time it's a girl so fine to make my jaw drop. She's got sad eyes with just enough resolve to get her through another day. The other suitcase drops down. Up swings the leg of her traveling companion, a certifiable-looking guy, and then he slides down into the car. I tip my hat, a beat-up leather cowboy hat I traded for some coffee. We get to talking, and by their reservations and his nervous tic, I get the feeling they're on the lam too. But we drink some whiskey, and things loosen up, and they shake the dust off their backs, and pretty soon they whip out a spoon. Well, by that time I don't have no more rules. I'm liquored up and she's starting to look like my future ex-wife.

She drawls, "You want some?"

I say, "What is it?"

She says, "A speedball."

I say, "Let's go. Let's celebrate. I'm on a desert planet far from earth, I'm a man nobody knows, and I think I'm in love."

So they cook it up over a lighter, and they draw up the bubbly brown cure, then crush up the shiny white, dissolve it in water, and suck that up too, in the very same tube, for a cocktail extraordinaire. I been jostled, rattled, and cradled by this train, and I got no yesterdays, no tomorrows, no time at all, so might as well go somewhere I never been before. Bill Burroughs, wait for me.

He holds me off, and she lays the needle on my hot, blue, healed vein, pounds it in with a tap, a flick, like a spike. They must have been working at dulling this one down since they left home, the way it hurts going in.

"Didn't pack no spares, did ya," I offer as a decoy from the pain. His fingers let go of my arm slowly as she pushes down the brown.

My heart, heavy, slides under a cold fog, and the back of my neck gets heavy and warm like a ton of honey's being poured on it, thick, smooth weight, and the tway-yay-yang's lower, slower than just solo coke, muted, like she put her hands on my ears. I can't talk. It makes my stomach swim to hear the low thick echo, the hum that squeaks up in your head with every word you say. You don't wanna hear that, you just want to stay suspended like shit in a bucket of warm champagne, your head floating, your body completely dissolved.

I must have flashed, because acrid tendrils of puke corkscrew up my nose. Night falls. In the sway of the train and euphoric dreams, we slow down, stop, speed up again. More voices down halls make desperate deals. Raspy whispers, trading something for balloons. More whiskey stings my lips, cigarettes burn fingers, unsmoked. Slow down, stop, speed up. Stars are out, shining like Christmas lights in the black black night. I'm riding my bike down the fire escape stairs of high-rises, *bonkety bonkslam* into the wall, bounce off floating, and down the next flight of Nerf stairs.

I feel hands pulling on my pants. I twist halfhearted, useless. No is the word I hear myself think? say? as I fall away into the dark and then light trying to push him off, arguing, dick, tired, no, sleep, wake up, get off me, no you fucker, come on baby, wake up to find the weight and stink of a stranger on me, furry legs between mine, pants around his ankles, my pants missing in action.

Numb is a friend in times of need. I open my eyes. He's not budging. Out cold. My head pulsates. Light streams into the car and lands on another guy sleeping in the corner, similarly attired, tiny dick like a nylon full of hair gel disappearing in his hand.

She's gone with the loon.

My body's coming back, smashed and bluish. Mingus is sleeping, like he didn't see nothing to get excited about, and there's nary a dog bite on my dance partner, so I figure I didn't put up a fight, or Mingy would have jumped in.

So it was all my fault. I deserved it, drunk girl at a frat party. Don't walk into the lion's den expecting tea and sympathy, Jack. Gotta stay awake at all times. How ya gonna protect yourself in that condition? Huh? All droolin' on yourself.

I slip my hand slowly under limp sticky dick, into my front pocket, quiet, careful not to wake him. My thumb opens the knife, oiled and easy it swivels. I slip it back under his body, grab his worm in the other fist, and slice through a soft chicken neck, feel the hot rush of thick liquid on my thighs, kick him off me. I'm looking around for anything, grab a hunk of metal, backhand swing across his head, which breaks like pottery. He's trying to stop the geyser spouting from his new gash.

For once I can think on my feet, I can spew like a fucking talk show host, I never felt so clear.

"People pay a lotta money for that, baby, I don't hear ya sayin' thank you." I kick him in the hip and he jackknifes into the corner. By this time the other asshole's starting to move around.

"Hey . . ."

I put on my steel toes real quick and lace them at the ankle in a double knot. He picks himself up, lumbers side to side in the narrow space like he forgot his train legs, holding out his hands to bounce off sloping walls.

He's all, "Whad're ya dooin' . . ."

Drunks are fun to taunt, so I say, "Come on, bitch, we had such a good time last night, don't you wanna go for another round."

"Yeah, tha's right, baby, you didn't have no complaints. . . ."

"Well, I changed my mind. That's a woman's prerogative ya know. Guess ya just can't trust us, can ya."

He lunges at me, I grab his arm and pull him past me, ramming his head into the wall. Then I spin him around and bust his balls, and when he doubles over, I grab the back of his head with both hands and slam his face down into my knee.

I'm yelling, "THIS IS GOOD," over and over.

He's on the floor and I'm crying and sweating and puking all over him. "Next time ask nice, fuckface," I yell. He's got a blank stare like he's never gonna register anything again. I don't care if he sees me cry. I don't care if anyone sees me cry anymore.

When the train slows down, I climb out and find a boxcar. I

need to feel mountains fly by, cool and green. I sit down on the floor in the open doorway, chest heaving, wind cooling sweat, dangle my legs over the threshold, looking out my back door.

Mingus says he's sorry he didn't help. Lying there with his face on his paws, he moves his eyebrows up anxious-like, as he turns his eyes to me and back to the eighty-mile-an-hour scenery.

"It's OK, boy. You're a lover not a fighter, I know."

I pull the 45 out of my jacket and squeeze off a round. I was so distracted, I forgot I even had a rod. The difference between a beating and a shooting is that a job with your bare hands is just plain more satisfying, even if it is a fuckload more work.

Sometimes a healthy brawl is the only thing that makes you forget your annihilation and the wind whistling over your nuclear shadow. And for a second, blood is the Great Red Hope that cleansing can happen. But then that awful filth comes back and hovers like a whiskey cloud that no sunshiny kill can burn off. It just clings, dark, gloating.

It's lonesome knowing there's no fix for your tragedies. I reach in my pocket for a smoke. The box is empty. Twenty friends to a pack, and they're all gone. A boy and his dog sniff the air for an oxygen rush.

OYSTER CULT

Gotta find her. Beeline for the Schmiegel, ask the barker where she went. He points down the street.

Ally's working the Cinema now where she said she'd never work, because here you got to do lap dances, and she never wanted to touch men.

When I first walk in, I remember how I hate customers trying to look respectable. I just want to yell, "Who do you think you're fooling. We all know you're getting ready to pay to polish your knob, ya lousy scum. So quit acting like you're still at the computer convention. You don't deserve any respect so don't act like you do. Just get on your knees in front of these women right now, shell out all your dough, apologize, say thank you, and lowcrawl outta here."

I know one of the babes hanging out front, and she gets me past the bouncer and downstairs to the dressing room. Stepping over two girls slouched in bikini thongs, I head for the bathroom, through half-naked ladies applying paint, the sound of puke. Then I hear Ally's voice.

"Hey!"

I turn around and look for her, she's nowhere, just this skinny girl with a tit job, and I look around and Skinny says, "Over here. It's me."

She walks over and hugs me, I step back and look at her. Satan eyes. Pinpoints. Where's my Ally. Where are the big black pupils on a green dish in a trapezoid eye that seduces with the promise of most sublime love. Where's that ass like a young Liz Taylor in *Butterfield 8*.

She slips her arm through mine, walks me upstairs and sits me down in the audience. "I'll see you in a minute."

Onstage some babe's moving stiff with unnaturally sagging tits and a tan, wagging her shaved choch at the audience. She's going through the motions, staring over the crowd, no eye contact. You can see every broken part of her heart. Some old fat white guy gets up and leans over her, titty grabbing and humping on her. She stiffens more and looks like she's gonna hurl, but he doesn't notice.

Then two premium babes, a redhead and a blonde, come strutting out in matching vintage satin one-piece bathing suits. They're stars. Pole tricks, flinging themselves circular in unison, Hollywood good looks, smiling. They love it here, laughing it up, flashing newborn lambs and doing gymnastics like Esther Williams to porno hip-hop. Gorgeous. Scanty applause, a few tips, but three guys follow them into the back where the real money's made.

Then Ally comes out. A little tired, but she hasn't lost it. Slow slither to an old X song, "My Goodness." She climbs over the guy in front of me to fling her tits in his face. When her set's over, she scoops up all the cash on the stage. Flashing ass, she glides through the curtain.

Then she comes out the side door and sneaks me in like old times. No vacancies in the Wet and Wild room, so into the Bangkok room, bigger booths. She pulls the curtain. I sit on the vinyl upholstered bench, thinking just for a second of the cum from the guy before me, glancing at the pile of Kleenex on the floor. She sits on the table in front of me.

"Ally. Why. Why why why why why."

"Why what, loverboy?"

"You know what I mean. You're high . . ."

"As a kite . . ." She hums the rest.

"Yeah. Well I came to get you. . . ."

"Get me? Honey, you know I'm with Pez. What do you mean, 'get'." She kisses me. Runs her hands under my shirt. "Still got some fine titties."

"SO WHAT."

She's talking, but my mind's in Inverness. An oyster farm on the coast, where me and Mom used to go and gorge ourselves on salty sea poontangs stung with lemon. They were shiny and held delicious promise of that one-in-a-million pearl. We shucked them, sucked the precious live things out, then we threw their flat white houses on a mountain of empty broken shells. No one ever came and collected them or used them for anything. They weren't pretty or shiny anymore, just cracked, dull, chipping in the sun.

THERE GOES MY BABY

Even if Ally's a mess I still love her. What's love if it's not sticking with a girl through hard times?

So I wait outside for her to get off work, and then I walk her home.

But she's lost it. Shooting skag has warped her once poet godhood. Now she sways like a loopy pendulum between grandiosity and suicide. She's stuck in the time warp of when I was bad. One minute she tells me she loves me, and the next she's got out the hammer.

We fight. I say, "You're destroying yourself. I only always loved you. Why don't you believe me?"

And in lipstick she scribbles poetry across shop windows about how I need her so bad I'm killing her. There's no point. She has her view of the world and there's no way she can see mine.

We get to her house, and tears start rolling down my face. I can feel my heart. It's a chest pain, a heart attack, a hole, a map burning up from the middle like at the beginning of an old cowboy TV show.

I tell her, I'm not crying about never *getting* no more love. I'm crying because *I* finally loved and it's never gonna happen again. She says no, it will, and I say no, I know everyone says that, but I don't think it can.

There's no hurt like loving a crazy person and watching her drift down the river and you're calling and calling and she just disappears in the fog.

I dig through her records until I find the one with her favorite country song, called "He Stopped Loving Her Today." When they came and put a wreath on his door and took her picture off the mantle, which was all he had left of her for the last forty years, and they took his old withered body to the grave on a creaky little wagon, that's when he stopped loving her. We dance all slow to that stupid song and cry.

I wake up with her on her bed, with my head in her million-dollar cleavage, and Pez comes home. We hear the door slam and Ally jumps up.

Old Pez comes waltzing in, like it's nothing that I'm there, like I'm not even a threat.

"Hi baby," Ally coos and lap dances all over the little fucker, way more desperate than she ever was with me.

Pez says, "Hey, Bub" to me, and starts laying out the works on the table.

Ally's getting the rubber hose and tying herself off, slapping her white arms with that tiny hand that used to take me to heaven. I get up off the bed, sidle up behind Pez, and sweep the stuff off the breakfast table.

She spins around. "WHAT THE FUCK ARE YOU DOING? I

guess you're gonna go out and score for us. Ally's about to get sick if she don't get some right now."

"Ya think that's somethin'?" I grip Pez around her scrawny neck and slam her up against the wall. "How do ya like me now?"

Her tenny runners are dangling, wiggling at the end of her skinny legs. She's coughing scratchy noises, slobber's coming out of her mouth, she's turning blue, veins bulging in her neck, temples. Now she's purple. She gets littler and littler until she's nothing, and she don't say nothing no more. I forget she's helped me and been my bro. I forget everything but the kill. But it's no good healthy numb, no zeroing out the wait for a never girl.

Mingus is barking. Ally pipes up. She's crying. "Jim, don't."

Aw shit. I sure can't handle no woman crying. And then I remember. But I can't remember the promise the girl made a long time ago. Something about a paper box.

There ain't no sense in loving Ally or killing Pez. Because guys that beat their old ladies and their kids and me, they are me, serial killer putting a hit on myself, my vein in the cross hairs. It doesn't fucking matter who started it, because I am them, that's why I beat the shit out of everyone including Ally, if only with words. I try to beat the rage out of me, but it's stubborn. It braces itself against the doorjamb and screams.

"Gotta go," I mumble and slam the front door, carry the bike down the stairs.

I'm riding away from the scene of the crime to what I lost. I know I left it out here somewhere.

I spin through Sixteenth and Mission, and the old guy says, "Outfits, outfits."

That's it. The only way to be loved by Ally and make her happy is to give her what she wants. Get the tiny balloons. Ride real slow back to her house. She's going to be so surprised. She'll love me and we'll float off on her cloud. We'll touch each other like aliens, all light, no elbows and knees to get in the way. Then she'll see me through those H-goggles and recognize me. She'll realize it was Pez she was looking at that whole time and *thinking* Love, she'll see she's been duped, see truth, Taylor and Burton, Monroe and DiMaggio, Dietrich and Piaf.

I get to her door. I hold her in my arms. I take out what she needs. I lay it down before her. I promise her everything. I'll be what she wants. No price too high. I give all to her that was ever me to be reshaped and gouged out and rolled up and smoked, to curl up next to like a shred of pink baby blanket that fits in your hand and no one can see, but you know it's there, secret dependence, secret reliable, secret selfless, invisible made for you and to be shared with none. I dive off the falls, my barrel don't last, my parts fall away, I do not mind. It's the flying makes the landing hard worth dying.

I says to the outfits man, "Thanx, yer lookin mighty styley yerself."

EXTREME

A murder spree's good work for broken hearts, but then you can't break roadkill, can you.

I ride by Frankie's house, house of love, house of comfort and superman powers and salvation and exhilaration. That's what I saw when I used to roll up to her stoop, to get my fill of what Frankie had. Course Frankie's in jail now. So there's no more salvation for me there. What I seen in New York was salvation. And what I done on the train. And what I saw in green eyes, a long time ago. It's not in a house, under Victorian gables, anymore. I guess there's one thing I learned, for everyone that lets you down, somebody's gonna lift you up, and then somebody's gonna kick you to the curb.

So what, I ain't scared. You gotta have balls to be balls out. Only a bold motherfucker rides into traffic naked, risking everything. That's the only way to delirium.

Now I know what Rosemary meant by keeping your heart open even though everyone beats the crap out of it. That's to tenderize it.

I take Mingus over to Mom's and we have steaks.

She says, "Where have you been? You don't call your mother for months?"

"I had to take care of some business."

"What business? You don't have any business."

"I had to find something." I kiss Mingus good-bye and put him in his very own yard. I whisper, "Look I'll miss you, but you won't be able to keep up. Your feet would just hurt a lot. I gotta lie low for a while, but I'll be back, OK? I promise."

She says what am I doing, I can't leave that dog here, she doesn't want a dog, they always die. "Now where are you going? And how long are you leaving this hound here?"

"I have to go for a long bike ride. Don't worry Mom, I'll be right back. You need some protection anyway."

She says she does not need protection and she doesn't like big dogs, and then she starts petting him and yelling at him to stay off the fancy rug and feeding him scraps off the table. I feel bad about lying. But he does have a big bark, and I will be back, someday.

I get the bike ready for the road, load it up with rain gear and a bedroll. Weatherproof it, fashioning fenders from a cut-up plastic water bottle. I throw my leg over the drop bars, get up on the seat and start pedaling. Through Boyz' Town, slow down at the Castro Theatre, wistful, covet James Dean marathons. Slow, suck seduction of Hot Cookie off greased sheets, up off the seat, torquing like a can opener, like a derrick, fists wrenching chrome pipe, scaling heights like a tractor, overlooking my city by the bay, heart hammering. Wind icicles perforate my lungs and freeze sweat as it beads.

I can hear the blood pump in my head and there's nothing like it at all. It takes a long time and it's a lotta work, but the view is laid out before me a long time as I slow ride over the crest.

The long broad boulevard slices through the middle of the city all the way to the Ferry Building, through the skyline flashing like teeth, to a bridge, to a village I cruised on a Stingray a thousand Sundays ago.

My fingertips rest on icy brakes. And then, swoop, down Portola, forty miles an hour with no shock absorbers, suicide visions of mangled collisions skull breaking open and run over by cars, if I die now, at least I'll die happy, blowing lights, tears streaming toward my ears as I bomb down the cliff, sail and soar like Da Vinci dreaming, pedals spinning faster and racing past cars full of families going home to steak dinner, ice metal wind like a wet sheet slapping, whipping past Stern Grove's cold eucalyptus filling my head with something you'd never find in New York City or any city but this, an aeronautic trance, a pilot lost in the cadenza of flight all the way to Merced Lake, lonesome and free.

Here in the avenues, the yellow sun is slanty on stucco, intense, like the last pleas of a boy before a leaving train. You see, it's me beseeching on the platform, waving 'bye.

I hit the highway that snakes down the coast. I stop in a Pacifica diner, looking out the window at gray waves seducing surfers to be sucked into undertow. Then I go in the phone booth to call her. Never mind. Pretty baby, so long. Go break some other heart in two, because I got the wind kissing my cheek, and that's all the love I want.